Family Occasions

FAMILY OCCASIONS

A Novel by

GEORGE R. CLAY

DAVID OBST BOOKS

RANDOM HOUSE
NEW YORK

Library of Congress Cataloging in Publication Data
Clay, George R.
Family occasions.
ɪ. Title.
PZ4.C62Fam [PS3553.L385]   813'.5'4   78–57137
ISBN 0–394–50188–8

Portions of this book appeared originally
in the *Ladies' Home Journal*, *Seventeen Magazine*, and *The New Yorker*,
and in *New World Writing*, a publication
of The New American Library, Inc.

Manufactured in the United States of America First Edition

24689753

For my Ann, and all of ours.

PROLOGUE

1923

Louisa Hooper hated taking naps, considered them a waste of perfectly good daylight, but toward the end of her eighth month Dr. Hallowell had insisted that she lie down for an hour each afternoon with her feet up, and at least shut her eyes. It had been impossible to find the time that last week at Loon Lake when she was closing the summer cottage, but once back home in Glenllyn, with the two older children in school, she had forced herself to go to her bedroom toward the middle of the afternoon.

On this particular day she had spent more than an hour after lunch organizing the children's winter clothes, getting the woolens out of cedar chests and moth bags in the attic, inspecting them, making piles to be mended or discarded or lengthened. The afternoon was warm, almost simmering, a late September reversion to midsummer. It had been stifling up there in the attic, under the slate roof, among the steamer trunks and war souvenirs and boxes of letters no one would ever read again, yet for reasons now forgotten, no one dared to throw out. When the clothes were all sorted she went to the little dormer window,

opened it wider and leaned against the sill, looking out through
the treetops, staring so intently at the maple pattern that her
eyes began to glaze and all she could make out clearly were
empty blue spaces in a blur of green: delicately etched holes full
of sky. Sweat was running down her cheeks, tickling slightly,
and dizziness came over her as though a hand had been placed
gently across her eyes. She gripped the sill and gave her head a
quick shake, waiting for the contraction. It came, a cramp that
spread as it tightened. Today, then. She walked to the narrow
stairs and climbed down sideways, one step at a time, gripping
the banister; then she closed the attic door, made her way down
to the second-floor telephone in Curt's dressing room, and gave
the operator Jim Hallowell's number. He was on house calls and
might not be back until late afternoon. She left a message to
have him phone her, then hung up, closed her eyes and sat very
still trying to think, to *think*. Suitcase. Bills. Potted plants (she
could leave a note for Bridgit). Birthday present for Peter. Had
Gabe and Rosalie asked Curt and her for dinner this weekend,
or was she imagining it? She should check the engagement
book, but suddenly she was half asleep, could hardly manage to
pull the shades down before climbing onto the bed. When
would Jim call back? Probably not while she was napping.
Would a contraction wake her? Would this heat ever end, the
sun ever cross the sky and sink, simply sink—

DAYLIGHT STILL SPARKLED through pinpoints in the window
shades when Louisa woke up, but the bedroom seemed cooler
and she knew from the unmistakable house sounds that Miss
Brunner had returned with the baby. Outside, across the street,
on the slope of Glenllyn station yard, she could hear the gossipy
spin of a lawn mower and, beyond somewhere, a bicycle bell—
tiny and faintly triumphant. Marlie and Peter must be at supper. Their voices, arguing, punctuated by an occasional chink of
china, floated up to her from the dining room. Feeling a new

wave of pain, Louisa gripped her pillow and concentrated on listening for Curt, trying to single out from all the other noises his footfall, the rustle of his newspaper, his cough.

Frowning, she sat up and swung herself heavily around, working her legs over the side of the bed and pointing her toes to where she had left her slippers upright so that she would not have to bend down. Finding them, she slipped her feet into them and moved methodically about the room raising the shades, standing sidewise before each window and just reaching out to the shade cord, so as not to have to press her front against the sill. Between windows, she paused to look over her shoulder. It pleased her the way, with each raised shade, a new shaft of late-afternoon sun seemed to overcome the room, like soft orange-colored columns being rammed into a box. When the last of the shades was up, she walked carefully across the carpet to her dressing room, holding her shoulders back as Jim Hallowell had told her she must. She stood then, her hand on the doorknob, and again she listened. All she could hear was Marlie's voice saying something to Peter.

They were still quarreling, their faces covered with chocolate, when Louisa made her way down the main staircase that led past the dining room into the front hall.

Seeing her on the staircase, through the open dining-room doors, Peter turned in his chair and waved a dessert spoon at her. "This is my third helping," he called. "Marlie has a secret to tell you."

"I have not," Marlie said into her pudding. "So don't talk about it." She was blonder than her brother, very delicate and precise, her curly hair kept back by a wide blue ribbon. "I don't want to talk about it until Daddy gets home," she announced, returning to her pudding, eating it in minute, ladylike spoonfuls.

"Ma will find out anyway. Then it will be a hundred times worse. A thousand times!"

"It will not. It will *not!*" The girl looked over at her mother, almost savagely. "Where's Daddy?" she demanded. "I have to see Daddy!"

But Louisa was only half listening. Unable to hold back a new pain, she had walked down past the dining-room entrance and into the hall, to hide her face from the children. She went to the screen door and latched it, then took Marlie's parasol off the hall table and carried it back past the dining room to the closet under the staircase. It wasn't until she had closed the closet door and, smiling, went into the dining room, that she realized Marlie was on the verge of tears.

"He should be home any minute, dear," she said, already leaving them. "Don't let Peter upset you so." She pushed through the swinging door into the pantry. "And use your napkins, both of you —you look a sight."

Bridgit was getting out the dinner plates; she seemed to be forever on tiptoe. Annie, beyond, stood planted before the stove. Both looked around, respectfully but with friendliness, too.

"Another one of those days," Louisa said.

"Miserable hot, Mrs. Hooper," the cook agreed.

"But the fan's a great help," Bridgit offered, her pinched, devout face all seriousness. "Would you be likin' something cool, missus? Shall I concoct an iced tea?" There was pride in the maid's voice, as if putting up with the heat were a talent she didn't expect others to share.

"Thank you, I think I'll wait for Mr. Hooper." Louisa paused, then said, "Did Dr. Hallowell phone?"

"Mother of God!" Bridgit blurted. "I'd clean forgot! Not half an hour ago—I wrote it down if I can only . . . It's here somewheres."

"It doesn't matter in the least. Don't worry about it, Bridgit," Louisa pleaded. "Really."

"To call before eight o'clock was all it said."

"That's exactly what I needed to know. Now tell me this: I know it's Thursday, but will either of you be in later on this evening?"

"I will, Mrs. Hooper." Annie was standing half in the pantry, wiping her hands on her apron. "I'll be up in my room writing letters, if you need me."

"Perfect," Louisa said. "Just leave supper on plates in the oven. Mr. Hooper and I can serve ourselves. Unless I have to leave before he gets home."

"Is there anything at all we can do?" Annie said. "Anything you—"

"Not a thing. As long as somebody's in the house." She had started up the back stairs when Bridgit, calling *"Here* it is, missus!" came running after her and triumphantly thrust a slip of white paper into her hand.

THE DOOR AT THE HEAD of the narrow stairway was ajar, but no sound came from the nursery, and Louisa knew before she reached the second floor that the baby was asleep. No matter how many times she told Miss Brunner to let her know—to wake her, if necessary—when Chris was ready for bed, the governess kept defying her. And always in the name of consideration. "I dit not like to disturb you," the German girl would say. "I thought of course you need your sleep." Louisa could hear her now, in the bathroom between the back stairs and Marlie's room, washing out the tub, and then she heard the bathroom door click shut. If she called the governess, it would have to be softly, lest she wake the baby, and Miss Brunner would merely turn the spigots on harder. And if she went to the bathroom door and opened it, Miss Brunner would be in Marlie's room—would go from there to the third floor, or maybe down the front stairs, always keeping one jump ahead. Louisa held the railing, catching her breath. She could sense Miss Brunner behind the bathroom door, could almost see the other woman pause and look up, preparing her next move, timing it. The water continued to splash into the tub, neither louder nor more softly. I'm acting childish, Louisa thought.

She let go of the railing and walked quietly to the nursery door.

In the hushed semidarkness of the large, square room, everything seemed to reflect Miss Brunner's neatness: the bare bureau, the closed toy box, the child's chair with the little clothes folded over its back and the small blue sneakers placed, just so, underneath. Everything but the willful position of Christy himself. The baby's rump stuck straight up in the air, as if he had been trying to burrow through the crib mattress when he was overcome with exhaustion. Louisa gave him a pat, then crossed the room and raised the shades to let in more air. The bathroom spigots had stopped running now, and behind Christy's infant snoring she could just make out the faint, concentrated rush of an approaching train. She wondered whether it was coming from the direction of Glenllyn Hill or out from Philadelphia. Raising one shade still higher, she stood gazing through the window screen and waited.

How ridiculously ominous it sounded, the muffled roar gathering into a pocket, growing imperceptibly, so that one second it was quite far away and the next it was on top of you. Now she could see it—the dark-red, gold-lettered suburban electric nosing primly up to the outbound platform. It coughed, jolted, and stopped, quiet except for a low throbbing. Louisa watched the conductor and brakeman jump from the two end cars, and passengers follow one another down the train steps. They huddled loosely on the platform, then drifted apart, disappearing behind the shed and reappearing in the parking space or walking toward the underpass. Louisa scanned the faces of the men who passed below on their way up Station Avenue. The train gave three shrill chirps, hummed nervously, then ground forward. She examined the deserted platform a moment longer. Then she adjusted the shade, glanced mechanically at Christy, and tiptoed out.

The bathroom door was open and the room was empty. She walked down the hallway toward the front stairs, not sure what she would do next. Maybe she should pack her suitcase. It was well past six—too late to telephone Curt at his office. He should have taken the five-thirteen, or at the latest, the five twenty-two.

Probably he had stopped at The Racquet for a drink. He would show up just after she had left, looking sheepish and smelling of peppermint.

"Mrs. Hooper?"

Louisa started as if she had been screamed at, then saw Miss Brunner standing in the doorway of Marlie's room. "You gave me quite a fright," Louisa said, forcing herself to smile.

"Excuse me, it was not my intention." Miss Brunner's fluid voice seemed unsuited to the stilted English she spoke. Louisa noticed that she had already changed into her street clothes. She waited for the governess to speak, but the German girl remained silent, impertinently courteous.

"What is it, Miss Brunner?"

"I wish to know, iss Marlie to stay up until her fadder comes home? I wout not ask this if Marlie has not chust now wished me to fint out." Louisa felt a sudden desire to slap the German woman's face. "She likes so much her fadder shout hear her prayers," Miss Brunner added, as if she knew more about Marlie's likes and dislikes than Louisa did—as if she had to plead for the girl.

Louisa started down the front stairs without answering. "You may go out now if you want to," she said when she had reached the landing. "I'll see that the older children get to bed."

"Chust as you wish." Louisa did not look around, but she could hear the governess climbing the stairs to her room on the third floor.

THE FRENCH DOORS between the front hall and the dining room had been closed. Through the curtained glass Louisa made out the thin shadow of Bridgit moving about, resetting the table. Marlie and Peter were out in the yard somewhere. Their laughter, soprano and clear, seemed to float on the September evening, rising weightless, higher and higher, then ceasing abruptly—caught, like a balloon in a tree. Louisa pushed open the screen door and called, "Marlie!" There was no answer.

"*Marlie!*" she called again, with an impatience that surprised her. Hearing a stifled giggling close by, she stepped out onto the terrace, her hand still grasping the knob of the screen. "It's bedtime," she said. "I'm not going to look for you." There was a rustle in the evergreens that grew against the fieldstone wall of the house, behind the tulip bed. Louisa closed the screen behind her and waited. "All right," she said at last. "I'll count to five. One, two—"

"No!" The girl had climbed from her hiding place onto the terrace step and was glaring at her mother, small and indignant. "That's not fair. You're supposed to count to *ten!*"

"I'm in no mood for games, Marlie. Come inside."

"Maddy said I could stay up until Daddy gets home."

"Her name is Miss Brunner—and *I* say you're to come to bed this instant! Please," she added gently, watching the child back away. "Please, dear, don't make me angry."

"Maddy said—"

"Marlie."

"No! I will not!" The girl turned and ran toward the kitchen courtyard. "I will not, not, not, not, not," she sang. The kitchen screen door slammed.

"Peter."

The boy had ambled to the twin maples in the center of the yard and, leaning against them, was whittling. Now he looked up at his mother gravely.

"Come in in fifteen minutes," she said.

"Sure, Ma." He snapped his Scout knife shut and nodded toward the kitchen. "Want me to catch her?"

"Catch yourself. In fifteen minutes."

She went into the house. Marlie was hurrying up the back stairs, tiptoeing, and so confident that she would not be heard. In a moment, the bathroom door closed quietly, then Marlie's bedroom door. Oh, God, Louisa thought, feeling Bridgit's message in her hand. Why did Curt have to pick tonight? She crossed the hall and, lifting the telephone, sat down.

Jim Hallowell answered, his buzz-saw voice droning "Weezie,

old dear"—so hulking and powerful a man that she could hear the push of unused breath between his chopped-off phrases. Louisa, listening to the vibrations rather than the words, imagined drops of perspiration trickling down his cheeks, somehow finding their way between the bulging folds of flesh on his neck and his wilted shirt collar.

"Are you standing up?" she interrupted.

"Hell kind of a question is that?"

"Sit down. You sound as if the heat's got you."

"Always got me."

She laughed. Then she did what she hadn't meant to do, what she had been concentrating on not doing. She said, "Will you be home tonight if I need you?"

"Now, Weezie, you know the routine. If I'm out, Dora will know how to get in touch with me."

"Did I get you up from the table?"

"Yes."

"How *is* Dora?"

"Dora's perfectly fine. What's got into you, Weezie? Curt not home yet?"

She shook her head at no one, then lied, "I think I hear his train now."

"There's no train for twenty minutes. Did he phone you he'd be this late?"

"Not exactly."

"When was his last bout—two, three months ago?"

"Less than that. You should know."

"Look, are you getting anything regular? Any pattern?"

"No. But I never do. You should know *that*, too."

"Tell you what. Pack your bag. I'll stop by after my rounds unless you call me first. Happy?"

"Unbelievably."

"Smile."

"Yes, Doctor."

"That's the girl. Goodbye." He added, "Brat," and hung up.

Marlie, in her blue cotton nightgown, was leaning over the banister. "Aren't you mad at me?" she called.

"Aren't I what, dear?"

"*Mad* at me."

"No, dear, I'm not mad at you."

"Oh." The girl sounded disappointed. "Can I stay up?"

"For a few minutes. In your room."

"No, in the playroom."

"All right, in the playroom."

"Till Daddy gets home?"

"We'll see."

"Till the next train?"

"All right, dear."

"Who was that you were talking to? Dr. Hallowell?"

"Please, Marlie, either go to your room or go up to the playroom, but do *not* stand in the hallway shouting questions down at me."

"I only wanted to know who you were talking to. I don't see what's so wrong with that." Her face drew back, but reappeared a moment later, over the third-floor stairway. "You always tell Peter!"

"What do you always tell me?" Peter asked, coming up behind her.

"Must you let that screen door slam?"

"Sorry, Ma. I really forgot." Standing on the stairs, he leaned over and kissed the top of her head. "I'll run the trains," he said. "That should shut her up." He started climbing the stairs two at a time, then stopped, called "Sorry" again, and walked up quietly.

Louisa watched him, disgusted with herself. She could still feel the place where his kiss had touched her hair. Eight years old, she thought. Only eight years ago—or was it eight seconds—he was inside me, hurting like this new one. Six years ago Marlie, two years ago Chris, thirty-three years ago I inside mine, thirty-five Curt inside his. Bridgit. Bridgit, with her lost message, could be either thirty-four or twenty-four, but Annie is forty-five flat, and that other one—who will have to leave soon or I'll lose my mind (maybe the day I get back from the hospital I'll fire her, because Curt will never do it, any more than he knows how to discipline the children, or himself for that matter)—thirty. I have to get up. Louisa, get up and pack.

SHE HADN'T FINISHED PACKING—hadn't begun, really, though her suitcase was open on the bed, and clothes (the entire contents of her closet) were piled, draped, hung about the room—when she saw Curt arrive. In the three-quarters of an hour since she had come upstairs, she had dusted and then scrubbed the bedroom closet—insanely, she had known, even while indulging her compulsion to complete the job before leaving for the hospital. She was waiting for the closet to dry, standing in front of the window arranging her shoes on the sill, when she spotted the taxi coasting down Station Avenue. At first she thought it was on its way to meet a train from the city, for it passed the house and went on to the station, but it circled the station parking lot and returned, coming to a silent stop in front of the house. It was a city cab, she saw.

As soon as Curt got out, maneuvering himself backward, then standing there, rocking a little as he searched his pockets for his wallet, she knew he was beyond the sheepish stage. Instinctively she listened for Peter and Marlie. They seemed not to have heard; their voices still rose and fell behind the clickety monotone of the electric train. But as she watched Curt, she heard the playroom door suddenly open and Peter, calling "I'll get some," run down the stairs, past her bedroom, along the hallway, and down the back stairs. Curtis was still searching for his wallet, diving his hands into the side pockets of his gabardine suit, when Louisa left the room.

She found Peter on the pantry floor, peering under the sink. He looked over his shoulder at her. "I lost a cork," he said. "We're using corks, Ma. For freight."

"Daddy's home," she said, hearing herself say it, watching the boy react to the taut way she couldn't stop herself from saying it.

Peter was on his feet at once, standing, she imagined, at inward attention, almost comically awaiting her command.

"The only thing I'd like you to do is keep Marlie in the playroom." The boy nodded. "Just keep her there."

Right after Peter had started up the back stairs, she heard the screen door slam and the hall closet opened and shut as Curt, humming tunelessly to himself, put his hat away. He walked into the living room and stood still.

"Wee-za!" he called thickly, in a voice that might have been either annoyed or anxious. She was about to go to him—had meant to go immediately—but when he called her name again, impatiently this time, crossing the living room and pulling himself up the stairs, she felt suddenly tired. She leaned against the pantry sink and listened, wondering how long it would take him to find her, and thinking, What a time to play games, what a foolish age for hide-and-seek.

He was coming back down the stairs now, stepping carefully, as if he were leaning on the banister. In the middle of the dining room he paused, seeming uncertain as to where she might be; then he took several more steps and pushed through the pantry door. He lurched slightly as it gave way before his weight. When it swung back toward him, he held on to it, smiling at her.

It was an absurdly grave smile—a smile of sympathy, of quiet understanding, almost of forgiveness. His wavy light-brown hair, finespun as a child's, looked as if it had just been brushed and combed for a party. Louisa looked at his thin, clean-shaven face —at the small eczema rash on his right cheek and the deep creases slicing down both cheeks—and she wanted to cradle his head in her arms.

He lifted his hand in an apologetic gesture and touched the rash with the tip of his forefinger. When he spoke, it was with infinite compassion. "Mussen," he said quietly, shaking his head. "Mussen do it."

"Do what, Curt?"

"Mussen do it."

"Curt, I don't know what you're talking about."

"Don'," he begged softly. "Please don', Weeza. Mussen do it."

He let go of the pantry door and started toward her, with that expression, like a monk about to bless a pilgrim, still on his face. He wasn't talking now but concentrating on managing the few steps across the narrow pantry. Louisa watched him but did not move. Then he was so close to her that she had to tip her head back to look up at him as he raised his hands and placed them on her shoulders. He stood there a moment, supporting himself, and through her thin summer dress she could feel that the palms of his hands were damp. Suddenly he began to shake her—feebly at first, then quite hard.

"*Curtis,* stop that! Stop doing that!" She reached up and pulled at his wrists until his hands fell limply from her shoulders.

He didn't look at her. He was half leaning against her, swaying. She could feel and smell his breathing. The smile of forgiveness had set itself on his lips. "Please don' leave me," he said, blinking as if something had got in his eye. Abruptly he swung himself around, grabbed the edge of the sink, and made his way out the pantry, then across the dining room and up the front stairs.

Standing at the foot of the stairs, Louisa could hear him in the bedroom, lunging from side to side, banging into things. Then, as she knew it would, the house grew quiet.

She waited a few moments and went up. She found him sprawled face down on the chaise longue, clutching her red evening dress grotesquely in his right hand. The rest of her clothes —those that hadn't slipped from his grasp—he had simply picked up and dumped back into the open closet. He had tried to hide her suitcase; when she saw one of its leather straps sticking out from under the bed, she sat down, and in spite of the pains, she laughed—silently, helplessly, until tears ran down her cheeks.

Finally she went over to him. Kneeling on the rug, she loosened his necktie and took off his shoes. Then she kissed him on the head, as Peter had kissed her, and left. As she closed the bedroom door, for the first time she heard Marlie upstairs, screaming and pounding on the door of the playroom.

"It's okay," Peter said. He was sitting on the staircase landing, guardian of the tower. "I locked her in. She can't get out."

"I'd better let her out now," Louisa said. "She doesn't understand."

"Sure." He handed her the key, then started down. "Think I'll open you a can of soup," he called from the second-floor hallway. "Jellied soup, Ma. That's what you need."

ALONG THE FAR WALL of the playroom, between wooden horses, four planks had been set up as a table for Peter's electric trains. Marlie was slumped at the foot of this table, not crying now but sniffling, her head lowered, the fingers of her right hand twisting a curl. When she saw her mother, she wriggled partway under the table and began whimpering between sniffles.

Louisa walked over to the table, bent awkwardly, and held out her arms. "Come here, darling," she said quietly. "Please." Marlie lowered her head, trying to hide her face. She said something.

"I can't hear you, darling. Come to Ma and we'll talk it over. Please come to Ma."

Marlie shook her head and wriggled all the way under the table. Louisa didn't know what to say. She stood there. After a while Marlie looked up, blinking.

"You *told* him to," she said.

"Told who, Marlie? What?"

"You told him to lock me in!"

"Daddy's sick, dear. He's asleep. I thought Peter would stay and play with you while I put Daddy to bed. I'm sorry he left you, darling. Please come out, you'll get your nightgown dirty."

"It's dirty already."

"Please, Marlie. It's long past bedtime."

"I'm coming out, but not because you want me to. You needn't hear my prayers, either. I can say them better without you."

"All right, dear."

"Leave the room first. I won't come out until you've left the room."

Halfway down the stairs, Louisa became aware of the pains again. She felt a lightheaded sluggishness, as if she had to hurry yet couldn't make herself. When she got to the kitchen, Peter had set the table there for her and put some jellied madrilène in a bowl. She remembered that Bridgit had set the dining-room table and that Annie had left supper in the oven, but she didn't have the heart to tell him.

"I got some eggs out," he was saying, "but you better cook them. I'm not much on cooking eggs. I've never done it. Here's the butter. Eat your soup first, though, before it melts. Would you like some saltines? There are saltines."

She shook her head. They sat down, she before the bowl of madrilène and he at the opposite side of the kitchen table, in Annie's green rocker.

"Cool you off?"

She nodded, smiling.

"Shall I see Marlie gets to bed?"

"She's already going. You should go, too."

"That clock's wrong. Fast."

She made herself eat the soup while he nibbled absently on a saltine, watching her.

"This is fun," he said. "Just you and me. I'm glad it's Thursday. Sure you don't want a saltine? Here." He pushed one across the green oilcloth, then watched her take and eat it. There was no sound but of their eating and the quiet ticking of the alarm clock on the sill above the sink.

"How about if I sleep on the sofa in the living room," Peter said casually.

"Why?"

"So you can sleep in my room." She looked at him, puzzled. "*You* sleep in my room and *I'll* sleep on the sofa. Don't you see?" he said.

"Peter—" she began, not sure how she would finish it, how it could be said at all, except directly. "Peter, you're not going to understand this, but I want you always to remember it, no matter how—how bad Daddy gets at times, or how discouraged I may seem to you. I want you to remember that I love him. And he loves me."

Peter blushed, seeming on the verge of either laughter or tears. "How about your eggs?" he said, talking louder than he had to. "Don't you want your eggs after I got the butter out and everything?"

"I'm not very hungry," Louisa said.

"Shall I clean up? Here, I'll rinse your soup bowl."

"No, darling, thank you. You go ahead upstairs. I'll do it."

Gripping the edge of the table, she watched the second hand on the clock above the sink. She waited, counting the interval between the pains, until she heard Peter reach the third floor, and then went to the telephone in the pantry and called. She heard the Hallowells' phone ringing and at the same time Marlie, from the head of the back stairs, shouting "Ma!" She concentrated as hard as she could on the ringing sound, wondering if it would ever stop. Then at last she heard it—Jim Hallowell's voice.

"Ma!" Marlie shouted again.

"Hello, Jim—Louisa. Thank God I caught you," she said into the telephone. "Hold on a second, would you?" Capping the mouthpiece with her hand, she called, "Marlie, I'm on the telephone."

"But I forgot to tell you my *seek*-ret!"

"I know, dear," she answered automatically. "I'll be right up."

"Are you ready to go?" Jim asked when she had returned to the phone.

"I will be by the time you get here."

"Nine minutes," he said and, without waiting for her to reply, hung up.

"WELL, DEAR?" Louisa stood beside Marlie's bed, thinking, Eight minutes left. "I'd love to hear your secret, but you'll have to hurry."

"Bend down," Marlie said. "I have to whisper."

"I have a better idea—you stand up."

Marlie scrambled out from under the top sheet and stood. Taking her mother's head, pressing her mouth so firmly against Louisa's ear that she could feel the child's lips move, Marlie whispered, "Maddy and I *both* love Daddy!"

"Why, that's wonderful, dear," Louisa said. "But it's not a secret, exactly, is it? Everybody in this house—"

"It is too a secret! She loves Daddy, but she isn't sure whether he loves her. Maddy said so!"

"Of course Miss Brunner did, and I see what you mean—it's a lovely secret. Now I'm going to tell you one. In a few minutes Dr. Hallowell is going to come and drive me to the hospital. And tomorrow we'll have a new baby in our family."

"I know." Marlie dropped to her knees, making the bedsprings jounce. She frowned at her mother. "Will it be a girl?"

"That's God's secret."

"But you already have two boys! Why do you always pray for boys?"

"I don't pray for boys, dear—"

"You must, or else why would God keep giving them to you?"

Louisa shook her head, feeling the perspiration on her brow and upper lip, trying to stop herself from breathing so audibly. "Well, this time you and I will both pray for a baby girl, to even things up," she said quickly. "Now give me a hug. I have to hurry and pack before Dr. Hallowell gets here."

After leaving Marlie's room, Louisa found herself unable to remember exactly how the child had phrased it about Miss Brunner—unable to think of anything but Jim's arrival: willing the metallic slam of his car door, then praying for it out loud, muttering "Please slam—please, God, please slam!" When she finally saw his gray sedan arrive—saw, through the screen door, how he jumped out of the front seat and hurried down the walk, leaving his car door open instead of slamming it—she laughed, or tried to, though it came out a groan.

"Why the raincoat?" he asked, picking up her suitcase. But she didn't know, couldn't think of the answer until halfway down the walk, his arm supporting her (or was he carrying her bodily?), when she remembered about the towel: that she had put on Curt's raincoat to hide the bulge of the towel.

"Plenty of time," he said gently, as if she'd asked a question. "No need to worry about a thing. That's my girl—in you go. Whole back seat is yours."

As he slid into the front seat and slammed his door, Louisa, taking a last look at the fieldstone façade of her house, saw a figure leaning intently out of one of the dormer windows. What a pretty young woman, she thought; then, with a shock of helplessness and despair, she realized that Miss Brunner—bathed, dressed, ready, two hours before, to take her evening off—had never left the house.

She began to weep uncontrollably between contractions—the fat, childlike tears mixing with the drops of perspiration. "Be there in a jiffy," Jim wheezed, raising his head and talking into the rear-view mirror. "Everything's arranged."

Hearing him say that, Louisa burst out laughing. She tried to stop herself—longed for the next contraction to grip and strangle the ridiculous sounds that kept coming from her throat.

"Hell's the big joke?" Jim was asking.

"Miss Brunner!" Louisa gasped.

"What's she done now?"

"That's just it—I'm not *sure,* I . . ." But he never gave her a chance to explain.

The car door slammed.

"Easy, dearie—wheelchair's right over here."

"Where's the telephone!" Louisa cried, no longer even trying to hide the panic in her voice—for the face hovering over her was a woman's, leering under what appeared to be a governess's cap.

"Doctor's going to meet us in Delivery," it said, as if Louisa were a frightened little girl. "Easy, now, *easy*—there's a love . . ."

CHRIS' LOG
1928-1942

CHRIS' LOG
1928-1942

One

WHENEVER I THINK about my father I begin with Juan-les-Pins—then comes the circus of M. Debreaux—then Paris; like having to say the Lord's Prayer from the beginning or else you lose your way. My parents had separated in the fall of 1928: that is, Mother had taken all four children to France and left my father home in Philadelphia, to see whether he could give up drinking. Peter went to a boarding school in Switzerland and Marlie to a kind of Episcopalian convent, I guess you'd call it, in Paris, while Johnny and I lived with Mother in Juan-les-Pins. My father came over that June, and we all sailed home together in August.

I was seven when we first went to France, and a lot of what happened there is pretty vague in my mind. I remember a few things—unrelated, most of them, pleasant and faded, like decalcomanias on a nursery wall. My father used to take Johnny and me on snail hunts in the fields back of Juan-les-Pins. Sometimes we'd find miniature artichokes. The main street of the village was lined with eucalyptus trees, and he said they smelled like Smith Brothers cough drops. Our weekly allowance was ten centimes, but he always gave us a little more to buy licorice shoelaces from the old lady with the mustache who sold candy on the way to the beach, because her son had been bayoneted by a Hun.

Every sunny morning the same people would show up at the beach: English and American governesses, mostly, with the children in their charge. Also a few retired French couples who seldom spoke and never went in swimming; a half-dozen resort-hotel chambermaids on their day off; and a larger, much louder group—perhaps fifteen factory workers and their wives, on vacation, who splashed and ducked and shouted strange phrases over their shoulders as they pranced headlong into the surf.

Promptly at eleven the prince would arrive at our beach umbrella, and Jeanne, our nurse, would buy Johnny and me home-baked tarts. He carried them on an enormous but very light round wicker tray: strawberry tarts, with a few cherry and blueberry ones. He was a White Russian and had great style, as though he really was a prince (which he may well have been) imitating servants who had once served him. He handed you your tart with a swirling motion, and you paid him by placing the money on a saucer at the edge of his tray. When he walked to the next umbrella—a large, composed young man wearing a rumpled blue serge suit and expensive black shoes—he moved almost dreamily, like a bishop blessing those who had been fortunate enough to gather along the Mediterranean that fine July morning.

Around noon the sand artist would ring his bell and everyone would go to look at the day's picture—we children running along the water's edge where the sand was hard-packed and the color of Wheatena; our nurses well behind, tediously slogging down the beach as though they were wearing ski boots. The sand artist worked in the shade of a clump of stunted pines, and each picture (a volcano spewing fire on a village, or maybe an expanse of wavy water dotted with sailboats) was as large as a living-room rug. After we'd looked and commented and looked some more, he would collect our coins in a Legionnaire's cap, shoving it aggressively at each adult and thanking each with a quick twist of a smile.

My LAST DISTINCT MEMORY of Juan-les-Pins begins on a Sunday afternoon, some two weeks before we left for Paris, where we would join Peter and Marlie and all sail home. I know it was a Sunday because that was allowance day, and I told my father I had saved up four francs, twelve centimes. My father and I must have been alone. He was a soft-spoken man with a thin face and mild gray eyes. He hardly ever laughed out loud, but he smiled easily, and he had a light strawberry rash, like a small birthmark the shape of Italy, on his left cheek.

"Well, Chris," he said, "since you seem to be the banker in the family, how about opening a foreign department?" I looked puzzled and he said, "Come on upstairs." After rummaging around in his top bureau drawer, he brought it out and handed it to me: a small metal box with orange felt material covering the bottom, and a rounded bronze lid decorated with running ostriches. "It's a toy tinderbox," he said. "Open it."

Inside was a pile of foreign coins he said he had collected after the war, when he was an officer courier with the Hoover Food Commission. He showed me how to tell which were Austrian and which Dutch, which Belgian and which German. The Swiss and Italian ones were easy to recognize. The hardest came from several Balkan states he said didn't exist any more. I spread them all out on his bed, and for the next hour or more played with them —putting them in little piles according to color, feeling their metal faces, even smelling them to see whether I could detect any difference between the silver and the brown ones. Every night before going to bed I would pick out a few coins at random and try to guess, without looking, what country they came from and whether they had a round hole, a square, a triangle, or no hole. When I got to know every coin just from the size and weight of it, I felt wealthy. It was something I had—a possession and an accomplishment—that no one could take from me.

One night I boasted about this to Johnny, and he threatened to take them. Johnny didn't do too well in school—until my father arrived, we had gone to an English grade school on the outskirts of Juan-les-Pins where we fed the chickens or played rugby at recess—but he was really smart at getting secret things if he suspected they had any special value.

To make sure he wouldn't get my tinderbox, I took it down to the beach the next morning and hid it under the sand a short distance from our beach umbrella. I felt good about my hiding place, and became especially friendly to Johnny as we watched the sand artist and talked in French to the Russian prince. After that, John and I wandered out the old stone breakwater and pretended we were pirates, that we had sailed over from North Africa and were the first white men to land on this rocky coast of France.

Toward lunchtime Jeanne came after us, distinctly annoyed that we hadn't told her where we were going. In her nervous, irrefutable fashion, she bustled us home, gargling angry French dialect the entire way.

It wasn't until late afternoon that I remembered about the tinderbox. Of course I never found it. I cried myself to sleep that night and went down every day I could to hunt for it, but Jeanne told me I was a silly little boy when I pestered her to remember exactly where she had placed the beach umbrella that morning. I asked my father if it was possible for a box buried in the sand to sink down and down and eventually wash out to sea, and he said yes, he thought so. For months afterwards, I had a recurrent dream: that I came upon a secret cave in an island far out in the Mediterranean, that I discovered there the tinderbox—only it had grown to full size and contained gold and rare jewels—and that I was the richest man in the world.

I KNOW WE WERE in the South of France for Bastille Day, because there was a fireworks display at Cannes; but soon afterwards we set out by rented touring car and chauffeur for our final weeks in

Paris. I remember stopping, that first day on the road, for a picnic lunch near a lemon grove. I expected the fruit to be yellow, but it was green and *smelled* yellow. When we got back to the car —an enormous, rectangular black box, with railings on its roof such as one sees nowadays on cabin cruisers, and a metal chest nearly as large as a steamer trunk attached to its rear end—a hissing, accompanied by a settling to the right, made it obvious that we had, as the French say, burst a tire. Georges, our chauffeur —a tall, silent, thickly built man who always looked both harried and self-righteous—heaved himself out of the car and lumbered around to see what he could do. This turned out to be not much, for it developed that the Antibes auto-hire company that had so proudly provided us with car and bonded, liveried chauffeur had failed to include a jack.

Mother wanted my father to "get to" a telephone (she didn't say how) and demand that the auto-hire company send another car; but the idea that, to everyone's surprise and admiration, Johnny came up with seemed more practical; this was that some-one should unstrap his bicycle from the roof rack, ride it to the next town, and borrow a jack. My own bike was safely in the cellar back home, but there had, for the previous several weeks, been discussion as to whether John's bicycle—his first, and much too big for him—should be taken along or left behind when we sailed, and I could see that he hoped its usefulness in this emergency might gain it the status of an invaluable family possession. Cer-tainly we all felt, as we watched Georges pump the valiant little thing up and over the next hill toward our presumed salvation, that a bicycle is a remarkable invention.

However, Mother felt this truth progressively less during the hour and three-quarters it took Georges to return. The next town, according to our road map, was exactly ten kilometers away— about six miles. "I knew you should have gone yourself," she said to my father accusingly. They didn't fight much in front of us, but when they did it was over the most trivial things.

"Too bad you didn't say so earlier," he replied.

"I *knew* it earlier, and so should you have," she said. "He's probably sitting in a café right this minute, buying wine with the extra money he plans to charge us for having to take a little exercise."

I half expected her, when Georges returned—still silent, still harried and self-righteous—to go up to him and sniff his breath. But the jack was in the handlebar basket, and perhaps she felt that for the moment nothing else mattered.

Between them, Georges and my father had us moving within twenty minutes, but it was already getting toward sundown. We had an objective much farther along the way to Paris, but now there was nothing for it but to spend the night in the town that had vouchsafed us the jack. As we sat parked there, waiting while Georges returned the jack to its owner, Johnny and I saw a wagon with a cracked canvas sign dangling from its tailgate, which read LE CIRQUE DE M. PAUL DEBREAUX.

THE QUALITY OF THE TOWN, the look and feel of the hotel where we took rooms that night, the business of registering, unpacking, eating supper—all these details have left me, along with the town's name. In my mind's eye I picture our hotel and the *mairie* as facing each other across a square, with a fountain in its center and streets leading off from its corners—narrow streets, with narrow shops on the ground level and balconies above them—but this may be a recollection of any number of small towns we stopped in during our nine months, or a simplified composite of them all. The only building I specifically remember is a high-windowed red-brick grammar school, just off the square; for it was next to this, in a gravel playground, that M. Debreaux was destined to perform.

I use the word "destined" because, from the beginning of the performance to just before the end, when we couldn't bear to watch him any longer, there was about M. Debreaux a trancelike quality, as if he were acting not from his own free will but under the spell of some lifelong hypnosis. When Johnny and I arrived at the playground (it was dusk, and yet our parents allowed us to go by ourselves, which makes me think the school must have been visible from our hotel), the audience consisted entirely of children. M. Debreaux, standing a dozen feet from his wagon and speaking in an old man's monotone just too loud for ordinary conversation, had already begun reciting the long list of his past achievements. He had been a featured vaudeville performer in Paris in 1905, 1906, 1907, 1908, and 1909. In 1903, he'd had the inestimable honor of being summoned to the court of the King of Spain for a performance on the occasion of . . . He had played before the noble guests at the wedding of the Princess of Saxe-Coburg-Gotha, in the year of Our Lord . . . In 1913, the mayor of Lyon had awarded him a medal. He had entertained a convention of international business leaders at The Hague, celebrating the twentieth anniversary of . . .

It was hard to concentrate on what he was saying, for he droned and his gaze was fixed a foot or so above our heads, as if he were addressing an audience of adults standing immediately behind us. He was a small man—no taller than some of the children who stood listening, restlessly but politely, just outside the feeble circle of light made by the acetylene lantern that hung sputtering from a pole on his wagon. His head was completely bald, and his shoulders, under a gray sweatshirt, sloped down from his short neck the way a gorilla's do. He had a paunch—not a large one, but you could guess that he was ashamed of it by the awkward way he kept clasping his hands in front of him, as if he wanted to hide it. His legs, covered by gray gym trousers tied at the ankles, were bowed, and he stood with his feet, shod in sneakers, planted far apart, in the stance of a Japanese wrestler. The very inexpressiveness of his face—or, rather, the fact that what expression it had was derived from creases and wrinkles and bone structure, and not from any play of feeling—gave him an ascetic quality that contrasted with his routine boasting.

Toward the end of his speech, two or three clusters of adults

—men of the town, all carrying musical instruments—paused beyond the half circle of children to listen, and though M. Debreaux neither turned toward them nor altered the look on his face, he at once repeated the list of some of his earlier achievements: *"Mille neuf cent six, mille neuf cent sept, mille neuf cent huit, mille neuf cent neuf,"* he intoned. But the men soon left and went into the school building, and when, after a minute, lights went on inside and the first tentative brassy sounds of a band tuning up came through the open windows, M. Debreaux finished his oration as if he had planned all along to end it there—as if these random notes had always been his cue.

He bowed briefly, acknowledging imaginary applause, then waddled back to his wagon and returned with his arms full of wooden milk bottles of the sort one tries to knock down for prizes at country fairs. Sleepily, he began juggling three of these. He made no attempt to impress us with his speed; on the contrary, he never varied his slow pace, but with inexorable regularity added one bottle after another until there was a great arch of spinning wood over him and it seemed that if he added one more bottle they must all knock against one another in midair. And as a matter of fact, when the last one was tossed, they did just that; with a single loud report, they banged together, and M. Debreaux gathered the lot of them into his arms as they fell, with the air of a bored cardsharp executing a fancy shuffle.

He bowed again—this time to real, if childish, handclapping and soprano shouts of approval. He kept his head lowered for a long time after the applause had ended—so long that it occurred to me he must be expecting coins to be tossed at his feet. I had none, and neither had Johnny. Finally one boy, better dressed than most of the others, walked over and dropped a ten-centime piece directly on the spot where M. Debreaux's eyes seemed to be fastened. As if a catch in his neck had been released, M. Debreaux snapped his head upright, and then he carried his milk bottles back to the wagon and returned with a unicycle and a small seesaw.

The band was going full tilt now, practicing some march or other, and M. Debreaux rode his unicycle around the seesaw, zigzagging this way and that in the gravel, trying his best to be performing in time with the music. When the music stopped, he pedaled up the seesaw, balanced for a moment at the fulcrum—arms extended, head erect, eyes closed—then, without opening his eyes, jumped to the ground, leaving the unicycle and seesaw as they had been, in perfect balance. The band started up again, and he lifted the unicycle down and repeated the act, this time pedaling with his hands, his legs sticking straight up.

For each of these feats, we children clapped as loudly as we could, and after each M. Debreaux bowed, keeping his head lowered until one of us had dropped some object on the gravel. Apparently there were few coins in the gathering, and one boy offered a slingshot, another a peppermint twist. Each time, M. Debreaux immediately indicated his acceptance by lifting his head and going on with his performance. It didn't seem to matter to him what was offered. He never picked any of the things up, and he never smiled or looked at us. He had not, since his introductory speech, uttered a single word. Presently he went through a tumbling routine—back flips, cartwheels, somersaults in midair—while the band played a maddeningly slow march, in a rhythm he could not possibly follow. At last he stopped and bowed, breathing heavily and blinking from the sweat that now ran down his bald head and collected on his lashes.

I was carrying a souvenir French flag, and I decided to add it to the collection at his feet, though I doubted whether he would perform any more. Now that he had begun to seem wearied, he looked old to me—older than my grandfather—and I thought that he must surely be through for the night. Before I could take him the flag, however, he lifted his head, and with a barely discernible smile on his lips, gazed at the phantom adult audience behind us. He rocked forward onto the balls of his feet and took a deep breath, filling his lungs so that his chunky torso seemed to inflate like a soccer ball, then let the air out slowly and rocked back onto his heels. *"Et maintenant—"* he said, with a ring of real showmanship in his voice. *"Et maintenant!"*

WITH THAT PUZZLING ANNOUNCEMENT, M. Debreaux went back and, this time, all the way into his wagon. I didn't even try to make out what he was doing there, for just then two things happened: my parents appeared—at the end of an after-dinner stroll about the town, I suppose—and the band took a break in its practice session. The lights of the school building dimmed, and the men walked out onto the sidewalk, stretched, glanced up at the sky, lighted their pipes, and looked with amusement at our little group on the gravel lot. Some of the musicians—six or eight —came over and joined us. I noticed, too, that a few other grownups were coming to join the crowd—couples from the hotel, perhaps, or townspeople finished with their supper chores and out to cool off in the evening air. My father asked Johnny and me how the vaudeville was going, and we answered, in whispers, that it was not a vaudeville, it was a one-man circus.

"Whatever he calls it, it's pathetic," Mother said. "At his age!"

The light from the lantern now seemed to have grown twice as bright as it had been, for full dark had fallen, and when M. Debreaux emerged from his wagon, he, too, was transformed. He had taken off his sweatshirt and gym trousers and was wearing a costume that resembled, more than anything else, an old-fashioned bathing suit—the kind with heavy black cotton trunks coming to below the kneecap, and a black-and-white-striped top with sleeves halfway down to the elbow. In the way of many retired athletes, he looked both stiff and supple, both flabby and strong. For a while, he waddled about on the gravel, setting up a pyramid of six tables—not card tables, exactly, but not much larger than that—with three on the bottom, then two, and one on top. Then he went back to his wagon and returned with an ordinary bicycle.

M. Debreaux climbed to the topmost table, pulling the bicycle up after him. I suppose he wasn't more than ten or twelve feet above the ground, but to me it looked like thirty. He stood beside his bicycle for a moment, in profile to the audience and facing the windows of the school, as if he were posing for a statue. Then, casually, he put his left foot on the left pedal, swung his right leg over, and sat down as if to ride. He stayed that way for some seconds, controlling the slight wiggle of the front wheel, establishing his balance. When he'd got the bicycle absolutely still, he lifted his feet gradually from the pedals and placed them, one behind the other, on the frame tube—the bar between saddle and handlebars—in front of him. Then he eased himself forward until he was crouching on this bar, lowering his head as he did so and keeping hold of the handlebars. When his forehead was almost touching the center of the handlebars, he straightened a leg—the left one—backward off the bar, and in a moment, without seeming to give himself any upward thrust at all, lifted both feet straight into the air and hoisted his head and shoulders from the handlebars.

There was a gasp from the crowd, but no one dared to clap. I looked at Johnny. He was staring not at M. Debreaux but at the bicycle, as if he was wondering whether he might not, with a little practice, make his own behave with the same uncanny obedience. Then we both looked at M. Debreaux, for he was lowering his body now, first dropping his torso to the handlebars, then doubling himself into an inverted crouch, then placing his feet in their single file on the bar. This done, he lifted his head and shifted his weight back onto his haunches.

He remained in this upright crouch on the bar for what seemed a long time—I would guess, now, more than a minute—panting, his face flushed. The bicycle's front wheel wiggled once, but he steadied it without even looking down. Gradually his breathing became calmer and his face less red. He raised his right hand from the handlebar and wiped the sweat from his right eye, then put that hand back and wiped the other eye with his left. He did not return his left hand to the handlebar, though; instead, he reached down and gripped the upright between the front wheel and the handlebars. At first, no one seemed to know what he had in mind, but as he began to lower one of his legs from the bar, a murmur rose from the spectators, who now realized with a shock that he was planning to thread himself through the V of the balanced bicycle and come up on the other side.

The crowd was much larger now, for all the members of the band and quite a few passers-by had joined it, but it was so silent you could hear the sputtering of the lantern, the men sucking on their pipes, and the occasional grunts of M. Debreaux. Suddenly, when he had backed and twisted himself halfway through the V, a loud bell began to toll the hour. M. Debreaux froze where he was, his hands gripping the bar and his feet together in the bottom of the V. When the bell had struck eight times and the last vibration had died in the air, he went on, working his way so slowly that he seemed hardly to be moving at all.

The bicycle was no longer upright. As M. Debreaux inched backward through the V, he had to tilt the bicycle farther and farther in the opposite direction to maintain balance. By the time he got his head through, the bicycle was at a crazily precarious angle, but there he was—he was through the V. You could tell from the way the crowd breathed that everyone knew the danger was about over. All he had to do now was right the bicycle as he straightened his body, then swing himself onto the seat.

It was while he was doing this—leveling the bicycle—that he lost control. In my mind's eye, I can still see the look of disbelief that came over his face as he felt the bicycle begin to ease away from him. By bending his knees and letting his arms out full, he held it steady for perhaps five seconds, but he must have realized almost immediately that the angle was too great for him to manage. With consummate skill—indeed, this was as expert, in its way, as anything he had done—he doubled up into a tight crouch and then sprang free of the bicycle, catapulting himself backward.

The crowd watched him do this as intently as if it were an integral part of the performance. It was only when he fell with a thump onto the gravel, and the bicycle and tables came crashing down, that the spectators reacted with the tidal movement that seems to grip all crowds when they see an accident—first the falling back with a terrified gasp, and then the closing in around the victim.

Two of the musicians helped M. Debreaux to his feet, and he stood between them, leaning on their arms, gazing at the circle of gabbling faces about him as if he didn't quite know why everyone was so excited. Then he seemed to understand, for the first time, that he was being supported. He shook himself free of the musicians and muttered something about his bicycle. A man brought it to him, and he examined it thoroughly: the seat, the pedals, the chain, the spokes, the various bars, and particularly the alignment of the front wheel. He stroked the front fender, then set the bicycle down and took his hands away from it. The bicycle stood by itself. Everyone was talking at once, but M. Debreaux appeared not to hear anything. As he walked around the balanced bicycle, examining (it seemed) its very soul, I could see that his right shoulder was badly scraped and torn, and that the gravel had made a bloody shred of the back of his shirt.

"*Eh bien!*" M. Debreaux shouted, cupping his hands about his mouth and addressing the crowd. "*Eh bien, mesdames et messieurs! Nous allons recommencer!*"

With that, he turned, leaving his bicycle still in balance, and began to set up the tables again.

"He can't!" Mother said—first to my father, then, louder, to the people standing close to us. "Stop him!" she said. "Why in heaven's name doesn't somebody *stop* him!" And without waiting for a response, she began elbowing her way through the crowd and presently burst into the circle of light shed by M. Debreaux's lantern.

At first it was impossible, because of the commotion that arose in her wake, to hear what she was saying to him, but her intent was clear enough from her gestures. She kept shaking her head and pointing to his shoulder, talking fast, while he only smiled sadly and waited for her to stop. Finally she did stop, and without even answering her, he went back to setting up his tables. Mother looked helpless for a moment. Then she plunged her hand into her pocketbook and pulled out a hundred-franc note—worth, in those days, about five dollars. She slapped it down on one of the tables and began once more to talk to M. Debreaux, who again interrupted his work to listen courteously to her.

Eventually she paused for breath, and he spoke to her patiently, as if he were explaining something to a slow child. *"Parce que c'est nécessaire, madame,"* he said, *"—eet ees nécessaire."*

Picking up her hundred-franc note, he held it out to her. She shook her head and turned away. He shrugged. *"Merci mille fois, madame,"* he said, and dropped the money onto the gravel, where it lay with the slingshot, the peppermint twist, the ten-centime piece, and the other offerings.

Mother made her way back to us. M. Debreaux quietly went ahead setting up his pyramid of tables. The crowd clapped and cheered him, but Mother could not bear to watch, and looking at his bleeding shoulder, even I was glad when we started back to the hotel. The last I saw of M. Debreaux, he had climbed onto the topmost table and was braced there, reaching down impatiently, while two of the musicians lifted his bicycle up to him.

FOR REASONS I STILL DON'T UNDERSTAND, my parents became much friendlier to each other after seeing M. Debreaux—a friendliness that lasted the whole time we were in Paris. They bought Johnny and me toy sailboats and took us (both of them, together) to the Luxembourg Gardens, where we could play with our boats in the shallow pond or roll our hoops along the paths until time for the Punch and Judy show. They took us to the carnival that was perpetually in session near Napoleon's tomb, and let us ride on the dromedary. Sometimes we went to a children's movie theatre that showed Félix the Cat cartoons, and Charlie Chaplin. The trolley which took us out to Versailles smelled strongly of garlic and hair oil—a combination that grabbed the back of my throat and felt peppery. Just before sailing home, we visited the Tomb of the Unknown Soldier. For years I was convinced that the Juan-les-Pins candy woman's son was buried there—the one who'd been bayoneted by a Hun. I remember my father saying that that tomb was so sacred, even horses wouldn't dare walk on it. He promised someday to show us a spiked helmet he'd captured from a Hun, a German officer, in the winter of 1918.

Coming back on the boat in August, he let me pick a number in the horse race one afternoon; our entry won five dollars and forty-eight cents, American money, which we divided evenly and spent exactly as we chose: I on a real stuffed bird that walked and pecked when you wound it, and he (of course) on a half-bottle of champagne.

Two

HARDLY REMEMBER Peter and Marlie joining us in Paris or returning with us on the boat, but I can never forget the way Marlie acted toward my father after we got back home. The thing that sticks in my mind is that she was always trying to protect him. This may seem odd, considering Marlie was only twelve years old, but in a way being that young helped her. Through our dining-room windows we could see across Glenllyn station yard to the railroad tracks, and every afternoon she watched for his train to arrive out from town. As soon as the grandfather clock in our front hall chimed five-thirty, she'd slip through the French doors into the dining room, climb onto the sill and sit watching, listening, determined to see my father before anyone else did, trembling to dash and open the front door before Mother could get downstairs. She knew that if she were with him Mother couldn't say anything, or at any rate couldn't say everything, no matter how much my father'd had to drink.

Sometimes, as a special treat, she would let me watch with her. I remember one afternoon in particular—early October, it was.

I hurried to get through with supper (Johnny and I ate at five, in the kitchen), and ran to the front hall. Marlie was already there, staring intently up at the clock, her eyes squinting with concentration. She had blond hair, cut short and parted on the right. One lock flopped down onto her forehead. She was forever playing with it, twirling it around her finger and tucking it under a silk bow that covered the left side of her head. I remember the dress she wore; my father had once mentioned, casually, that he liked it, and she changed into it almost every afternoon to meet him. It was of blue velvet, a party dress with puffed sleeves and a lace-trimmed yoke that stuck out beyond her shoulders, making them look absurdly broad.

"We're four and a half minutes early," she said to me. "Oh, well . . ." She took my hand, led me into the dining room and carefully closed the curtained glass doors.

It was a high-ceilinged room, at this hour dimly lighted by silver sconces with half-shades that hung at intervals along the soft-green walls. The table was set for four. Glass and silver gave off a subdued glow, as if waiting for the candles to be lit before coming fully to life. The napkins at the two end places were freshly starched and folded in the shape of a shield; the other two, Marlie's and Peter's, lay stuffed in their dented silver rings.

Marlie tiptoed over to her place, picked up the knife, and showed me its handle. "See that," she whispered. "That's the Hooper crest. That means it's Daddy's. You can always tell." She ran her thumb along its blade, then placed the knife back beside her plate. She beckoned and I followed her to the windowsill. We both climbed up, using the radiator, then sat with our legs dangling and our backs to the heavy off-white folds of the damask curtains.

"I suppose it will be late as usual," she said. "What a nuisance." She began talking in a low, patient voice, going over the rules to make sure I understood the game she played each night with my father. After he got off the train, we would see him cross the station yard, then Station Avenue; then he would come in our walk. He would stop at the terrace steps, take out his keys, and twirl them three times. That was when we were to dash for the door. If we opened it before he could get his key into the lock, we each got a peppermint.

"He has to be on the train," she said, "so don't worry about *that.*" She spoke emphatically, as though she were answering a question. "He promised me he'd telephone if he took a different train. He *promised.*"

I nodded, gazing at the far end of the room and listening as hard as I could for the sound of the train. Along the left-hand wall a folding screen, burnished in gold lacquer, hid the swinging door to the pantry and cast a diagonal shadow in the direction of the mahogany sideboard. The sideboard stood centered against the wall opposite us. It was flanked by two corner cupboards, one dark pine and the other cherry. In the dimness I could just make out the features of my great-grandfather Hooper's portrait, hanging in a carved gilt frame above the sideboard. The frame was oval and his face was almost square. The flesh-colored paint outlining his jaw shimmered, moving forward off the canvas and then receding, moving forward and receding.

"Chris?" I looked around. She was unrolling the curl. It came to the tip of her nose. "The thing to do is close our eyes, then we can hear better. Daddy taught me that trick. Try it, Christy, go on. Are they closed?" She reached out and touched my face, brushing her fingertips lightly over my eyelids. "Now don't worry. There's nothing to worry about because he promised. Here, I'll hold your hand, that'll make you not be worried." I wasn't worried in the least, but I didn't dare tell her that. She found my hand. Hers was warm and slightly damp. It was hard to keep my eyes closed; my lids kept twitching to open. Outside, in the pantry, we could hear Bridgit moving about—shutting the icebox door, turning a spigot on, off again, walking into the kitchen.

I coughed.

"*Shh!*" Marlie pinched my hand. "Hear it, Chris? Hear the train?" I tensed my whole body and stopped breathing, trying to hold back the tickle in my throat. At first I couldn't hear anything. Then my ears caught a faint drone way in the distance. We both squirmed around and knelt on the sill. We lifted the curtains, letting them fall over our backs, and stared fixedly into the hazy, bluish air.

Our yard was a bed of brown- and pumpkin-colored leaves, and maple leaves covered the front and kitchen walks. It was a shallow plot bordered along the avenue by rhododendrons. Between the brick terrace and the rhododendrons were two maple trees: the trunk of one grew almost horizontally and had to be supported by a thick chain fastened to its upright twin. A dogwood tree stood at the head of our front walk, and across the avenue, just inside the barberry hedge enclosing the Glenllyn station yard, were buttonwoods—tall, stout ones paralleling the avenue. We could see through their mottled branches to the gas-lit train platform and, beyond, to the farther slope of the station yard with its shaggy tufts of dead grass and its dried-out forsythia bushes bordering St. Martin's Street. The station itself was partly hidden by the shedlike platform on our side of the tracks. Only its square brick tower was visible: tower, steep slate tower spire, and iron-arrow weather vane.

The drone of the train was getting louder. A car, dark blue with flared fenders, coasted silently past our windows down Station Avenue to the parking lot. Marlie took a handkerchief out of her pocket and wiped the steam off the panes with a circular motion. The damp glass squeaked. She giggled. The drone of the approaching train filled the air; then a wide beam of light splashed along the tracks, making them gleam dully, and the front car of the suburban electric glided past the platform shelter and into sight. Marlie knelt upright and began bouncing up and down. She turned, saw me looking at her, and frowned. I smiled, but she had turned away again and was looking for my father among the passengers piling down the train steps.

"Do you see him?" Her voice sounded loud in the still dining room. The train chirped and moved slowly forward. A line of automobiles, their headlights weak against the dusk and leaf smoke rising from fires along the avenue, followed one another up the hill. I was afraid to say I hadn't seen him. I was about to lie, to say *I think so*, when Marlie drew her breath in sharply.

I saw him. I saw him at the same instant. It couldn't have been anyone else. He was cutting across the station yard: a slight, lively man in a chesterfield coat and bowler hat. His coat was unbuttoned and the bowler was pulled jauntily over his right eyebrow. He walked with a loose, unhurried step, grasping a folded newspaper as if it were the handle of a tennis racket.

When he reached the barberry hedge he picked a place where the bushes had been clipped back. He edged through, lifting his arms and turning sideways, then started across the avenue, beating time against the side of his coat with the newspaper.

"I'll tell you when," Marlie said. "Don't you dare move till I tell you."

At the foot of the terrace steps he clamped the newspaper under his arm, pulled his coat aside and dug into his trouser pocket. He brought out his keys. They were in the palm of his hand. I could see them glint in the porch light. He jiggled them, caught the chain and then let go of it, dropping his keys on the walk. He bent over to look for them, stepping backwards in the bent-over position. He reached down, picked up the keys and stood. He twirled them three times and started up the steps.

"Now!" Marlie gasped the word, squirming out from under the curtains and climbing down off the sill. We both ran to the front door. We could hear him on the other side of the door, whistling under his breath. Marlie put her hand on the knob. When his key clicked, she twisted the knob and yanked.

"We won!" she shouted. "We beat you, Daddy—we beat you and we didn't start until you twirled three times, did we, Chris?"

He was standing on the mat, leaning toward us, swaying slightly, pointing his key at the place where the lock had been. A foolish, half-amused expression came into his eyes. He reached up and scratched the back of his head, tilting his bowler so far forward I thought it would fall off.

"Why," he said in a soft, astonished voice, "this must be where I live." He stepped into the house, closing the door behind him. "And you must be Marlie Hooper—*Miss* Marlie Hooper! How *do* you do?" He took off his bowler, flourished it in the air and made a low, sweeping bow. Marlie giggled and curtsied. My father bowed faster and faster, saying, *"Miss* . . . Marlie . . . Hooper!"

"Oh, Daddy!" she cried. "Stand up straight! You look silly!"

"Silly, Miss Hooper! *Silly!"* He jammed his hat onto his head, gave the rim a flick and turned as if to leave.

"No, Daddy!" Marlie screamed; before he could turn back, she had lunged at him and thrown her arms around his waist, crying "No, no, no, no!" She tugged desperately at his sleeve, then collapsed on the floor making high, broken sounds like a person moaning and shivering at the same time.

My father and I both looked at her. Neither of us moved—we just looked. It only lasted a moment; then he stooped down and lifted her gently from the floor. She flung her arms around his neck, burying her face in his shoulder and sobbing uncontrollably.

"There, dearest." He stroked the back of her head, coaxing her in a monotonous, soothing singsong. "There, there, I was only fooling, sweetness, only fooling, I would never leave *you.* Here—see? Here's your peppermint."

I stood quietly to one side, waiting to find out how my father would handle her this time. He kept coaxing her, trying to get her to look up at him; then the second she did, he popped the peppermint into her mouth. She smiled. All at once she started to laugh. He was tickling her. She squealed and giggled as hard as she had been sobbing before.

"Faker!" He pinched her nose. "Who's your friend?"

"What friend?"

"That fellow standing behind you. The bum with the black mop on his noggin."

"That's *Christy.*"

"By gosh, so it is! I'd better say hello, hadn't I?"

"No!" She threw her arms around his neck and began fake-crying.

"No?" My father tickled some more, making her wriggle and squirm until she couldn't hold on any longer. She fell from his arms and rolled backwards onto the rug. "*Woops*-a-daisy!" He swooped me into the air before she could scramble to her feet. He held me high over his head and brought me down quickly, pretending to almost drop me. I clamped my legs around his waist and we hugged. He gave me a peppermint and another hug. As he pulled me close for a second hug, I smelled the whiskey on his breath.

IT WAS EASY TO TELL when he'd been drinking, because that was when he played the bowing game. It became a kind of ritual—though he never again pretended he was going to leave Marlie. After tickling her and hugging me, he'd go to the foot of the stairs.

"Hey!" he'd call up the stairwell. "Anyone else live here?"

When Johnny showed up, my father might go to the kitchen for cookies and get his fist stuck inside the box, complaining that he couldn't pull it off. He'd walk around the dining-room table as if he were in horrible pain; then, groaning theatrically, he'd promise us the whole box if we could only remove it from his hand. After that, he'd take sugar lumps out of his pocket and toss them in the air for us to catch in our mouths, like puppies.

"Is that you, Curtis?" Sooner or later Mother would call from some far corner of the house: the attic or the sewing room or the linen closet. We'd hear a door slam, then her footsteps coming along the second-floor hallway.

It was the sound of her high heels, sharp and definite as a rebuke, that invariably made my father see himself as a clown. All dignity and purpose then, he would hang his chesterfield coat in the closet under the staircase and solemnly pull the light chain.

"Where's Peter?" he'd ask me, matter-of-factly.

"Playing with his trains, I guess."

"Peter is always playing with his trains," Marlie would say. "He never meets you at the door the way I do, does he, Daddy?" She'd slip her hand into his and stand very still, waiting for Mother to come down the stairs, watching as if she were ready to defend my father against the world.

Three

PETER SEEMED TO BE PART of the world that Marlie felt she had
to defend him against, not so much for what Peter said or did as
for his ability to pretend that my father didn't exist. He was an
awkward, overgrown boy who, as far as I could tell, spent most
of his time either reading or running his electric trains. He seldom
bothered with Johnny or me, and Marlie, because she was a girl,
annoyed him. In a way he pretended the whole family didn't exist;
but he ignored my father differently from the way he ignored the
rest of us—more deliberately. And when he did pay attention,
that was deliberate too. Like the evening my father showed us his
German helmet.

He was putting Johnny and me to bed because it was Thursday,
Sigrid's day off. (Sigrid was the governess after Jeanne, who'd
stayed in France.) With Marlie perched on the arm of his chair,
my father read us a story about a battle between two armies of
lead soldiers. It made me think of Paris and the Tomb of the
Unknown Soldier, then of the German helmet. After he had
finished reading I asked him when we could see it. "Right now!"

he said, slamming the storybook shut. He sent Marlie to the attic
and told her where she could find it, in a square wooden fruit
crate, wrapped in brown paper.

He lifted it out carefully and handed it to me. It was covered in that shiny black patent leather they use for dancing
shoes, and it had visors both back and front, with a rusty
spike jutting out the top. It was the heaviest headpiece I'd
ever held, much heavier than a varsity football helmet. I remember how it pressed my head down when I tried it on—
how the leather mashed against my nose and smelled sweaty.
No wonder they lost the war, I thought. My father said that
he'd captured the helmet from a Hun, but that the Hun was
already dead when he captured it. Maybe he'd killed the Hun.
He couldn't be sure. Nobody could be sure. Ever.

"What's a Hun, anyway?" Johnny asked.

"That's another word for German," my father said. I heard a
slight sound over by the bedroom door, and looking up expecting
to see Mother, saw Peter instead. I guess he'd come down to get
a look at the helmet.

"But is Sigrid a Hun?" I asked. I had asked my father, but I
was looking more or less in Peter's direction.

"You bet!" Peter said, and came into the room.

"She is *not!*" Marlie said. "She isn't, is she, Daddy?" Peter held
his hands out for the helmet, so I gave it to him. He stuck it on,
went over to the mirror on my bureau and posed in front of it,
looking like those pictures of Napoleon where his hand is under
his shirt scratching his stomach and his feet are at right angles,
with the front knee a little bent. Johnny and I burst out laughing,
Peter looked so young and so old at the same time. Also because
he was doing what, for us, would have been unthinkable: making
fun of the war. He made a ghastly fierce face at himself in the
mirror, but Johnny and I were the only ones amused.

"*Is* she, Daddy?" Marlie asked again.

"Sigrid a Hun?" My father blushed, cleared his throat and
shook his head thoughtfully. "No. No, Marlie, she isn't. She's

German, but not all Germans are Huns. Only soldiers can be Huns. German soldiers."

When we'd finished prayers, Johnny and I asked if we could play with the helmet again tomorrow. My father said no, only on Thursdays when Sigrid had her day off, because it might make her sad to see it, especially if she'd lost a father or a brother or an uncle in the war.

SIGRID WAS STRICTER than Jeanne had been—partly, I guess, because she could speak better English and it's easier to be strict when you're sure you're being understood—but I liked her anyway. I liked the way she looked—the way she blushed so easily and had bright golden hair done up in braids coiled on the top of her head like two upside-down Indian baskets. Marlie told me we used to have another German governess, named Maddy, when I was a tiny baby, and her hair was the same color as Sigrid's, only short and curly. On Thursdays, when she was dressing to go into town, Sigrid let Marlie and me watch her take the hairpins out and untwist her braids. Marlie loved this. She would stand close to the governess, murmuring, "It's beautiful, Sigrid—just *beautiful!*" and would ask timidly if she could touch it. Sigrid's loose hair was so full and long that when she moved about the room it swayed lightly from side to side across her buttocks. She slapped her buttocks whenever she couldn't find something or was in a hurry. "So now!" she would say, and give them a sharp slap with the flat of both hands. I asked her why she did this, and she said, "It helps me to think with my head, Chris. In Churmany everyone slaps his buttocks when they wish to think." I liked the way she softened "Churmany," and "buttocks" had a wonderful sound, like a milk horse trotting.

ONE THURSDAY AFTER SUPPER I was coming into the living room just as my father was getting up off the sofa.

Mother stopped knitting and looked up at him. "Curt," she said, "what are you going to do?"

"I think I ought to apologize to the poor girl, Louisa." He smiled—a gentle, tentative smile, as if he were asking permission.

"I don't."

"Oh, yes."

Mother didn't answer. She knitted as fast as her fingers would go. My father left the room. Mother tried to keep knitting, but I could tell she was listening to every step he took. He reached the second floor, walked around the stairwell and started up to the third, where Sigrid was.

Suddenly Marlie turned on Peter. "It's all your fault!" she said.

"This is Thursday," Peter said quietly. "We're allowed to play with it on Thursdays."

"It *is*, Ma—it's all his fault! I warned him in plenty of time she hadn't left yet. He deliberately marched around her, wearing it. Not just *by* her but *around* her, making drumming sounds!"

"Shut up," Peter said. "I mean it, Marlie."

Mother dropped her knitting and covered her face with her hands. She didn't make a sound, but her shoulders were shaking. I felt strangely fascinated, and at the same time weak and numb. She had rich dark-brown hair, parted in the middle and waving on each side, gathered up in a large knot at the back. I couldn't take my eyes off the knot, which bobbed up and down at the nape of her neck as her shoulders shook.

After a minute or so she took her hands from her face, asked Peter for a handkerchief and dried her eyes. "Nobody's to blame," she said, "and Daddy is right to explain it to Sigrid. These things will happen. So let's forget it—let's please, *please,* just forget it!"

IT WAS EXACTLY a week later, when Marlie and I were watching her undo her hair, that I saw the photograph on Sigrid's trunk in front of her art books. Sigrid had a small room that looked even smaller than it was because of the sharp angle of the dormer window opposite the doorway. Her trunk, a compact black metal chest covered on the top and sides with travel stickers, stood directly under the window. On it was a row of foreign art books, neatly arranged between square wooden bookends in which the initials "S.W." had been carved, then painted red. Against the left-hand wall, where the ceiling reached full height, was a cream-colored dresser with glass drawer pulls, and next to that a straight chair with a rush-bottom seat. The chair had to be moved in order to open the closet door. Aside from the white iron-frame bed opposite the dresser, the rag rug and the pink wastebasket at the foot of the bed, there was no other furnishings. Sigrid made her own bed and kept everything meticulously dusted. Not an object was ever out of place. If she sat on her bed, she straightened the tufted spread before leaving. When she had completed the lengthy ritual of combing and braiding her hair, she searched for stray wisps, even kneeling to inspect the rug for them.

She was doing this, with Marlie helping her, when I happened to look over and see the photograph in its silver frame. I walked across the room and looked at it closely. It was of a man sitting on the barrel of a cannon. He was in American uniform—the kind with the turned-up collar and leg bindings —and his left foot rested against the wheel of the cannon. He had no cap on. A strand of wavy light-brown hair had been raised from his forehead, perhaps by a passing breeze, and seemed to be pointing like a direction sign at a fluffy cloud over his right shoulder. The photograph had been tinted here and there. The soldier's eyes were blue dots and his thin, fine face was splotched pink.

Even before I took the picture off the trunk I knew, of course, who it was. I was holding it up to the light from the window when I felt Sigrid standing over me.

"Let go," she said quietly, and lifted the frame out of my hands.

"Daddy doesn't have his rash," I said.

"No." She opened her top dresser drawer, threw the picture inside and slammed the drawer shut. "Now"—she slapped her buttocks—"you must go, Chris." Her face suddenly looked ugly, with a sickly sweet smile twisting her lips. "Or Sigrid will miss her train. Run down to Marlie's room, yes? Maybe when Sigrid comes back from town she brings you a present. Marlie!" She placed a hand on my sister's shoulder. "You stay a moment. Go on, now, Chris—no fussing. Go to Marlie's room—run, or no presents!" She pushed me out into the hall and closed the door behind me.

I had hardly reached the bottom of the third-floor stairs when I heard Marlie running behind me. She rushed into her room, pulled the door shut, then tiptoed across and closed her bathroom door. Without saying a word she crawled under the bed, beckoning me to follow.

"Why're we hiding?"

She didn't answer right away. "Cross your heart and hope to die," she whispered when I was under the bed. "I'm going to tell you a secret. It's the biggest secret I ever told you in your whole life, so cross your heart and hope to die."

I rolled on my side and crossed my heart.

"Now. Remember that picture?"

"In Sigrid's room? The one I just saw?"

"Of *course*, silly."

"How could I forget it in about two minutes?"

"Oh, stop, Christy, and just listen to what I'm telling you. I gave Sigrid that picture. If anyone asks you anything, like Bridgit or anyone, maybe even Mother, you tell them *I* gave her Daddy's picture. Promise?"

"If you say so. Okay."

"What do you promise?"

"What you said. I won't tell anyone about the picture."

"No, that's wrong. If anyone *asks* about it, you say I gave it to Sigrid."

"Okay."

"Cross your heart and hope to die."

"I already did that!"

"Do it again."

"Cross my heart and hope to die."

"All right."

"But why is it a secret?"

"That's all I'm going to tell you. I don't want to talk about it any more."

We crawled out from under the bed.

"Now!" Marlie slapped her flat buttocks. "We're going to play. We're going to stay right here in my room and play until your suppertime."

JOHNNY AND I DIDN'T EVEN KNOW Sigrid had left us until Mother picked us up after Sunday school and we saw this stranger standing next to our car, smiling in a way that managed to be both nervous and arrogant.

She was a dumpy woman with tightly curled reddish-brown hair that looked as if it might uncoil with a faint twang if it hadn't been held so close to her perfectly round head by a hairnet. Over the net, stuck directly on top of her head, was a lacquered, syrup-colored straw hat with a narrow yellow ribbon around it. Her behind stuck not only out but up, and her ankles, below the hem of her flowery green dress, lapped over the edges of her low-heeled walking shoes.

"This, boys, is your new governess—Miss Browning," Mother said when we were so close to the car that it would have been rude if somebody hadn't said something. "Miss Browning—Johnny, my six-year-old. And Chris—eight last month."

"Husky lads," Miss Browning said, giving each of us a birdlike nod.

"Jump in, you two." Mother opened the back door. "Annie has a roast waiting for us in the oven."

"Hop to, John!" Miss Browning chirped, with a flap of her chubby arms. "Into the auto with you, posthaste—*hup!* Christopher—*hup!*" She clapped her hands sharply, at the same time climbing, herself, onto the running board, wrenching herself into a curious half-twist, and hoisting her behind onto the front seat. "All settled?" she asked. "Close the door, then. No slamming, mind—little gentlemen *do* not slam."

"Miss Browning is from England," Mother said. "She hasn't even been in this country a month. Isn't that exciting?"

"You mean she's real English, from *England?*" Johnny asked, probably thinking of the pink country on the map of the world up in our playroom.

Miss Browning bounced forward on her seat, then bounced herself again, this time to a sideways perch, and looked back at Johnny. "English from England, British from Britain," she babbled, "six of one, half-dozen of the other." She bounced once more, landing face-front.

SEVERAL TIMES THAT FALL, after Sigrid left, my father stayed away three or four days in a row. Mother always told us he'd gone to Delaware or Maryland on a business trip, yet every night she and Peter would wait up for him. One night I awoke with a headache. Mother wasn't in her bedroom; half asleep, I groped my way downstairs, clinging to the banister. When my eyes became accustomed to the light, I saw Peter talking in a low voice to Mother. I couldn't hear everything they were saying, but I knew it was about my father. Peter was sitting in the armchair opposite the sofa, leaning forward, his enormous feet spread and pointing out. His elbows were resting on his kneecaps and his cheeks were cradled in the palms of his hands. As soon as he saw me, he straightened up, narrowing his eyes.

"It's Chris," he whispered.

"Chris! What is it, dearest?" Mother got up, and keeping her face averted, hurried out to the pantry to fix me an ice pack. Peter didn't say anything except, impatiently, "Sit down, sit down!" Before going back upstairs I noticed that the clock on the mantle said ten minutes past three.

The day after my father came home, instead of joking or roughhousing with us he'd keep looking for things to do for Mother; he was constantly jumping up to pull out her chair or hold a door open for her. But on his second or third day the whole cycle would begin again: his playing the bowing game when Marlie met him at the door; then, after a couple of weeks, not showing up at all; and finally Mother and Peter talking together, that private way, in the living room.

One morning (in November this was, the week before Thanksgiving), I noticed that Peter was sitting in my father's chair, at the opposite end of the breakfast table from Mother. Mother said grace. Then she told us, with no particular emphasis, that my father had gone to New York. She cleared her throat and said, "Kids, Daddy's in New York."

"On business," Peter added, looking at Marlie, then at Mother, then at us.

"I thought he only went to Wilmington and Baltimore," Johnny said.

"This is a special trip," Mother explained quietly.

Marlie giggled. I looked across the table at her. We all looked. She giggled louder and louder until she was shaking her head, bouncing up and down with tears in her eyes, and still she couldn't stop giggling.

Suddenly she got up and ran through the living room, onto the porch.

Peter wiped his mouth and threw his napkin onto the table. He pushed his chair back.

"Don't!" Mother said. She shook her head slowly. "Finish your cereal."

Four

MARLIE DIDN'T GO TO SCHOOL that morning, and she was in her bedroom when the rest of us got home. Just before supper was announced, Mother asked me to run upstairs and see if she felt like joining us. I had expected her to be in pajamas, but when she unlocked the door I saw that she was completely dressed.

"Everyone thinks you're sick—"

"*Shh!*"

"I was whispering."

"Hurry *up*, Chris!" She pulled me into her room, closed the door and turned the latch. I stepped on something soft. Looking down, I saw it was a sweater; then I noticed the rest of the room. Every bureau drawer was open part or all of the way. The closet was open too, its entrance choked with clothing boxes. Dresses were piled across the foot of her unmade bed. Other dresses, skirts and coats were heaped on the windowsill.

"What the heck have you been doing all day?"

"Oh, Chris!" Marlie burst out laughing. She hugged me, then

ran across the room and threw herself onto the bed. "Come here," she said, pushing some dresses aside and patting her quilt. "Sit here. What did Ma say? Is she upset? I guess she thought I was dying or something."

"She wants to know if you're coming down for supper."

"Oh!" Marlie sat up and glared at the door. "What if I really *was* sick! What if I were dying of some horrible disease—I bet she wouldn't even bother to check on me herself. She'd send someone else up, and they'd find me dead; then she'd have me carried out under a sheet so she wouldn't have to look at me, and the only reason she'd go to my funeral would be because it would look suspicious if she didn't!" Tears began to fill Marlie's eyes at the thought of herself so tragically neglected; then abruptly her mood changed. She jumped from the bed, scooped up an armful of skirts and carried them to her bureau.

"Oh, well," she said, "what do I care? I don't have to stick around *this* house much longer!" She jammed the skirts into her bottom drawer and turned. "Didn't you even hear what I said, goopy? Won't *you*, even, miss me? Oh, Chris!" She burst out laughing. "You don't believe me. Look!" Grabbing my hand, she dragged me over to her closet. She kicked aside the cardboard boxes, reached to the back of the closet and pulled out a suitcase. "See this?" She unsnapped the locks and threw the lid back. I saw that the suitcase had been packed so tightly that the inside straps wouldn't buckle.

"Now do you believe me?" she whispered triumphantly. "This is why I pretended to be sick all day! I had to *pack!*"

"But Ma said—"

"It doesn't matter *what* Ma said"—Marlie put the suitcase back in the closet—"nothing she says matters. The only thing that matters is what *I* say." She went over and sat down on the edge of her bed. "Now listen: Daddy's gone to New York—never mind why; just believe me that it's not on business the way Peter said at breakfast. But I'll tell you a secret if you swear not to tell anyone—not even Johnny. Before he left, Daddy promised he'd come back and get me. I'm not exactly sure when, but as soon as everything's arranged. Like the school I'll be going to, and the house we'll live in, and"—she lay back on her quilt, gazing up at the ceiling—"and so forth."

She closed her eyes and smiled a long, slow smile. "Oh, Chris," she murmured. "I'll learn to cook for him, and sew, and we'll play tennis and—know what?" She began describing the life they would have together: the things they'd do, the places they'd go. I found myself hardly listening to her words at all, catching only the excitement that rose from her inflection like a prayer. "And you know, Chris—you know what he'll say? He'll open the door to our town house, a heavy oak door, all carved, and I'll be standing there all dressed up, and then—"

I began to feel silly, standing at the foot of her bed. Clearing my throat as loudly as I could, I said, "Supper's ready. Are you coming down, or what?"

"Gosh, I almost forgot!" She opened her eyes wide and sat up. "You'd better get out of here while I neaten up!"

"What'll I tell Ma?"

"Say I'm feeling much better, that I'll be down as soon as I've dressed. And, Chris—if you dare to even hint about my leaving, I'll never speak to you again."

"Are you really, I mean *really*, going away?"

"Of course, dopey! Now beat it—I'll tell you more later."

I SENSED SOMETHING CRAZY in the idea of Marlie's going to live with my father in New York, but as her own conviction never seemed to weaken, I began to believe it myself. Each day became the day my father might send for her, or return himself to take her away—to "rescue" her was the way she put it. She became so certain of it that she would sometimes grow sentimental at the thought of leaving the rest of us, of never seeing our yard or our house or her own bedroom again. She would walk about her room, touching the furniture, fingering the curtains, running her palm over the tufted bedspread. She'd get her photograph album and sit in the Windsor rocker, turning the frayed black pages lovingly, smiling at the lopsided, overexposed snapshots of Johnny in his two-piece bathing suit, sticking his tongue out at the camera; Peter standing stiffly on the terrace steps, one clasp of his corduroy knickers dangling; me shinnying up our maple tree.

"What goopy, wonderful brothers," she'd say; then she'd flip the pages over and pull the travel folders, which she had collected while we were abroad, out of the flap on the inside back cover of the album. She'd spread the bright folders across her bed, arranging them fussily: the summer resorts on the top row, the winter resorts on the bottom.

"Let's look for me," she'd say, picking up a summer folder and examining it for pictures of girls her age. Not finding any, she might point to a lady with short blond hair who was playing tennis. "There I am, grown up," she'd say. "And that's Daddy. He's winning, but he's letting me almost keep up with him because I'm a lady."

"It doesn't look much like Daddy."

"You don't understand, Chris—I'm older, and he's younger. We're just about the same age."

"Who says so?"

"*I* say so. It's my game!"

Sometimes it was hard to tell how much of what Marlie said about my father was part of her game, and how much was the truth. She claimed that he wrote to her all the time. I looked through the mail one entire week to see if he'd written to her. She never got any letters from anybody. When I asked her about it, she said he sent the letters in care of her best friend at school, a girl named Trishy Sturgis, because he didn't want Mother to know he was "in contact" with her. Several different times she told me he'd written promising to come for her, but she invariably got a note the day he was supposed to arrive, giving some important-sounding reason (once, I remember, he'd been summoned to the White House to advise President Hoover) why he couldn't make it.

My father never wrote to anyone else in the family. That was why I was so surprised when he actually did come back, and Marlie was the last one to find out about it.

HE CAME BACK TOWARD THE END of our Easter vacation, on a Saturday. John and I had just been to Miss Wood's afternoon dancing class. We were dressed in our blue serge suits, starched white open-collar blouses, short pants and patent leather pumps. Miss Browning called for us at the Glenllyn Cricket Club at four o'clock, and she seemed even jumpier than usual. She kept edging the car over to the English side of the road. Finally she parked for a moment and told us, "Your da is home."

"Our what?"

"Your daddy, your daddy! He's home for a visit. A short one."

When she finally turned down Station Avenue there he was, natural as could be, trimming the dogwood tree at the head of our walk. We opened the car doors before Miss Browning had come to a stop.

"Take it easy, kids," he said when we tried to climb up on him. Stooping down, he kissed each of us with a strange formality. "I'm glad to see you, Johnny," he said. "How are you, Chris, dear?" He smiled weakly for a moment, seeming ill at ease. Then he said "Gosh!" and pulled us both to him, Johnny's head to one shoulder and mine to the other, and rocked us.

"Come into the house," he said, standing up and unrolling his shirt sleeves. "I think Bridgit has tea for us."

He looked exactly as I knew he would. He was wearing the same baggy gray-flannel pants he had always worn on Saturdays, and his shoes were shiny only on the toes, the way they used to be after he took a face towel out of the hamper and rubbed them off and threw it back before Mother could catch him. I wanted to take him aside and ask whether he had come back for Marlie, but I was afraid that if they had arranged a secret meeting place, my suspicions might upset their plans.

He sat forward on the sofa, holding the teacup over his saucer so he wouldn't spill tea on the rug. When he sat back, he picked up the saucer along with the cup and held them both to his mouth and sipped. That was something Miss Browning had taught us never to do. I wondered for a moment if she was going to correct him; then I looked at my father and saw that his hand was shaking so badly he could hardly keep the cup to his lips. It rattled against the saucer as he set it down again. He didn't see me looking at him because he had to concentrate so hard on what he was doing. When he'd sipped enough of the tea so it wouldn't spill, he placed the cup and saucer back on the table with both hands.

It was five-fifteen by the time we had finished tea. When the hall clock chimed the quarter hour, my father stopped in the middle of telling us about a circus clown he'd sat next to on the New York subway and looked questioningly at Miss Browning.

"Mrs. Hooper said she'd be back at about half-past five," Miss Browning said, fidgeting with her handkerchief, pulling it out and tucking it back into the sleeve of her dress. "There's an in-town train in eight minutes."

"Well,"—my father got up—"would you tell Marlie I missed her? Peter, too."

"It does seem a shame. It does seem . . ." Miss Browning fluttered across the rug and gazed vaguely out the living-room windows. My father went to the hall closet. He came out with his chesterfield coat. I felt, for that second while he was fishing for his coat sleeve, that he had never left us—that he was just stepping out for a minute, maybe to get an evening paper at the station. I meant to ask him something important—I was sure there was something terribly important I had to ask him—but before I could remember what it was, he had kissed us and started out the door. We followed him as far as the terrace, and stood watching.

He waved at the head of the walk, and turned and waved once

more before disappearing down the steps to the underpass. I kept my eyes on the far platform, waiting for his bowler hat to appear. I had seen it and was waving with both arms, trying to catch his attention, when I heard Miss Browning gasp "Peter!"

I turned and through the screen door saw Peter walking calmly down the stairs. "Daddy just left!" I cried. "Hurry, before the train comes! Hurry, Peter—he's at the station. *Hurry!*"

Peter looked at me, then looked past me. He had a faint smile on his face. He didn't come out of the house. He stood inside the screen door and watched the train platform. He never took his eyes off the platform until my father's train had come and stopped and started up and disappeared over the trestle bridge. Then he went to the telephone and gave a number.

"Ma?" His voice was quiet, but not a whisper. "All clear. Bye." He walked back upstairs without saying another word.

Marlie didn't come home until the following afternoon. She had spent the weekend at Trishy's house. When she heard that she had missed my father, I thought she was going to commit suicide. She stayed in her room for two days without eating. Mother did everything she could to coax her to be reasonable, but Marlie was convinced Mother had given orders that she wasn't to be told about my father. She refused to believe that Peter was the one who'd been supposed to let her know. Even when Miss Browning swore on a Bible that she'd heard Mother telling Peter to give her the message, Marlie refused to believe it.

"Why did you do it, Peter?" Mother asked. "Oh Peter, Peter —*why* did you do it?"

"I forgot," Peter said.

The day before Easter vacation ended, Marlie went outside and rubbed her face and her neck and her arms and legs with poison ivy. She had to stay out of school for three weeks with bandages on, before it cleared up.

Five

I NEVER ASKED MOTHER whether my father might visit us again, and she never brought the subject up. Nobody did. Marlie's suitcase was no longer packed, hidden away at the back of her closet. She didn't tell me it wasn't. I saw it one day, by the attic door, and when I lifted it it felt empty. She never spoke of getting letters from him either. Every now and then, toward early evening, I'd see her slip through the dining-room doors, and I knew she'd be sitting on the windowsill listening for trains—no longer in hopes that my father might be on one of them, but just to listen.

Mother was particularly gentle with her after the business about the poison ivy, and didn't insist on her going to school if she didn't feel like it. Everyone knew there was nothing really wrong with her, but Mother said she looked anemic and let it go at that. I got to like the days Marlie stayed in bed; it gave me an excuse to come home early from school and visit her, which was almost like playing hooky. The first time I did it she started right in lying about my father again, but differently from the way she had before: as if she wanted to stop but couldn't yet bring herself to.

"I have something to show you," she said in a bored voice as soon as I'd closed the door behind me. She tiptoed to her dressing table, unlocked the center drawer and pulled out a thin box wrapped in tissue paper bound by rubber bands. Inside was the photograph of my father sitting on the cannon—the one I'd seen in Sigrid's room. "Remember this?" Marlie said, getting back into bed and propping the picture beside her, against the pillow. "He left this for me when he was here at Easter time. There was a note with it saying I could give it back to him when I joined him. I burned the note." From the automatic way she spoke, I could tell that Marlie knew I wouldn't believe her, and didn't really care. Yet when I reached out to pick up the picture, she shook her head. "You can look at it all you want to," she said prissily, "but I'll have to ask you not to touch it, because I shined the frame just this afternoon and I'm almost out of silver polish."

"Can't I even—"

"Out the window!" she screamed, piercing the false sickroom atmosphere with a terrifying suddenness. "Quick, Chris—look out the window! Is it Peter? *Is it Peter!*" She dove out of bed, brushed past me and ran to the window while I stood watching, too flabbergasted to move. When I finally looked out the window myself, all I could see was a middle-aged man with a cane walking down our hill toward the station. It occurred to me that Marlie might be pretending to be frightened, just to hear herself act; but she couldn't have faked the dead whiteness of her face or the perspiration on her forehead.

"Why didn't you look when I told you to?" she asked, breathing heavily. "It sounded *exactly* like Peter!" She had hardly climbed back under the covers when she thought she heard Peter again. After that, she stayed at the window. "I'll keep watch while you're looking at the picture," she said. "Only hurry, because I *know* he'll be home from school any *second!*"

Each time she showed me the picture, she'd start worrying

about Peter the moment she took it out of the box. It was the only memento of my father remaining in the entire house, she claimed, and Peter would do anything to destroy it—he'd break the lock on her dressing-table drawer, if he suspected that that was where she kept it.

"How would he find out you even have it?" I asked.

"He's been spying!" she shouted. "Don't you understand—he's been spying for Mother!"

"What makes you think that?"

"Why else does she let him sit in Daddy's chair? And why is he always watching everyone, then sneaking off to have those long talks with her?"

THE SPIRIT, AT LEAST, of what Marlie said about Peter was true: ever since my father had left, he had acted as if he and Mother were running the house together. He never played with his electric trains any more. When he wasn't in school or reading in his bedroom, he helped Mother about the house, performing all my father's chores. He carried wood up from the cellar, turned over the tulip beds, and as spring wore on, put a kerosene torch to the tent caterpillars in the sassafras tree by our kitchen courtyard.

If Mother was marketing, he would constantly be listening for the sound of our gray Willys-Knight. As soon as he saw it coast down our hill, he would run out to help Mother bring in the groceries; then the two of them would go upstairs to the small sitting room off her bedroom and talk. When she'd finished telling him about her day, he would give her an account of his: not only the chores he'd completed but what classes he'd had in school and the marks he'd gotten on his homework. In a year or so, he would be going to St. Matthew's, a New England boarding school, where he planned to win all the scholastic prizes. Then he would go to Princeton and Harvard Law School, after which he would become rich and famous, and finally would be appointed to the Supreme Court. He talked over these ambitions with Mother as solemnly as if they were on the brink of materializing, and the seriousness with which she listened must have confirmed his opinion. At least that's the impression he gave the rest of us, especially at Sunday lunch when he got to serve the ice cream.

"Has Johnny been a good boy today, Miss Browning?" he might ask. "How good a boy has Johnny been? Two scoops' worth, or three?"

"I get as many as you!" Johnny shouted. "I don't care what Miss Browning says, I get as many scoops as he gets, Ma!"

"Johnny," Mother said gently, "there's no need to raise your voice."

"Then why's he think he's such hot stuff?"

"He's only trying to get your goat. Now calm down and act your age."

"How come he gets to serve dessert in the first place? He's not so much older than we are."

"He's a whole lot older than you are, my darling."

"But he's only a brother. He's still only a *brother!*"

Another time, when she and Marlie were shopping, Mother phoned to say they would be late for supper and for us to go ahead and begin without them. The trouble started because Miss Browning wasn't there either, so Peter was in charge, and Johnny and I were having a water-pistol fight. As we sat down to supper, Johnny filled his pistol from the pitcher. Peter told him to squirt the water back. Johnny did, but he filled the pistol again—this time from his milk glass.

"All right, give it here." Peter held out his hand. "If you don't, I'll have to send you to your room. There's a pretty good dessert."

"You're not my boss." Johnny sighted the pistol across the table at me. "Just because Ma isn't home yet, that doesn't mean you can boss us around."

"Better hand it over, Johnny. I'm not kidding."

"You do anything to me and I'll tell Ma." He squirted once into his milk glass, testing the pistol.

"Ten seconds to hand it over, Johnny. One. Two. Three. Four . . ." Peter didn't slow down after five, the way Mother usually did. He counted at the same steady speed. When he reached eight, he stood. "Nine, and—"

"No!" Johnny screamed, squirting the milk directly at Peter's face. Peter shook his head, blinking. A hard, bright look came into his eyes. He reached out and with one swipe wrenched the pistol from Johnny's hand; then he pushed his own chair back and started around the table.

Johnny clung to his chair. "I won't leave!" he yelled. "You can't make me—I'll tell Ma! I won't, I won't, I'll tell Ma!" Milk was dripping down Peter's face and his yellow forelock was sticky with it. He tossed his head, flipping the wet hair out of his eyes, then wiped across his cheek with the back of his wrist. Bridgit pushed halfway through the swinging door from the pantry and stood watching, but Peter didn't even notice her. For a moment he seemed to consider slapping Johnny. He lifted his hand and came down with it, but instead of slapping he lifted Johnny, chair and all, and carried him up the front stairs. Johnny never stopped screaming. I heard a door slam, then Peter's slow strides coming back along the second-floor hallway and down the stairs.

Peter said nothing as he came into the dining room. He sat at his place and looked up at Bridgit. "You can take Johnny's plate away," he told her. "He won't be joining us for dessert either, so help yourselves to his share out in the kitchen."

"Sure it's brown betty, Mr. Peter," said Bridgit, "and there's more than enough to go around."

When Mother came home, Peter didn't wait for Johnny or me to tell her what had happened. He told her himself immediately.

"I trust your judgment," Mother said as he helped her off with her coat. "But I also know how the others must feel. You've got to take that more into account, Peter. Especially when it's hardest to. Chris, go tell Johnny he can come down."

"Don't forget to give him back his water pistol, too," Marlie said.

THINKING BACK, MOTHER TRIED to treat us all equally—she just needed Peter more. If she didn't have anything to keep herself busy, like shopping or committee meetings, I noticed the way she would start inventing things to do. First she might neaten the porch, which Bridgit had already neatened; then she'd begin carrying stacks of magazines from the porch to the attic. On her way down from the attic she'd pause by the small oval mirror in the second-floor hallway, and if she thought she was alone, she'd look at herself—not a quick glance, but for too long a time: as if she couldn't force her eyes away from their own image. Toward the middle of the afternoon she would suddenly drop everything and drive over to Country Day for Peter. They'd play a few holes of golf at the Cricket Club, then come back and talk in Mother's study until supper.

She must have been thinking a lot about the past—about how things had turned out the way they had—because it is from this period that I remember her telling us, usually at mealtime, stories of her own girlhood: things that had happened when she was as young as Marlie, or younger—even Johnny's age. It was my first proof that she had not been born a grownup, and I never tired of listening.

At other times, though, especially after we moved up to Loon Lake for the summer, it was as if Mother had to get out of the house and away—from all of us. More and more frequently she took walks by herself through the pine and laurel woods that encircled the lake, or drove around the countryside alone, hunting for antiques. She had lots of friends on the mountaintop, and they kept asking her out, but they reminded her of summers she preferred to forget, and she couldn't face their pity. Twice, during August, she thought up excuses to make the four-hour trip back to Philadelphia to see Grandfather.

Grandmother was at their cottage in Maine, but Grandfather ran a bank and had to return to the city quite often, and (as I learned later) Mother wanted to talk to him about getting a job in a brokerage firm. He was already giving her a handsome monthly allowance, and offered to double it if that was the problem, but she wanted to learn about the management of money and in the end got her way. She had already tentatively lined up

a job with a firm called Charles D. Barney and Company, and she
started in that September when we returned from Loon Lake.
Not long ago I met a lady named Mrs. Burke, who had been a
telephone operator at the same brokerage house, and she said
Mother had used all her charm and her social contacts to outsell
the men, who had both admired and (a little) resented her, calling
her the "Bond Queen of Philadelphia."

This whole side of Mother I know almost nothing about, but
it must have been important to her because she worked hard at
it—not only studying about securities, but even taking a Dale
Carnegie correspondence course so that she would develop more
self-confidence and would be able to speak out to executives. After
Johnny and I went to bed, she and Peter would go to the living
room and do whatever Dale Carnegie's course required for that
day's homework: often as not acting out some imaginary scene,
with Peter playing the skeptical businessman and Mother trying
to sell him on some new "issue" or to explain to him why he
should revise his "portfolio." Lying in bed, we could hear Peter
shouting, "No, no! Not interested, my dear lady, simply not
interested!" and Mother, all collected calmness, saying, "Sir, it's
your wife's interest I have in mind, and your children's."

Although she made a lot of new friends in town, Peter could
tell (we all could) that Mother was seeing too many different men
to take any one of them very seriously. At home, Peter became
more indispensable than ever; but Marlie's nose (as Mother put
it) was "way out of joint," so she made a special effort to give
Marlie treats—like shopping, and going places with her. For
example, when the Barnum and Bailey circus came to Philadelphia, Mother got opening-night tickets for Marlie and Trishy
Sturgis, but not for Peter. She planned to take the girls only, and
made a little too much point of it, but that was all right. Johnny
and I knew we'd get to go later, and Marlie seemed really pleased.
The performance was for eight in the evening. Mother had to
spend the afternoon in town working, and the plan was for her
to leave the office early and get home by five-thirty. She and the

girls would drive back to town, have supper there, then go to the circus from the restaurant.

She got out from town after five-fifteen, expecting both Marlie and Trishy to be in the front hall waiting to jump in the car and go; but I was the only one around.

"Where's Marlie, Chris?"

"Upstairs, I think. Taking a bath."

"A *bath!* We have less than fifteen minutes. Why on earth is she taking a bath now? Where's Trishy?"

"Trishy's not here."

"Why on earth not? I spoke to Mrs. Sturgis yesterday afternoon and she—Marlie!" Mother went to the bottom of the stairs. She was starting up when Bridgit hurried through the pantry door and tiptoed across the dining room.

"Miss Marlie's in the kitchen," Bridgit whispered. "She says she's not goin' to the circus at all."

"Oh, she does, does she! Well, Bridgit, please tell her I want to speak to her this minute! *Marlie!*" Mother didn't wait for Bridgit. She brushed past the maid and started for the pantry door. Just before she reached it, the door swung open and Marlie appeared, carrying a plate of supper.

"Why don't you answer me when I call you?" Mother said, stepping back so that Marlie could pass. "What's this about your not going to the circus? Do you realize what time it is? Marlie! *Look* at your mother when she's speaking to you!"

"Calm down, Ma. I'll look at you as soon as I've put my plate down."

"Honestly, Marlie, this is the meanest thing I've ever heard of, it really is. I rushed back here from work, thinking you and Trishy would be ready to leave the minute I arrived. Where's Trishy? Why isn't Trishy here?"

"I didn't ask her."

"That's no answer."

"It's the truth."

"I don't care whether it's the truth or not. Why *didn't* you ask her? You knew perfectly well we were going to the circus tonight, just the three of us. And to dinner first. We planned this weeks ago. And don't tell me Trishy couldn't come, because I saw her mother yesterday afternoon. Marlie!"

"What?"

"Put your knife and fork down and look at me! Now don't eat another mouthful until you've told me why you didn't ask Trishy!"

Marlie put her knife and fork on her plate and took a drink of milk. She looked at Mother over the rim of her glass and kept looking while she was putting the glass down. "Are you sure you want to know?" she said. "Because it's your fault, and I don't think people really like to know things that are their own fault."

"*What's* my fault? What are you talking about?"

"That Polly Cameron said what she said to Trishy."

Mother turned to Johnny and me. "Look, will you kids leave dessert and beat it for a few minutes? Go play on the porch until I call you. Go on, Johnny. Bridgit will save your rhubarb for you, dear."

"They don't have to leave," Marlie said. "They'll find out for themselves sooner or later anyway. Anyway, there isn't much to tell. It's just that I was going over to ask Trishy at recess and I heard Polly say something to her, that's all. Polly said—" Marlie suddenly stopped talking. She picked up her milk glass and drained it.

Mother waited. After a half minute, she said, "Yes, dear?"

"Polly said I wanted to be friends with Trishy because I haven't any father and she has more money—that Trishy's family must have more, or why else would you have a job? That was all. So I turned and walked away. That's all."

Mother put her hands out and leaned against the back of the chair next to Marlie. She stayed that way for a moment, seeming to gaze at the back of her hands. Then slowly she pulled the chair out and sat down in it. She picked up the pepper shaker, examined it briefly, then set it down again.

"And that—and you think that that was my fault?" She looked at Marlie. "Is that what you honestly think, my darling?"

"No," Marlie said. "As a matter of fact, I guess it isn't. Not entirely, anyway."

THIS KIND OF SCHOOLYARD CRUELTY never fazed Peter, and it was harder on Marlie than on Johnny and me because our friends weren't old enough to care what other kids' parents did; but, indirectly at any rate, it must have been hardest on Mother. Good as she was at her job and much as she loved it, you could tell she sometimes felt she was a failure at everything else—as a daughter, as a wife, especially as a mother. Each year she insisted on taking the entire summer off to be at Loon Lake with her family; but it was there, on the mountaintop, that she seemed most discouraged.

Johnny and I noticed it, particularly that second summer after starting her job, and so did Marlie; but Peter must still have been too full of his own importance to see what was going on. Otherwise he wouldn't have taken it so hard, that afternoon on the Loon Lake golf course, when Mother ran into one of her old beaux.

"Old beau" was the term Mother herself used after he had left the golf course; but I could tell from the moment I saw him—

standing a little behind her on the eighteenth green—that he knew Mother, and knew her pretty well.

Mother was watching Peter line up his ball for a putt. Then she must have felt the man's eyes on her, because she turned and looked directly at him. He was tall, with bushy eyebrows and a long, bony nose, the tip of which seemed to nestle in his luxuriant black mustache. His ears were so flat and their color blended so perfectly with the bright tan of his lean cheeks that you had to look twice to make sure they were there at all, and he held himself with a military erectness that belied the gentle, almost pleading expression on his face. There was nothing said—not even a smile exchanged between him and Mother—but the way they kept looking straight into each other's eyes was so personal that anyone could have told they wanted to be alone.

"Who the heck is that guy?" Johnny asked, leaning his bike against the big pine tree near the caddie house.

"Search me," I said. "But I bet you a double-decker against a single-decker Peter misses his putt."

Johnny didn't take my bet. He already owed me two ice cream cones—that was why we had ridden out to the golf course in the first place, to see if Mother would advance him his allowance.

They had begun walking off the green before they saw us: Mother and the caddie first; then the man, saying something to Peter and smiling while Peter deliberately kept two or three steps behind.

"What are you two bums doing out here?" Mother asked, kissing us as if she hadn't seen us for days. "I thought you were at the beach . . . Francis, I want you to meet my swimming champions. This is Chris—Mr. Wagner. And Johnny."

Mr. Wagner took a step backwards and squinted at us as if he were appraising livestock. "Born 1921 and 1923 respectively," he said. "And you, young man, must be a few weeks from your ninth birthday," he added, smiling at Johnny. "Toward the end of September, if I'm not mistaken."

"How in the world—" Mother began.

"I have an obsession for vital statistics, Louisa. My store of useless information about my friends is staggering."

"But you haven't lived in this country for—how long has it been, Francis? Ten years?"

"I have spies," he said, and winked at Johnny and me.

"Are you a golf pro?" Johnny asked.

"He *should* be!" Mother said, laughing. "He's done wonders for my game. I haven't broken seven on the eighteenth in I don't know how long."

"You didn't break seven today, either," Peter said. We had forgotten he was there. He stood about ten yards away, adding up the scorecard. Now we all looked at him as he stuck the pencil stub behind his ear and hoisted his golf bag onto his shoulder. "You took two drives."

"By gosh, you're right," Mother said. "I'd completely forgotten. Well"—she turned back to us—"where are you kids off to? The lake?"

"But can I have next week's allowance, Ma?" Johnny begged. "I really need it."

"Sunday is allowance day, Johnny."

"But I owe Chris two cones."

"I think you'd both better wait. Besides, I haven't any change."

"Allow me." Mr. Wagner dug into his trouser pocket and came up with a fistful of golf tees, matches and coins. "Let an old expatriate atone for his past sins of omission," he said, holding out a quarter for Mother to take.

"Johnny knows perfectly well what our arrangement is," Mother said.

"It's a gambling debt, Louisa—a debt of honor!"

"Well . . ." Mother was about to take Mr. Wagner's money when Peter shouted, *"Catch!"*

He flipped a quarter end over end at Johnny. "That's a loan, kiddo," he added. "Till Sunday."

Mr. Wagner closed his fist. He jingled his change for a moment before sticking it back in his pocket. When he offered to give

Mother and Peter a lift home from the golf course, Peter said, "We've got our own car."

"Francis, it was wonderful," Mother said quickly, "just wonderful, seeing you again."

"Don't send me off for another ten years," Mr. Wagner said. "You have a daughter I haven't seen since she was three or four years old." As if it were the most natural thing in the world for him to do, he leaned forward and gave Mother a kiss on the cheek; then he waved goodbye to the three of us, jumped down the grass bank and started walking, his long back straight as a general's, toward the club's parking lot.

When he'd disappeared behind the caddie house, Mother told Peter she thought he'd been more than a little rude, flipping the quarter to Johnny that way.

"I don't like your taking money from strangers," Peter answered. "Kissing them, either."

Mother looked at Peter—annoyed, but amused too. "He's hardly a stranger," she said quietly. "He's an old Philadelphia beau of mine. As a matter of fact," she added, blushing under her suntan, "Francis Wagner and I were nearly engaged before I met your father, and I suspect that his being up here on the mountaintop isn't exactly a coincidence." She studied Peter for a moment. "But that's not the real point, Peter, and you know it. The point is, I don't like your telling me what to do and what not to do. It's a terrible habit you've been getting into lately. I have half a mind to stop off at the Loon Lake Inn on our way home and make you apologize to Mr. Wagner."

"I'll apologize to you instead." Peter put his arm around Mother's shoulder. "Sorry," he said, squeezing her. "Come on, Ma. Let's be friends."

"I expect my eldest son to act like a man," Mother said. "Not like a child—a fifteen-year-old baby."

THAT FIRST MEETING took place the Friday before Labor Day. Between then and mid-September, when Peter went back to boarding school, Mr. Wagner was around quite a lot: not necessarily even taking Mother out; just dropping by.

It was pathetic to see how helpless Peter was to do anything about it, or even to make Mother take his loathing for Mr. Wagner seriously. Whenever he could, he insulted Mr. Wagner, either directly or indirectly; but just as he had apologized to Mother on the Loon Lake golf course, something always compelled him to beg her forgiveness for the way he had acted: as if, by keeping in her good graces at whatever cost, he might miraculously outlast Mr. Wagner. I could see that Mother interpreted Peter's apologies as assurances that he would eventually come around; even if he rebelled a little at first, she was confident that he would (as I overheard her saying to Aunt Rosalie) "work it out of his system." Marlie was the only one she really worried about.

By the time he left for boarding school, even Peter had realized this: that Marlie, and not he, was the decisive one. He realized it on his last evening home—the Saturday he went with Mother and Mr. Wagner to *Macbeth.*

Although Mr. Wagner had gotten tickets for her, too, Marlie had flatly refused to go. Peter finally agreed to, but he didn't get his hair cut, as Mother had suggested, and he wouldn't wear his tuxedo, though they were dining at The Barclay beforehand.

The three of them drove off just as Johnny and I were going up to bed. Miss Browning fiddled around for a while—I could hear her pigeonlike movements overhead—and then went to bed. The last thing I heard before falling asleep was Bridgit and our new cook, Kathleen, unlocking the kitchen door, closing it carefully and locking it again, then tiptoeing up the back stairs.

It seemed as if I'd been asleep for about ten seconds when a strange sound, like hailstones, woke me up. I threw back my covers and swung quietly out of bed, so as not to wake Johnny. As I was feeling for my slippers, I heard a pebble skit across the bedroom floor. I took the chair my clothes were on, dragged it over to the window and climbed onto the sill.

It was Peter. For some reason it had to be. He was crouching near the roots of the big maple, looking for more stones to throw. I tried to whistle, but my lips were too dry. It didn't matter. He saw me—my white pajamas—as soon as he raised his head.

When he stood up, he looked like a grown man: something about the way the moonlight struck across the breadth of his shoulders and on the top of his enormous, shaggy blond head. It seemed, almost as I watched, that he was growing—if I leaned out the window a little farther, I might touch the top of his head. I couldn't make out the expression on his face. I waved to him but he didn't wave back. He lifted his arm and pointed stiffly toward the kitchen door.

It was a relief, after the way he had looked in the moonlight, to see his face through the glass panes of the kitchen door: ordinary as ever. "Cripes!" he said, catching the door just before it banged against the wall. "Chilly out there. What's the matter with turning on some lights?" Leaving the door for me to close, he charged across the kitchen to the light switch, flicked it on, then kept going, into the pantry. I heard him open the refrigerator.

I was still trying to get the door shut—you had to hold the latch back while you turned the knob, and I wasn't tall enough to do both at once—when he came back into the kitchen with a drumstick in his hand. "Here," he said, pushing me to one side, "hold this. But don't eat it."

"I wouldn't eat your stinking food if you paid me," I said. He smiled, and that made it worse. "Didn't you get enough to eat at The Barclay?" I asked. "Were you scared to order what you wanted?" I expected him to lose his temper when I said that, but instead he smiled again—friendlier than before.

"The Barclay!" he said, taking his drumstick back. "That fancy dump!"

"You should have ordered the most expensive thing on the menu," I said. "That's what I'd have done."

"They beat me to it. They *wanted* me to."

"Who?"

"Both of them."

"What did you have?"

"I don't know. Some lousy omelet."

"What's an omelet?"

"Scrambled eggs stuffed with something."

"How can you *stuff* scrambled eggs?"

"Never mind."

"I don't see how—"

"Never *mind*, I said. It's not important." He sat heavily in the green rocker, stretched his long legs out in front of him, and began gnawing on the drumstick.

I looked at the alarm clock on the sill behind the sink. It said not quite ten-thirty. At first I thought it had stopped. "Hey!" I said. "Where's Ma and Mr. Wagner?"

Peter shrugged, his mouth full of chicken.

"Then what the heck are you doing home?"

He ripped a last shred off the drumstick, leaned sideways and tossed it at the sink. It glanced off and fell to the floor, but he ignored it. He took out his handkerchief. "Chris," he said pleasantly, mopping his face, "it's none of your damn business what I'm doing home, but it just might develop in you an incipient respect for William Shakespeare, so I'm going to tell you anyway."

He began sucking his fingertips, wiping each finger after he'd sucked it. When he'd finished all eight fingers and both thumbs, he looked up at me. "The jerk dressed like Macbeth was approximately nineteen years old," he said. "Furthermore, Lady Macbeth sounded like Miss Browning in one of her more puzzling humors." He jammed the handkerchief back into his pocket and belched. "In short, it was an amateur production, and a lousy amateur production at that. It stank."

"Was the lousy *production* the reason you came home early?" I asked.

He didn't answer right away. He rocked back in the chair and stayed that way, bracing one foot against the edge of the table.

"I'll have to admit," he said finally, "the lousy company had something to do with it. I can't stand that guy's face."

"Did they see you leave?"

"They saw me leave. They wished me a safe trip home. Chris"—he rocked suddenly forward, as if he were coming at me through the air—"you've always been the one in cahoots with Marlie. How do you think she feels about Mr. Wagner?"

I thought it a silly question, but he looked as if he really wanted my answer. "She refused to go to the play tonight, didn't she?"

"Yes," he said, "she refused. Tonight." He stood up and came around to my side of the table, then crouched down so that his head was level with mine. "Chris," he said, fixing me with his man-to-man look, "I'll make a bargain with you. While I'm away at school, make her hate him." He spoke very deliberately, never taking his eyes off mine. "Make Marlie hate him, and you can have my electric trains."

"She already does."

"Not enough." He stood and walked over to the light switch. "Not nearly enough." He flicked the light off. "Good night, Chris. Remember my offer."

Seven

I HAD NOTHING AGAINST Mr. Wagner, and wasn't going to do Peter's dirty work even if I could have; but I was surprised to discover how right he had been about Marlie.

For the first few weeks after Peter went back to school, she tried to ignore Mr. Wagner, much as Peter had used to ignore my father. But she wasn't quite indifferent to him, even during September; more than once, when he was playing catch with Johnny and me in the yard, I would see Marlie, her face half-hidden by the chintz curtains, peeking down from her bedroom window. Neither Mother nor Mr. Wagner put pressure on her—if anything, they went to the other extreme, supplying her with excuses for not joining us. "Marlie probably has homework to do," Mother would say on a Sunday afternoon, "but how would you two like to drive down to the Wissahickon with us and feed the ducks?" Or else Mr. Wagner would show up on Saturday morning with four tickets to the Penn football game. "All I could get," he would say, holding them up for us to count. "Who'll volunteer to stay home?"

He and Mother sometimes played golf at the Cricket Club, and because he lived way over on the Main Line, he changed and showered back at our house whenever he was taking Mother out to dinner afterwards. She would usually take a lot longer to dress, and he'd wait for her on the porch, reading her financial magazines. I got the impression that he hoped one of us would come chat with him, and I was just as curious to find out what he was like, so I'd wander out and say hello. The first time I did it, he looked up from his magazine and said, "What's your favorite car?"

"Same as yours," I said, referring to his maroon beauty parked at the end of our walk. "Lincoln."

"Let me see," he said, flipping back a few pages. "That's the Ford Motor Company." He scanned the columns, found what he wanted, and looked up smiling. "Your car is selling surprisingly well, for a luxury vehicle in these depressed times," he said. "And Ford is doing better than most of its competitors. Which means that the Lincoln will probably be available when you get ready to buy one."

"What's that?" I asked, pointing to what seemed to be a line of different-sized smokestacks.

"That's a graph," he said. "A *bar* graph."

"What's it for?"

"Well, it's to show you how things compare. Like companies. In this graph—see—they've given a different bar to each automobile company, and the higher up its bar pokes, the more cars it has sold during the first nine months of this year. So you can tell at a glance how each company's sales are doing. In *comparison*—in comparison to all the other companies shown. Does that make sense? Now . . ." He kept talking and I kept nodding, but all the while I was pretending that he was my father. Not my real father, but that he was married to Mother and living in our house. Only more than that. I didn't know how much more I wanted it to be, or whether he would keep me from pretending far enough.

Now he had found a piece of paper and was drawing a bar graph of Peter and Marlie and Johnny and me, one bar to each, showing our ages. Then he did a second bar graph showing our heights. He held the pencil tightly, but his touch with it was light and very precise as he shaded in the bars. He sat up straight, with his head cocked on one side. Everything about him seemed so different from my father. Daddy had always had a rumpled, comfortable look, as if he had reached sleepily for his pants and found the coat to them thrown over a bathroom chair. His shirt sleeves, even when his coat was on, were rolled up. He didn't like cuffs about his wrists. Mr. Wagner didn't look uncomfortable, exactly, but he looked vaguely *European*—as though a valet had polished his shoes, selected his necktie and laid out his spotless, well-pressed, dark-blue pinstripe suit. I doubted that he could ever have killed a Hun. Instead of a collar with buttons, such as Daddy always wore, he had on a tie pin, a thin gold one, and his cuffs were clasped neatly about his wrists by diamond-shaped gold cuff links initialed "F.O.W. Jr." His heavy brows were joined at the bridge of his nose by a sprout of dark-brown hair. He wore heavy-looking tortoise-shell glasses, and above them, his high forehead was divided horizontally by the curving line which his golf cap had made, so that the suntanned face and neck looked like a mask of health hanging from his white scalp and thinning brown hair. I wondered whether he actually did have a valet. I knew he had a chauffeur—at least I'd seen one, a couple of times, come for Mother in the Lincoln when Mr. Wagner couldn't come for her himself.

"What's new money?" I asked.

"*New* money?"

I nodded. "You know—like some families have new money and some families have old money." I knew Mr. Wagner was not only rich, like Grandfather, but "wealthy"—which I took to mean *rich* rich. I had also gathered, from remarks made at various times by Aunt Rosalie and others, that there was something wrong with the *way* he was rich, and what was wrong had to do with his money being new while ours wasn't, and with his family not being "old Philadelphia" like ours.

"That's slang," he said. " 'New' has nothing to do with the money itself—when it was made at the mint. It has to do with how recently your family got hold of it."

"Is it all worth the same?"

"New or old, a dollar is a dollar."

"Then what difference does it make?"

"Well, that's tricky to explain. You know what feeling superior means—feeling you're better than someone else?" I nodded. "Some people feel superior to others if their family became rich first."

"That seems silly, kind of."

"Well, I agree with you—but then a lot of ways we feel don't exactly make sense, like when we're glad for no reason, or sad. If I had 'older' money than someone else, I can imagine it would be great fun to feel superior. *Feeling* it isn't so wrong—what's wrong is letting *them* know you feel it. But of course you don't feel superior in nearly as satisfying a way unless you know that they know you're feeling it. It gets pretty complicated, so the best policy is to forget the whole thing and stick to graphs and charts."

I didn't want to give the impression that I wasn't paying close attention, so I nodded and waited a few seconds, with my lips pressed together, before asking what I really wanted to know: "Mr. Wagner—did you ever kill a Hun?"

"A what?"

"A Hun. You know, in the war."

He shook his head and smiled apologetically. "I wasn't in the war at all," he said. "I was just too young to make it. But your father probably killed a Hun or two, didn't he?"

"How did you know? There's a German helmet right upstairs in the attic, with a *huge* spike coming out the top."

"That's wonderful," he said. "You should feel really proud."

"I do!"

"But not superior," he said, and rumpled my hair.

WHEN I WENT UPSTAIRS to wash for supper, Marlie knocked on the bathroom door and opened it, waiting until I had finished drying my face.

"What did you and Mr. Wagner talk about?" she asked, blushing.

"Graphs. Money. That kind of stuff."

"Graphs! What's that?"

"They look like smokestacks, only they measure things like how many cars different companies sell."

"Graphs . . ." She said the word to herself, trying it out. "Did he talk about anything else? He used this bathroom to change in, and look what he forgot." She held up a shaving brush. "Isn't it beautiful! Feel it. It's so big and soft! Do you think I ought to give it back to him? I guess I will. Go *on*, Chris, you haven't told me anything yet. What else did you talk about? You couldn't have talked *that* long about graphs. I don't really like him, though, do you?"

"Sort of."

"Graphs," she said. "I'll have to remember that—graphs."

HE GAVE MARLIE A PRESENT for her birthday, on the fifteenth of November, but he made no special point of it, and Mother didn't say anything when Marlie thanked him coldly and carried the present up to her room without even opening it.

After he had left the house, she called me into her room. That was when I found out what he had given her: a portfolio of color reproductions. All twelve prints were propped up about her room, against her bureau, her dressing-table mirror, the backs of chairs.

"Do you think the ladies are beautiful?" she asked shyly. I looked at one picture of a lot of ladies with rippling hair, dancing outdoors in their nightgowns.

"Sure," I said. "Their faces, anyway."

"Well, you know what? I'm not saying this to be conceited,

because I know it's not true, and anyway, he was probably trying to flatter me because—you know . . . But in this note that was with them, Mr. Wagner says I look like Botticelli's ladies. Here —read it. He says he's seen the original paintings in Italy and that if the artist—that's Botticelli—if he were alive today, he'd want to paint me."

"You do look like some of them," I said. "Except for the hair. Your hair's nicer."

"It is?" Marlie leaned forward, peering at herself in the mirror. "Do you really think so?" She turned around and gave me a hug. "Oh, Chris," she cried. "You're *such* a loyal brother!"

Mother gave several dinner parties that fall, and Marlie was allowed to eat with the guests if she wanted to. Until her birthday she had preferred having supper, those nights, in the kitchen with Bridgit and Kathleen, or else in her own room; but now she seemed to like being considered grown up. When I came in to say hello after school, she'd be brushing her hair or filing her nails. As soon as the clock struck six, she'd say, "Better scram, Chris, I have to dress." If Trishy Sturgis was around, Marlie would treat me like a kid. "Don't you wish you had younger brothers?" she'd ask. "They're really more darn fun."

She and Trishy both went to Miss Rollins's eight-to-ten o'clock dancing class at the Cricket Club. The last dance before Christmas, Mr. Wagner came to dine with mother and brought Marlie a corsage of gardenias to wear with her new evening dress. Mother had given her the dress for her birthday. It was the most expensive one she had ever owned, and she started getting ready for the dance at five o'clock in the afternoon.

She was taking her bath when supper was announced, so Mother told Kathleen to fix her a sandwich and a glass of milk. Mother took the tray up. We had finished dessert and were leaving the table when Mother came down the stairs. "Kids," she called in a stage whisper over the banister, "if you want to see something that really is *something,* hold your seats!"

Johnny and I stood in the hallway. There was a rustle at the head of the stairs, and then Marlie started down. Instead of stepping awkwardly and all in a rush, the way she usually did— holding her shoulder straps and calling for Mother to fasten the rest of the clasps up the back—she carried herself absolutely upright. Only her neck was bent slightly forward as she reached out and lifted the front of her full, powdery-blue skirt off the stairs.

She walked down slowly, but there was no shyness in her manner. At the landing, she paused. Her shingled hair was soft and looked almost golden: not the lemon-honey color of girls who are very blond, but darker, so that the top strands seemed more golden in contrast to the light brown underneath. Her eyes, gray or blue depending on what she wore, had become clear blue from the color of her gown; and although she had no make-up on, there was as much color in her cheeks as if she had just come in out of the snow. She was taller than most girls her age, but there was nothing thin about her. Even at fourteen, her body had begun to fill out.

The light, as she turned, caught some silvery-blue threads, making the material from her waist up glimmer and twinkle. Johnny whistled, or tried to. Marlie looked down as if she had commanded us to be there. She smiled over the banister, bent forward to look for the next step, and started down again.

She was still coming down the last few steps when the doorbell rang. Mother started to answer it, but Marlie, in a voice so different from her own that I thought she was playing one of her games, said, "That must be Mr. Wagner. I'll get it, Mother, shall I?"

She seemed to float across the hall, the bottom of her gown barely brushing the nap of the carpet. She opened the door. Mr. Wagner was standing on the mat, looking down and scuffing the soles of his shoes. Under his left arm he carried a white box. When he looked up, an expression of surprise crossed his face.

"Good evening, Mr. Wagner," Marlie said, still playing her game. "Won't you come in?"

He reached up slowly with his right hand and took off his hat.
He exchanged a glance with Mother, then looked again at Marlie.
He stepped into the house and bowed slightly; then with mock
astonishment he murmured, *"Miss* Marlie Hooper!"

The color left Marlie's face. She tried to say something, but
closed her eyes and shook her head. I thought she was going to
faint, she was squeezing the doorknob so tightly. She made a kind
of gasping sound, then picked up her skirt and ran to the stairs.

"Marlie!" Mother went to the banister, but Marlie didn't look
back.

Mr. Wagner shut the door. "What did I do, Louisa? Is she all
right?"

Mother looked up the stairwell. When Marlie's door slammed,
she turned to Mr. Wagner. There was a smile on her lips. "You
underestimate your charms, Francis," she said. "The girl has a
crush on you. Don't worry about it, she'll be all right."

"What should I do with this?" he asked, putting the box on
the hall table.

"Here, Chris." Mother handed the box to me. "Wait a few
minutes before you take it up. Tell her it's her corsage."

When I opened the door, Marlie was lying across the foot of
her bed, kissing something. "It's me," I said. "I brought you the
flowers. They're to put on your dress."

She raised herself on her elbows and looked around at me. I saw
what she had been kissing: it was the picture of my father sitting
on the cannon.

"Don't tell anyone, Chris," she said, half crying and whispering
to keep herself from crying more. *"Please* don't tell anyone."

"I wouldn't, Marlie. Do you want me to leave this here?" She
was biting her lip so hard she couldn't answer except by shaking
her head. "Are you going to the dance?" I asked.

"I can't," she managed to say. "I just can't . . ."

$\mathcal{E}ight$

CHRISTMAS DAY WAS AS LOVELY that year as any I can remember. When Johnny and I woke up, snow was coming down in crowded flakes that seemed to join each other near the treetops, so that by the time they had settled to the ground they were as big as pieces of torn bread. No one had broken the smooth white surface down our hill. The station, with its tower and weather vane, might have been a barn, for the tracks leading from it were hidden under a drift and the station yard had been transformed into a gleaming field. The rhododendrons bordering our own yard looked like a giant white caterpillar constructed for a carnival. The tree trunks, the terrace, the lattice-work fence enclosing our kitchen court, the garbage pails, the birdhouse sitting on its brown pole at the far end of the yard—all had been crusted by the fallen flakes.

Johnny and I shut the windows, grabbed our wrappers and ran down the hall shouting "Merry Christmas! Merry Christmas, everybody!" Opening Marlie's door, we yelled, "Time for stockings!" Then we raced upstairs to Peter's room.

"Get the hell out of here!" Peter pushed outwards with both arms and swiped at the air, then pulled the pillow over his head. We ran down to check on Marlie, then came back again to Peter. They grunted and hid under the covers, but each knew we would never stop until they were both on their feet, with their faces washed and their wrappers on.

Finally all four of us went into Mother's room and forced her to sit up in bed. Peter rounded up some cardboard boxes to put the stocking presents in, while Marlie brought a damp cloth and made Mother wash her face to keep awake.

If Marlie was still punishing herself with Mr. Wagner's remark, she didn't show it. He hadn't been back to the house since the night of her dance, and Peter, who had returned from school two days later, hadn't seen him since September. For those few hours on Christmas morning, it was as if Mother had never met Mr. Wagner. The four of us sat, as we had done every Christmas since my father had left us, in a half-circle around Mother's bed, and unwrapped our presents in rotation. Johnny still partly believed that his stocking came from Santa Claus, but seeing how the rest of us scrambled across the bed to thank Mother all the time, he did too. Mother must have been kissed a hundred times that morning. She sat there in bed—her thick brown hair loose about her shoulders; her soft cheeks, tan even in winter, still creased with sleep—smiling as if she were having a wonderful dream with her eyes open.

We piled the tissue-paper wrappings on the hearth and arranged our presents in our boxes. Mother watched us sadly. "Why are you doing that so soon?" she said. "I haven't finished yet. I have three more to open." She pulled a present out of the heel of her stocking and turned it slowly in her hands, as if she were trying to keep us from leaving.

"Come on, Ma," Johnny said. "We have to eat breakfast so we can go to the living room."

"I know. Don't rush me, darling. Stockings are the best part of Christmas." She let her head drop back against the pillows and looked absently at the still-wrapped present. "I wish you had two stockings apiece, or three." Her eyes closed and her voice trailed off.

"Shall I open it *for* you, Ma?"

She blinked and sat up. "I'll do it, Johnny," she said. "I'll do it right now."

AFTER BREAKFAST AND OPENING our main presents in the living room, around the tree, it was time to start out for Grandmother and Grandfather's house. They lived in town on Delafield Place: a quiet street with uneven brick sidewalks wide enough for a line of small trees, each one circled by its own guard fence. It had stopped snowing. Before we arrived, the brick had been shoveled, then swept clean of slush, and so had the gray-veined marble steps that led up to the white front doors of Delafield Place's four-story brick houses.

Mother parked behind the Ashmeads' Ford and the Bouviers' Plymouth. "Looks as if the Hooper family is late again this year," she said. "Everyone get their presents straight before we move an inch. Johnny, what did Aunt Rosalie and Uncle Gabe give you?"

"Nothing."

"Nothing?"

"Modeling clay," Marlie said. "Remember, Johnny? In the yellow box with the animal pictures on it?"

Mother made each of us in turn name all our presents. "Now," she said, opening the car door. "I forgot to mention this before, because . . ." She paused, turning to face Peter, then Marlie. "Well, because nothing. I just didn't tell you. Mr. Wagner's going to be here." Marlie frowned, then looked down at her lap, but Peter stared right back at Mother, expressionless. "Anyway, he *is* here," she added. "So"—she opened the door—"come on, kids, get a wiggle on. I just saw Mims peeking through the curtains."

Mims was Mother's old Alsatian governess. She had a wide,

wrinkled face and thin lips that were always either pursed reflectively or smiling. On family occasions, she hovered near the music room and kept peeking through the curtains until Mother and all my aunts had arrived. We saw her peeking now; then, a moment later, saw the front door open a crack.

"Wee-*sa*, where are your ruppers?" she called from the dark interior, in her guttural monotone that in forty years had not entirely mastered the English inflection.

Inside the vestibule, we hugged her and wished her a merry Christmas. "Gootness, not so hard," she said. "Merry Christmas. You'll break me; you're growing too big. Look at your mother— no ruppers or galoshes. Peter, you should take better care of her. Here"—she thrust a crisp new dollar bill at each of us—"it's not much, just a little something for the moofies. You know where to leave your coats. Well, Weesa"—she turned to Mother—"it *is* a merry Christmas for you, isn't it?"

"It certainly is, Mims. Kids, run upstairs to your grandmother. I want to talk with Mims a minute."

As we trooped up the wide, dark staircase with the wine-colored carpeting, Mother followed Mims into the music room and shut the curtained glass door behind her.

We left our coats in the dressing room off the second-floor hallway, then knocked on Grandmother's door. For the last few years, Grandmother had stayed in bed a lot. We weren't sure what was the matter with her, but we knew that whenever we visited, we were supposed to see her first of all.

"Johnny?" Peter looked over his shoulder, his hand on the doorknob. "Present?"

"Tarzan," Johnny said, remembering the trade name on the trapeze and rings that Grandmother and Grandfather had given him.

Peter knocked. There was a feeble answer that might have been "Come in." He opened the door, and the four of us filed into Grandmother's bedroom as quietly as if we were used to entering rooms that way.

"Come in, my dears, come over here and kiss me," she said. "Marlie, bring that pillow with you—the one on the wing chair, dearest—Mims never props me high enough. She thinks I read too much. Down a little. Perfect. My, but you're turning into a pretty young lady. Give me a kiss. Merry Christmas."

The bedroom was large, and being at the front of the house, still bright with late-morning sun. The enormous double bed had been made. Grandmother rested on her chaise longue. She wore a light-blue dressing gown with a ruffle at the neck. Her feet, under a white knitted throw, came all the way to the end of the chaise longue. She was a tall woman; even lying down, or half lying as she was now, she gave an upright impression. Her hands, which she lifted from the knitting on her lap to hold my face as she kissed me, were thin, with long fingers and long, beautiful nails. There were light freckles on the backs of her hands and on the bridge of her thin, almost transparent nose. Her lips were thin, and her chin stuck out sharply. Her hair, once auburn, was now almost entirely soft gray, but brushed back boldly from her high forehead, it waved and shone like a young person's.

"Are you feeling better, Grandmother?" Johnny asked.

"Better, Johnny? I'm feeling as young as you are. Well, perhaps that's overstating it. Let's say as young as Peter. Peter, your mother tells me you've won an English essay prize at school."

I listened to her talking to Peter, then to Marlie. Without looking directly at the curtains, the bedspread, the pictures on the walls, I had the feeling that everything bathed me in blue and white and peach. Those were Grandmother's colors. Even the furniture seemed to go with her. The dressing table between the windows, the highboy, the writing desk in the corner stood like so many graceful ladies, delicate and proud, on slim legs carved about with shells and sunbursts. There was a table by the wing chair, and on it I saw one of Grandfather's cigars, still wrapped. I tried to imagine him in the double bed under that wide canopy, surrounded by those valances and side-curtains.

"Tell me, do you like Mr. Wagner?" Grandmother hadn't

asked anyone in particular, but her question stunned us. For a moment no one answered; then Marlie, twisting the dark-blond curl that always flipped out from under her barrette, whispered, "I don't know."

"We had ice cream with candy on top," Johnny shouted. "And there was a man with a gun—Joe. Joe has a gun."

"Good heavens!" Grandmother exclaimed. "What on earth are you talking about?"

"He means Joe, their watchman," I said. "We went to his mother's house for lunch a couple of weeks ago."

"Joe's?"

"No, Mr. *Wag*ner's!"

"Dear me, how confusing." Grandmother glanced at Marlie briefly, then turned to Peter. She looked at him for what seemed to me a long time. The trousers of his blue serge suit weren't quite long enough to cover the red socks above his crepe-soled shoes. His coat was tight too; it barely buttoned over his heavy chest, and the wristbones of his huge hands stuck out below his cuffs. Though he had brushed his hair hard before leaving the house, it still curled over his ears and down the back of his shirt collar. Even his brows, above his small, piercing blue eyes, seemed to need cutting. There was a strange expression on his face as he stood there waiting for Grandmother to speak: faintly defiant, but embarrassed too, like a boy who has been called to the teacher's desk and is waiting to deny whatever he will be accused of.

Grandmother watched him affectionately, but as if she knew exactly what he was thinking. Quite suddenly she smiled. "Give Francis Wagner a chance," she said. "I think he deserves more of a chance from you, Peter."

"Grandmother, thank you for the Tarzan set," Johnny said.

"You're *most* welcome, Johnny. You certainly must have liked it. No grandchild of mine has ever before thanked me three times within ten minutes for the same present. Give me a kiss, now, all of you, and run along. You can't spend the whole day gossiping with an old lady."

LEAVING GRANDMOTHER'S ROOM was like stepping into another world. We could hear Paul and Gibby Bouvier and Tim Ashmead chasing up and down the hallway overhead. Hoppy, Tim's sister, was leaning over the fourth-floor banister, giggling and threatening to drop a water bomb. Johnny and I wanted to go play with them, but first we had to say hello to our aunts and uncles in the drawing room.

The drawing room was all the way at the back of the second floor. Its double doors were closed, but as we were walking down the hallway toward them, Uncle Timmy came prancing out, slapping his stomach and shouting "Ho-ho-ho! More people with dirty ears! How's my favorite niece?"

He hugged Marlie and danced her around, knocking a picture frame askew. "Merry Christmas! This is absolutely terrible— never *seen* such dirty ears!" He lifted Marlie's hair and seemed to be reaching into her ear. "Aren't you ashamed of yourself!" he cried, pulling out a quarter. "Really disgraceful!" He inspected all our ears, shaking his head sadly, pulling out dimes and quarters and dropping them into our pockets.

Everyone in the drawing room was making just as much noise as Uncle Timmy. They shouted "Merry Christmas!" and hugged us, stood back and looked at us and then hugged us again. Uncle Gabe was laughing his queer, contagious laugh that sounded like a locomotive picking up speed. Uncle Cort lifted me over his head to see how tall I'd grown. All my aunts tried to outshout one another: Aunt Rosalie asking me where Mother was, while Aunt Hell pleaded with Uncle Timmy to stop looking in ears and act his age, and Aunt Netty pulled at her shoulder, crying, "Let him alone, dearie—it's *Christmas!*"

"Where's Grandfather?" I asked Aunt Rosalie.

"I don't know, Chris. He was here a minute ago. Where's Popsie, Gabe?"

"Downstairs with Francis. I think Francis wanted to talk to him." Uncle Gabe gave Aunt Rosalie a big wink. "Alone."

"He'll be up in a few minutes," Aunt Rosalie said to me. "Why don't you go play with Tim and Gibby?"

"Can I go too, Aunt Rosalie?" Johnny asked.

"Yes, sweet one, you too."

We wriggled our way out of the drawing room and ran down the hall shouting "Hey, *Gibby!*"

The third and fourth floors were our favorite parts of the house. We could chase around all we wanted to, dropping water bombs onto Delafield Place, letting each other down on the dumbwaiter, and talking back and forth on the voice tube. Mims, as usual, was sent up to scold us. "Lena *neets* that dumbwaiter!" she said, standing in front of it. "Lena neets to send food to the pantry. Hurry up and wash, now—lunch is retty, lunch is retty!"

The grownups ate in the dining room while the rest of us— grabbing, throwing, crying, spilling, laughing—sat at small tables set up in the long, narrow living room. At least twice (it seemed) Uncle Timmy charged in to inspect the nearest victim's ears. Mims shuffled about, poking her nose over our shoulders to see if we had enough stuffing or gravy or cranberry sauce. The mince pies were brought on, and ice cream—three flavors, shaped like halved watermelons. Speeches were being made in the dining room. We could hear Uncle Gabe's voice above the others, shouting, "Francis! Let's have a speech from Francis!" Fred, Grandfather's chauffeur, was shuttling back and forth in a butler's uniform—clearing away the dishes, folding up the tables, showing his new false teeth in a broad grin.

They had finished in the dining room too. For ten seconds the house, the whole house, was quiet. Then Uncle Timmy, his left arm around Mr. Wagner's shoulder, appeared at the entrance to the living room. "Look at my ears, Uncle Timmy!" Johnny yelled. "Mine too!" someone else shouted. "My ears are worst!" "Uncle Timmy, look, look!"

Uncle Timmy smiled, shaking his head. "I don't want you to show me your ears," he said. "I want you to *lend* them to me for a very important announcement, about this bully gent on my left." Mr. Wagner looked puzzled for a moment; then he frowned and whispered something to Uncle Timmy, but Uncle Timmy paid no attention to him. "This bully gent on my left is *no longer* to be known as Mr. Wagner," he shouted. "The assembled Hoopers may call him what they like, when the time comes: Pop, Pater, Old Soak. I can't do anything about *that*. But for the rest of you ragamuffins, I now officially christen him—*Uncle Francis!*" Picking up a glass, he shook a few drops of white wine over Mr. Wagner's head, shouting "Hooray for Aunt Louisa and Uncle Francis!"

"You *promised* me, Tim Ashmead!" I heard Mother say. "You gave me your word you wouldn't!" But by that time the other grownups had begun crowding out of the dining room, cheering and slapping Mr. Wagner on the back. I saw Marlie go up and hold out her hand to him. It was a tentative, uncertain gesture, more dutiful than affectionate, but instead of shaking her hand Mr. Wagner pulled Marlie to him and gave her a fatherly hug. Peter had seen it too—he was watching from halfway up the staircase. I was trying to make out the expression on his face when the lights went out.

"Where's the magician!" Uncle Gabe bellowed. "Let's have the magician."

Someone threw open the doors to the music room, and there, in front of a spot-lighted blue table decorated with silver stars, stood a thin, wiry man with a grim smile that lifted the points of his waxed mustache. He was wearing a bright-green high-peaked cap with a silver half-moon on the front, and a long green robe. We cheered and clapped and scrambled for places on the floor while he bowed, lifting his cap and showing his bald head.

"Ladies and gentlemen, boys and girls," he began, in a surprisingly high-pitched voice. "I, Ali, greet you!"

Nine

I T WAS GROWING DARK by the time the magician had finished. The lights were on in the second-floor hallway when we went to get our coats. Mother didn't drive us home. Aunt Rosalie explained that she wanted to come out alone with Mr. Wagner. The Bouviers dropped Johnny and me at the house. I think Peter and Marlie must have gone ahead, in the Ashmeads' car. In any case, I remember that Peter was the one who opened the door for us.

"Two more guests!" he shouted over his shoulder. "Glad you could come to the party, old man, awfully glad you could make it!" He slapped Johnny on the back, almost knocking him down. "Matter of fact, I'm a guest myself." He slammed the door so hard that the lamp on the hall table shook. "We're all guests. Host and hostess haven't arrived yet. Busy necking. What can I get you? Ginger ale? Whiskey? Worcestershire sauce? *Marlie!*"

"What?" Marlie answered in a flat voice, from the pantry.

"Two more glasses of Worcestershire sauce. *Where's Kathleen!*"

"Don't yell," Marlie said. "Kathleen's in her room." She came through the pantry door, carrying ginger ale on a tray.

"But Kathleen's maid of honor," Peter complained. "Hasn't anyone *told* her yet? Marlie, go up like a good girl and tell Kathleen she's to be maid of honor."

"You'd better get well before Mother gets here, that's all I can say."

"Well? Get *well?* Christopher, do I look sick? Fine thing, making other guests submit to medical scrutiny. 'S this?" He took a glass from Marlie's tray and sniffed it. "Oof! Horrible stuff! Better go find something . . ." He burped. "Excuse me, guests. Be back shortly." He went to the sideboard in the dining room, picked up one of the decanters and pushed through the swinging door into the pantry. We heard the refrigerator door slam.

"Why's he acting so funny?" Johnny asked.

Marlie didn't answer. She carried her tray into the living room and set it down on the coffee table. She went over and plugged in the Christmas tree lights.

"Is he really sick?" I asked.

"He's tight," Marlie said quietly. "He was tight before we left town. All the time everybody else was watching that magician, he was locked in the fourth-floor bathroom with a pint of whiskey. I think he got it from Fred. If Mother comes back and catches him, she'll—I don't know what she'll do. She'll *die.*"

Peter had started singing at the top of his lungs: "Here comes the bride, big, fat and wide! Here comes the groom, mar-ching to doom! Here comes . . ." He stopped, and we heard him climbing up the back stairs. He walked down the second-floor hallway and on up to his own room on the third floor. The door slammed. In a few moments it slammed again, and he began to come down the stairs. On the second floor, he dropped something, swore, dropped something else and swore again.

"Kath*leen!*" he howled.

Kathleen waddled out of her room at the back end of the third floor. "What is it you want, Mr. Peter?" she answered.

"It's *you* I want!"

"I'm comin', Mr. Peter." Puffing and gasping, she hurried down the stairs.

"Faster! Faster, Kathleen! You're the maid of *honor,* Kathleen!"

Our cook exploded in a high, girlish giggle that ended in an old woman's cackle. "Yes, Mr. Peter," she sputtered. "Sure I'm right behind you."

The two of them clomped down the main staircase to the front hall. Peter came into the living room, crushing a large, badly wrapped package under his right arm. In his left hand he held his drink. Kathleen, her matted gray hair sprouting loose hairpins, stood timidly behind him, holding two smaller packages.

"Don't be bashful," Peter said to her. "Come right in. Host and hostess be here later. Let's cheer the guests up a bit. Marlie—" He put his glass down and walked over to her, holding the large package at arm's length.

Marlie pretended not to notice him. He plunked the package down in her lap. "Merry Christmas," he said. "From Daddy. From your own father. Whom you seem to have forgotten, but who has not forgotten you."

Taking the two smaller packages from Kathleen, he tossed one to Johnny and the other to me. "Merry Christmas from Daddy," he repeated. "Merry Christmas from Daddy."

"Where's yours?" I asked.

"Mine?" he said, picking up his drink. "Oh, *mine* . . . Guess I must have dropped it," he mumbled, and stamped back up the stairs.

Kathleen stood in the middle of the living room, a sad, kind smile on her face. "Sure it was a grand time yez had, with all the cousins and all," she said. "I have twenty-two first cousins meself, so I know."

Nobody answered her. Johnny and I were unwrapping our presents. Marlie hadn't touched hers, except to shove it off her lap. She sat gazing blankly at the porch doors.

"Would you be wantin' me to set the table for supper, Miss Marlie?" Kathleen asked. "Or shall I wait for the missus?"

Hearing her name, Marlie turned. She looked at Kathleen in a frightening way—as if she had never seen her before. It was the same dazed expression that had come over her the moment she'd realized that she had missed my father's visit.

"I'll make up some sandwiches," Kathleen said gently, and left the room. Her shoes squeaked with every step she took.

"What did you get?" Johnny asked me, opening the blades of his Scout knife.

"Same," I said.

"What's this for?"

"Punch holes in leather. Like belts." He nodded. We both looked at Marlie.

"Why don't you open it?" Johnny asked. "Go on, Marl—it's from *Daddy.*"

She fingered the loose package. Then she slipped the string down around the white drugstore paper and took out a cheaply made brown kangaroo.

"It's a trick," she said, letting the kangaroo fall to the floor. She picked the paper up and examined it. "Peter bought it," she said. "He bought it himself, at that drugstore in the Suburban Station, when he was coming home for Christmas vacation."

"Maybe Daddy sent him the money," Johnny said.

"Why? Why, after all these years of not even *writing!*" She threw the wrapping paper aside and ran out of the living room and up the stairs. "Peter?" she called. I heard her walk down the hallway to Johnny's and my room, back through her own room, then around the stairwell to Mother's. Four or five times she called his name: not loudly and not softly; just the way you do when you expect somebody to answer from nearby. It wasn't until she started up the stairs to the third floor that she shouted his name. She shouted it twice, in rapid succession: "Peter! *Peter!*" Then a door opened and banged against a wall.

I didn't know at the time, and I don't know now, why I

followed her. I remember deciding to tell Johnny that I was going to get ready for supper, but it wasn't necessary. He had taken off his belt and was punching holes in it.

Even before I reached the third floor I saw them. Peter's bedroom door was wide open. He was sprawled in the red leather armchair next to the bookcase, his profile to me. His eyes were closed, his feet stretched out in front of him, and he was humming the bridal march: "Dum-dum-dee*dum,* dum-dum-dee*dum . . .*"

Marlie stood, her back to me, watching him. "You did," she was saying in a low voice. "You did, didn't you?"

Peter stopped humming, opened his eyes for a second, then closed them again.

"Peter!" Marlie crouched down and shook his shoulder. "Please answer me, Peter, you've *got* to answer me, you've got to!" she begged. Peter opened his eyes and smiled—a sleepy, teasing smile. "I know where you bought it," Marlie said quickly. "Just tell me if he sent you the money, just tell me . . . *Oh!*" She stood and turned away from him in disgust.

Peter slapped his palms down against the leather arms of his chair and hoisted himself up. He stood unsteadily, one hand on the bookcase. He looked at Marlie and smiled again. " 'S the difference?" he asked. He patted her on the top of her head. "Time for beddy-bye," he said. "Night-night." He wheeled around and stumbled toward his bed. Taking off his coat, he dropped it on the floor, then flopped onto the bed and lay there for a few moments, humming "Dum-dum-dee*dum,"* before his breathing became deep and regular.

Even when I heard her, Marlie was so quiet that at first I didn't realize she was crying. She was seated on the edge of the red armchair, bending forward with her face in her hands. I felt ashamed, spying on her; but when I turned to tiptoe back downstairs, the banister creaked.

Marlie jerked her hands from her face. The whole upper half of her body became rigid. She stared at me, at first in real terror.

Then she realized who I was, and an expression of relief came into her eyes. I started to say something, but she had already twisted sideways, throwing herself against the arm of the chair, and begun to cry—not quietly any more, but out of control, the way Johnny sometimes cried.

Finally she managed to get her breath and look up at me. "I love Daddy!" she sobbed. "I love him, Chris—you *know* how I love him!"

"Mar*lee? Mar*lee!" It was Mother's voice, coming from the first floor. Marlie closed her eyes and pressed her hands against her ears. "Come down to the living room, dear," Mother called. "And tell Peter to. Mr. Wagner's going to open a bottle of champagne. Is Chris up there? Marlie! *Ou*-hoo, *Mar*lee!"

For a moment I was sure that Peter had won: that Marlie was going to break down completely.

"Do you want me to tell them you're sick?" I asked her. "You can sneak down to your room and get into your pajamas. I'll say you ate too much."

Marlie didn't answer. Instead, she jumped up from the chair, ran to Peter's bureau and started tugging his comb through her hair. She dropped the comb, wiped her eyes with her handkerchief, then leaned closer to the mirror and pinched her cheeks.

"Do you want me to do that, Marl?"

"I don't know what you're talking about." Without looking at me, she ran to the banister and shouted, "Be right down, Ma! Be right down, Mr. Wagner!"

Ten

Between Christmas and the end of the first week in January, when Peter went back to boarding school, he was just the same toward Mother, maybe worse.

"Come on, now, Peter, snap out of it," Mother said when he refused to go to the New Year's Eve dance at the Cricket Club. "All week you've been acting like a spoiled child. How about setting some kind of an example for your brothers?"

"How about the example *you've* been setting with Mr. Wagner, all last fall while I was at school?" Peter said, leaning his chair back on the living-room rug the way he knew Mother hated him to.

Mother didn't answer right away; she just stared at him, speechless. Then she spoke slowly, trying to control her voice: "That remark is so disloyal and so—so *mean*—that I can't believe you meant to say it, Peter, and I'm going to forget that you did. We were talking about the New Year's Eve dance. At some sacrifice, I have paid for your subscription."

"I never asked you to."

"You never asked me to, true. You never asked me to give you a monthly allowance, or to do a great many other things which I do, and which I will continue to do, because I am your mother and you are my child. That's not the point, and you know it."

"The *point*—you're always talking about the point! The point is, you're going out tonight with Mr. Wagner and you don't want me lurking around when he comes! That's the real point."

"Peter, I think you had better go to your room. I think you had better go to your room and stay there until you're ready to apologize."

"All right by me." He got up, went to the piano, took a cigarette out of the silver box, stuck it behind his ear and walked upstairs.

Mother leaned her head back against the sofa and shut her eyes. "Want an aspirin?" Johnny asked. "I know where Miss Browning keeps them." Mother shook her head, rolling it from side to side against the sofa back, without opening her eyes.

THE WEDDING WAS IN APRIL, a few days before Peter's Easter vacation began, but the school let him come home early. All of us (including Mr. Wagner, looking cautiously cheerful) went to meet him at North Philadelphia Station the afternoon before the wedding. The engine shot past, then the Pullman cars and the coaches—coach after coach, each moving a little more slowly than the one before. Red-capped porters filed along the platform, spacing themselves. Groups of people there to board the train pressed first to the right, then to the left, dragging their suitcases with them, trying to guess where the doors would be when the train finally came to a complete stop.

I climbed onto a bench and stood behind Mother and Mr. Wagner so that I could see better. There was a sharp screeching sound as the train couplings jarred; then conductors, slamming back the metal doors, shouted, "Watch your step . . . Watch your step, please . . . Let the passengers off first . . . Stand back, please . . . Watch your step!"

"See him, kids?"

"Not yet, Ma."

"I hope he's wearing a suit. I wrote him to be sure and wear a coat and pants that match."

The porters began picking up bags and moving ahead of their newly arrived passengers toward the stairs that led down into the station waiting room. People going on to Washington or Chicago were still jostling on the platform, crowding into the emptying cars. Others, come to say goodbye, were bending down to look through the train windows, waving, tapping on the gritty panes, making faces, shouting advice.

"What's a wooden nickel?" Johnny asked me.

"Oh, there isn't any such thing. Telling somebody not to take any is just a way of saying don't be a sucker."

The platform was almost clear of coach passengers now, and still we hadn't spotted Peter.

"Maybe he came by Pullman," Marlie said. "Shall I go see?"

"I'll go." Mother walked quickly down the platform toward the head of the train, where the parlor cars were, while Mr. Wagner looked anxiously after her, as though he wasn't quite sure what he was supposed to do in a case like this, when he both was and wasn't in charge.

He pulled a train schedule out of his pocket and began examining it, not looking at Mother, who was still hurrying down the platform away from us. Conductors at each car stood with one foot on the station platform and one inside the train, making departure signals with their arms. "All bo-*wurd!*" one of them shouted—and I saw Mother run up and grab his sleeve.

"All aboard, lady!" he said.

"Is this the train from New York?" she shouted over the sound of hissing steam. "The four thirty-two from New York?"

"Yes, lady—get on if you're getting on. Otherwise, stand back!"

Mother stepped back, but then worked her way from window to window of the nearest parlor car, hurrying so that she could check them all. The train couplings jolted and the cars lurched; then their wheels began to grind forward as train doors were slammed shut. Mother had found another conductor whose door was still open. She shouted something we couldn't hear. The conductor shrugged, shouted something back, motioned for Mother to move, then slammed the door in her face.

"I wonder what in the world your mother hopes to—"

"She's looking for Peter," Johnny said helpfully.

"Yes—so I see." Mr. Wagner gave Johnny's shoulder an affectionate squeeze.

Mother was running back towards us now. "Francis!" she called. "Francis—go check, will you? Please check with the stationmaster!"

"The stationmaster, Louisa?"

"There might have been some mix-up in the schedule. That conductor was very rude—did you hear what he said to me? I've half a mind to report him—Francis, *please!* I'm positive there was a mix-up!"

"I'll be glad to check, but the train did come, my darling. We *saw* the train."

"Well, check anyway. I'm going to phone the house on the chance that he arrived earlier and took a local. Marlie, watch them for me, would you, dear? Kids, don't move an inch. I'll be back in five minutes. Come on, Francis."

Mr. Wagner came back first. I saw him walking toward us, comparing his vest-pocket watch to the platform clock, glancing wistfully down the train tracks in the direction of New York, as if he expected to see Peter tramping along the railroad ties with a suitcase in each hand.

Mother trudged up the platform steps a minute or two later, discouraged and out of breath. "He sent a telegram," she said. "It arrived just after we left the house."

"Will he be on the next train, then?" She shook her head. *"Not on the next one?"* he asked again, making sure.

"We don't have to wait. He's coming later."

Mr. Wagner nodded. "That's it, then," he said. "Let's go, troops."

When we got home, the telegram was lying, unopened, on the hall table. Mother picked it up.

"Say when he's coming, Louisa?" Mr. Wagner asked, with an edge of annoyance to his voice.

She shook her head. "He just says he's taking a different train and not to meet him, he'll get the Glenllyn local from North Philadelphia."

"But you haven't even opened it."

"They phoned it in first," she said, offering him the sealed telegram. He shook his head. "Kathleen read me the message over the phone," she added, looking as though she might burst into tears but still didn't want him to comfort her.

"There's really no excuse for—"

"Francis!"

"Oh, all right, darling. I'm sorry."

"He might have missed his train in New York," she said stubbornly. "I think it was extremely responsible of him to telegraph us not to meet him." He cleared his throat and looked as if he was about to reply. He opened his mouth to speak, but shut it again and smiled ruefully. "Don't *look* that way," Mother said. "What would you have done if you'd missed *your* train in New York?"

He shrugged. "I suppose I wouldn't have missed it," he said quietly. "Not on an occasion like this."

Mother threw the telegram back onto the hall table and walked upstairs. Mr. Wagner fingered it. Then he dropped it, picked up his hat and walked out the door.

It occurred to me that he might not come back—certainly not for the party the Bouviers were giving him and Mother that night.

But he came back about twenty minutes later with a paper bag in his hand. "Here," he said, handing the bag to Marlie. "You'd better all eat this before it melts. Do you think your mother might like some?"

"*Sure* she would," Marlie said. "Boys, go tell her." Johnny and I ran upstairs and knocked on her bedroom door.

She was lying on her bed.

"Come down," Johnny said. "Mr. Wagner brought us ice cream. Chocolate!"

"Ice cream—at this time of year?" She sat up and started buttoning the front of her dress. "That man is the limit!" She reached for her shoes. "Tell him I'll be right down. Tell him a plate of chocolate ice cream would be the *pièce de résistance.*"

"The what?"

"Just say I'd love some."

PETER HADN'T COME HOME by the time Marlie and Johnny and I had finished supper. Twice Mother thought she heard him and hurried to the front door. When she had dressed for the Bouviers she came downstairs and sat in the living room, staring into the fire, unwilling to leave the house yet. Mr. Wagner had brought his evening clothes with him, in a suitcase. He dressed for the party too, and joined Mother in the living room.

Mother looked up at him as he sank down into the leather chair by the fireplace. "I can't understand it," she said. "I just don't know what to think. He should certainly be here by now."

"We have his telegram, so we know he's on the way. Let's relax and have a little confidence in him."

"We should—we should. But I have this awful feeling, this foreboding. After the way he behaved last January. I know it's silly, but . . ."

"Is there anyone you can telephone? Anyone he might be staying with, here or in New York?"

"If it were the school's vacation, yes—but the rest of his class is still at school. Getting him permission to come home early was like pulling hen's teeth."

"You know, Weezie, he's really pretty grown up for his age. Not mature, maybe, but very competent. Self-assured. I'd say he can take care of himself, don't you agree?"

"Alone? In New York? At sixteen? Suppose—just suppose—" She didn't finish. She leaned forward, covering her eyes with her hands. Mr. Wagner half-stood and seemed about to go to her, but changed his mind and sat down again. For a minute or two they both sat glumly staring into the fire: he in his tux and she in her yellow-silk evening dress. Mr. Wagner checked his watch.

Mother saw him and smiled. "Well," she said, "I suppose we really should leave."

Mr. Wagner didn't answer, but he did go to the hall closet and get his coat. He put it on cautiously, as though it were lined with pins. Then he got Mother's fur wrap and placed it carefully over his arm.

Mother went up to him. She let him arrange the wrap about her shoulders. He went to the hall table and picked up his hat. His hand was on the doorknob.

"I can't go, Francis!" Mother said. "Francis, he's my own—" The telephone rang. She wheeled around and picked up the receiver. "Hello!" she shouted. "Hello—*hello!*" She closed her eyes. "Oh," she said in a flat voice. She slumped into the chair by the telephone. "We'll be right over, Rosalie. We're leaving now. No. No, everything's fine. We'll be right over. Goodbye."

She hung up, but held the telephone in her lap, staring at it as if she expected it to ring again. Then slowly she set it back on its table, got up and went over to Mr. Wagner. Without a word, she pulled his face down to hers and kissed him on the mouth.

His hat slipped from his fingers and fell to the rug. There was lipstick on his face. Johnny and I giggled.

"Where's your handkerchief, my darling?" Mother said, reaching into his breast pocket. She wiped the lipstick off his face, then picked up his hat and placed it, cockeyed, on his head. "My paragon," she said. "My paragon of punctuality. We're going to be awfully late."

PETER CAME HOME the next morning, in plenty of time for the wedding, and he behaved beautifully: wore a suit; sat quietly through the brief ceremony at St. Mark's Church; went to the reception and looked friendly. I think he even wished them well as they drove off on their honeymoon. I asked him whether he'd changed his mind.

"About what?" he said. "Oh, that. Hell no. But I promised someone I wouldn't cause any trouble today."

"Who?"

"Never mind who. The person I stayed in New York with last night."

He didn't have to tell me who that was. Even Mother had guessed. I could tell by the fact that she never asked Peter about it—never once brought the subject up.

Eleven

MOTHER QUIT HER JOB, of course. She and Mr. Wagner went to White Sulphur Springs for their honeymoon and a couple of months later they took a second trip, this time with Marlie, to Canada. That was in the middle of June, right after school. Mother wanted to send Johnny and me to a camp in New Hampshire, but we talked her out of it. We loved Loon Lake, and convinced her that Miss Browning would be able to take care of us well enough, with Peter's help.

All that summer, but especially the first part, Johnny and I felt free as the wind—as the wind in your face when you're twelve years old and coasting downhill on a bike. We would usually jump on our bikes right after breakfast and meet at somebody's house or at the beach. If we saw a cluster of friends' bikes at the Cooks' or the Townsends' or the Grays', we coasted in; if we didn't, we kept on around to the head of the lake. Most of us gathered at the beach, around a big rock outside the Sweet Shop, by nine or nine-thirty. Then we'd decide whether to go swimming or play games on our bikes—like follow-the-leader, or no-hands coasting down the Lakeview Hotel hill, or bike polo with croquet mallets on the hard-packed baseball diamond back of the village water tower. If we swam, we'd practice up for the Water Sports. Canoe tilting and underwater distance plunge and backstroke were my favorite events, because I was good at them. I could spend an entire morning practicing holding my breath and fluttering—you were allowed to flutter your legs in the distance plunge, but your arms had to be straight out in front.

It was quite a contrast—after three or four hours of shouting, choosing up sides, arguing about rules, splashing, ducking, being chased—to come home for lunch and see Peter sitting up in our rickety tree house reading (of all things) Greek; or tinkering with the engine of the secondhand Model A Mother had bought so he could do errands when she and Mr. Wagner were off on a trip like the one to Canada. While they were on their trip he played a lot of golf, but as soon as they got back he seemed to drop the game and stick pretty much to the big porchy summer cottage with the wisteria trellis and the sloping back lawn with the apple trees forever thudding and the deep crowded flower beds. He stopped playing golf because he hated meeting Mother and Mr. Wagner on the fairway and being asked to join them. Mr. Wagner was even becoming fatherly about the whole thing, showing Peter his "magic" grip and offering to pay for golf lessons.

So Peter decided to try tennis. He came to this decision the first week in August—not to play tennis *with* anybody (not Peter), but against the backboard, and so early in the morning that he had the courts entirely to himself.

I know because I was there. He'd wake me, shake me impatiently at five-thirty in the morning and offer me ten cents an hour to be his ballboy. Ten cents an hour—that was a fifth of my weekly allowance every sixty minutes. We'd grab a quick breakfast (I never understood what all the rush was about, but Peter managed to intensify nearly everything he did in a way that defied argument), jump into the Model A and drive up to the Lakeview Hotel courts.

The hotel itself—a multidormered, shingle-roofed, buff clapboard affair with green shutters—straddled the summit of a pine hill overlooking the whole of Loon Lake. The tennis courts, eight of them side by side, were hidden (that was the effect) halfway down the back slope of the hill, at the end of a path worn through the underbrush. There was a shed-roofed grandstand facing the first court and a green-painted, white-marked backboard behind the last one; but at six o'clock in the morning it was hard to believe that anyone but ourselves could possibly know that all this existed.

They didn't know, as far as Peter was concerned. The courts were his, all eight of them, and the grandstand and the backboard and the high wire fence, with the pine forest just outside. Looking clumsy as ever in his spotless white ducks, cable-stitched V-neck sweater and Keds, with his William J. Tilden racket and his string bag of fifteen used tennis balls, Peter strode, flat-footed, across the courts each morning, taking full possession.

Solemnly he arranged the balls in triangles on the surface of the eighth court—the one with the backboard. Then he rallied all fifteen balls against the backboard exactly once, before taking his sweater off and hanging it on the near net post. He went through these motions ritualistically, without talking. Except for our sneakers scuffing the clay and the dead, hypnotic thud of tennis balls pounding the backboard, neither of us made a sound. Peter hardly looked at me; he addressed himself to the backboard, always to the backboard, as though he'd sensed some enemy behind it and was challenging him to a hopeless match.

Hopeless, because Peter couldn't play—had never once won a set from anybody, even Marlie, so far as I knew. When he practiced serving, he invariably foot-faulted, dragging the toe of his sneaker over the back line, scraping a hole in it and caking the toe of his sock with reddish dust as he swatted angrily at the descending ball. Even I, though I could hardly swing his bludgeon of a racket, could have told him that his feet were wrong for the backhand; that he shouldn't stiffen and stand so straight when he hit a forehand; he shouldn't lunge so at the ball; he shouldn't *stab* at it.

I could have told him, and perhaps I would have, if I had ever worked up enough courage to break the silence. But my job was to run after the balls, bring them back in the net bag, and arrange them in triangles at three-foot intervals across the court. When I had every little lobed triangle in place, Peter would turn from glaring at the backboard and, squatting angrily, would clutch the nearest bunch in his big left hand.

Though he checked his wristwatch before and after practicing, there was no definite quitting time. Our sessions all ended in the same way: with the appearance of another person. *Any* other person—the old Armenian who kept the courts in shape; a bellboy off duty; hotel guests out for a walk. Peter and I had a signaling system: if I heard or saw anyone coming, I was to swing the ball bag in a circle over my head; if he did, he was to grab his sweater.

One morning we were surprised by a frail, vellum-skinned gentleman wearing a white visor cap and brown linen plus fours. He had a leather case slung around his turkeylike neck, and was standing not ten feet beyond the wire fence, peering into the treetops through binoculars, looking for birds. Neither Peter nor I had heard him approach and we both spotted him at the same instant. Peter grabbed his sweater; I ran for the tennis balls. We were off the courts and halfway up the path before the man had even lowered his binoculars.

A few mornings after that, the one thing we had never anticipated happened: there was someone on the courts when we arrived. Because of the way the path curves around and in back of the grandstand, you don't see the courts until you're practically on them. I might have heard the faint scuff and thud sounds if I hadn't been thinking about canoe tilting. As it was, neither of us saw her until we were most of the way across the first court. Peter stopped walking and stuck his arm out to halt me. We stood there and looked at her as though she were an optical illusion: if we blinked hard enough, surely she would vanish.

But the girl—for she was a girl, fifteen or sixteen years old—had no intention of vanishing. She was wearing one of those white tennis dresses with a short frilly skirt and a round sailor hat with the brim pulled down in front to make a visor. She was on the eighth court, practicing her serve. She would serve three balls from one side of the net, throwing them so high that she had to stand on the toes of her sneakers, racket poised for what seemed like ten seconds, waiting for the ball to drop within range. If two of the three balls went over the net she would get the third—walking up to it with an easy, long-legged grace, unconscious that she was being watched—and serve again. When all three balls were on the opposite side she would walk around the net, pick them up smoothly with her racket and begin serving from that side. She did this perhaps three separate times while Peter and I retreated, stepping very gradually backwards into the shadow of the grandstand, Peter's arm still out stiff as though to prevent me from dashing impulsively forward. Then, just as we reached the grandstand, she looked over and saw us.

Nothing happened, except that Peter and I stood there (I, at least, feeling we'd been caught red-handed) while she peered at us as though we were at a great distance, on the far horizon, and she were wondering whether or not she recognized us and should wave or speak.

Before she did either, Peter turned his back on her and hurried up the path. But the next morning she was, almost literally, lying in wait for us. We had crept down the path listening, this time, for any sound from the courts. There were none. With a renewed sense of early-morning ownership, we walked around the grandstand and there she was: sitting on the bottom row of seats, contemplating a new can of tennis balls. On the bench beside her was a book, opened and face down, as though she had come prepared to wait for us all morning if necessary.

"I was hoping you might come again," she said in a vaguely British accent, without looking up. Then she took a deep breath, as if she were about to deliver a rehearsed speech, and raised her

eyes. "My name," she began matter-of-factly, "is Linda Mayewski. That is Polish, and I am Polish," she said, patting the book
beside her, "just like the girl in here. I work at the hotel. In the
mornings I am what is called a 'companion' to Mrs. Phipps, an
old lady who likes for me to read to her the fashion magazines,
and in the afternoon, while Mrs. Phipps rests, I have a job tutoring French and sometimes Latin."

She paused, frowning down at the still-unopened can of tennis
balls in her lap. Then she held the can up to her cheek, gave the
key a twist and smiled, her eyes lighting up with unselfconscious
delight as the hiss of compressed air, escaping with a minute
explosion, lifted a strand of her light-brown hair. She had silky,
almost weightless hair, cut in a pageboy bob, and features that
were delicate but not doll-like. When she spoke she looked directly at you, without blinking, in a way that made her seem both
vulnerable and oddly commanding—like those wide-eyed, fearless
princesses in medieval tapestries containing unicorns.

"That," she concluded, "is why I must play tennis at this funny
hour, and why I have no one with which to oppose." Her speech
over, she placed the can on the seat and for the first time smiled
at us: a frankly hopeful smile, divided equally between Peter and
me.

Peter seemed paralyzed, as if he had not only never been
spoken to in that way before but never been spoken to at all by
a girl, which was not quite true (he'd gone to all the same dancing
classes Marlie had). His gaze dropped to his feet, then shifted to
the courts, fixing finally on the distant backboard.

Somebody, I felt, had to say something soon—anything, so
long as it was kind. "He doesn't speak English," I blurted. "He
only speaks Greek. You know, *old* Greek. Like in Homer."

The girl looked at me, puzzled; for a moment I was afraid she
might take a deep breath and deliver her introductory speech all
over again. Instead, she looked thoughtfully at Peter, then said to
me: "Is he your brother?"

I nodded.

"Could you ask him, in old Greek, would he like to have a game of practice tennis? Could you say: It is tiresome to play with one's self—so little hitting for the much hiking after balls."

I turned to Peter. He hadn't moved a muscle; he stood, bull-necked, his eyes magnetized by the backboard eight courts away. I willed him to turn; I used all the telepathy I could muster to get him to turn and say something nice to the girl, even if he had to lie about how he couldn't or wouldn't play tennis with her. But Peter didn't budge. I glared at his stubborn back, at the cable stitching of his sweater stretching like coils around his heavy shoulders.

Finally, out of sheer exasperation, I hurled at that lumpish back the only phrase I could think of that was even close to Greek. "Gallia!" I shouted. *"Gallia est omnes divisa in partes* tres!"

I turned and looked apologetically at the girl, but she didn't speak to me—she just blushed, the redness starting at the base of her neck and seeming to rise, like a vessel filling with the color of embarrassment: flowing upwards through her cheeks and forehead to the roots of her hair. She picked up the can of new balls in one hand, her racket in the other, and walked, without looking right or left, straight toward the farthest court.

Peter still stared at the backboard. When she crossed his line of vision he said, quietly but distinctly, "Please stay."

She stopped, looked at him, holding his gaze for a few seconds, then nodded solemnly.

"Let's rally here by the grandstand," he said. "We won't need the court with the backboard."

They didn't seem to notice when I slipped away. At the first turn in the path I called "See ya!" to Peter, and he waved with his racket, and I left.

Twelve

NEVER CHASED TENNIS BALLS for him again, which was all right with me; I didn't need the money all that badly, and the August Water Sports were coming up soon, so Roger Townsend and I had to start practicing canoe tilting. Roger was my paddler.

The South Landing boathouse stored the poles and outsized pontoon canoes used for tilting, built with woven rope platforms across their bows. Roger and I were friends with Andy, the boathouse keeper, so he showed us the ledge on which he hid the key when he went off duty at six. Starting a week before the Water Sports, we met on the landing every evening after supper, and for an hour or so before sundown went through our paces.

A tilting pole is a fifteen-foot length of bamboo with a round, flattened, canvas-covered buffeter on one end. Tilting technique, the object of which is to knock your opponent off his platform and into the water, is difficult to perfect unless you have an opponent, but Roger and I did pretty well, considering. He would try to throw me off balance by stopping and turning the canoe as abruptly as he could, while I jumped about the platform making lunges at the air. After we'd had enough of that, we would imagine opponents in a variety of positions—coming at us head-on, broadside, off each quarter—then plan and practice executing our defense strategy. Finally we'd go through our offensive signals. I'd shout "One!" if I wanted Roger to feint a head-on attack and swivel right at the last second, "Two!" for swivel left, and so forth.

We felt pretty confident after nearly a week of practice sessions, so we decided to cut the final one down to half an hour and spend it entirely on attack signals. Roger was already at the landing when I arrived.

"Something's in there," he said in a low voice, nodding toward the boathouse. I knew Roger from school, as well as up here at Loon Lake. He was as brave as I was about most things and braver about some, but partly because he had a crew cut that was always a little long and made his hair seem to stand on end, he looked perpetually scared. There were certainly noises coming from inside the boathouse: random creakings and knockings. Roger was probably thinking of that bear that had been seen earlier in the summer, rummaging through garbage pails. I was, anyhow; but I wasn't going to let him know it.

"We'd better take a look," I said without much enthusiasm. "It might be somebody loosening the platform on our canoe. Got the key?" Roger opened his palm and showed me the key. I took it from him so he wouldn't have to pretend not to want to hand it to me.

The moment I turned the key and the big iron lock clicked, the noises inside stopped. I swung the wide, rotting boathouse door open a crack and looked in. Except for a few stripes of light where the wall boarding had separated, it was pitch-dark at the back of the boathouse; but directly in front of me I could see our big pontoon canoe, untouched, right where we had left it the evening before.

"Here goes," I whispered, then swung the door all the way open, at the same time bracing myself to make either a running dive into the lake or a dash for my bike on the path behind the boathouse. But nothing jumped out at me. There was nothing to hear but the screech of the rusty door hinges and nothing to see but piles of waterproof cushions, paddles stacked against the walls, and canoes nested in double-decker racks.

"Must be back there," Roger murmured, meaning at the far end where the rowboats were kept—the only portion of the boathouse we couldn't see clearly. I stared into the irregular patch of darkness until my eyes could distinguish one hull from another, but I still couldn't make out anything alive.

"See if there's a flashlight behind Andy's deck chair," I whispered.

"There isn't," Roger whispered right back, without even checking. "Look, Chris, we know our signals. Why don't we just skip—"

"Okay," I said. "Agreed." As I was swinging the big door shut I saw the toe of a man-sized sneaker poking above the bow of a rowboat, and toward the stern, a pair of extremely wide, fearless-looking eyes staring at me. I didn't know whose the sneaker was, but the eyes belonged to Linda Mayewski.

"See you at the beach tomorrow," Roger said, already on his bike.

"When's the tilting?"

"Middle of the morning," he called over his shoulder. "Around ten-thirty."

As I picked up my bike and wheeled it along the path, I noticed the loose boards, four of them, at the corner of the boathouse. I wondered why people called it necking when necks didn't have all that much to do with it. Or maybe they did, for all I knew. Peter might be able to tell me—though I'd have to be careful not to mention that I'd seen Linda in the boathouse, in case it made him jealous to know she was fooling around with someone else.

Roger and I won the junior canoe tilting, and I also won the fifty-yard backstroke and came in second in the underwater distance plunge (ten to fourteen years old). As we were walking back to our seats after being given the medals, I saw Peter—not in the crowd around the judge's platform but way back at the edge of the woods where the path up to the Lakeview Hotel begins. I couldn't understand it; Peter hated the beach—especially things like the August Water Sports. When I got to my folding chair I stood up on it to see over the crowd.

It was Peter all right, and he was actually clapping for Roger and me. He saw me on the chair and clapped even harder. He was in his white ducks and V-neck sweater, and he must have walked down from the hotel courts, because standing right beside him was Linda Mayewski. As soon as I saw her, I knew who else had been in the boathouse the evening before. At the time I'd half-recognized the sneaker from the way the toe was worn through, but I just couldn't believe it.

"WHAT'S IT LIKE, to walk up there and get all those medals?" Peter asked. We were sitting in the car outside the Sweet Shop, waiting for Johnny.

"It feels—it feels just right," I said. "That sounds conceited but I mean after practicing so much, it feels as though you really —as though there would be something wrong if you *didn't* get it."

"You practiced, all right. I can testify to that."

"It was you in the boathouse, wasn't it?"

He nodded. "I'm in love," he said, with a wonderful simplicity. "Chris, I'm in *love.*"

I decided not to ask him about necking. "Is it a secret?"

He shrugged, then thought for a moment and nodded. "Kind of—though Ma knows something is going on. She disapproves."

"How can she?" I asked. "She doesn't even know Linda."

"Not who Linda is, but what she is. Rather, what she isn't. Ma knows that Linda isn't ever going to be a Philadelphia deb."

"Is that important?"

"To some people, nothing else is important."

"What makes you think Ma feels that way?"

"She said she'd heard I was going around with a Lakeview Hotel waitress. I explained that Linda wasn't a waitress, she was a lady's companion, but Ma keeps bringing the subject up and referring to Linda as 'that Polish waitress.' "

"But suppose she were?"

"Were what?"

"A waitress instead of a lady's companion."

"Good question," Peter said, "and *touché*. It would make absolutely no difference whatsoever."

"I don't think Ma could really—"

"Oh, yes, she could. You'll find out."

"But don't you think—"

"Let's drop it. Here's Johnny."

TWO DAYS LATER, Linda was killed in a car accident. She was being driven down the mountain by one of the hotel guests—not the woman she worked for but a friend of the woman's—when their brakes gave way and they plunged over the embankment at a turn. The driver wasn't hurt. Linda was killed instantly.

Thirteen

INSIDE HIMSELF PETER WENT WILD, but it was a quiet kind of wild and had nothing to do with getting back at anyone. It had to do with himself, with (it almost seemed) becoming someone different from the way he had been before he'd met Linda—becoming a new person, sort of in her honor. Like going to the Water Sports ceremony, and clapping for Roger and me—that wasn't the old Peter at all. Neither was his telling me, outside the Sweet Shop, that he was in love. Peter had always been secretive, almost sneaky with his thoughts, yet here he was telling *me*, his kid brother, that he was in love. And after Linda died, he didn't stop being in love. He did, of course, in that the way he was in love had to change, but he refused to go back on his new self and become all closed up again. For example, he cried. I don't mean in public or at home in the living room when people were around, but all of a sudden it would come over him—the realization that Linda was no longer alive, that he would never be able to hold her hand again—and he would go off by himself and cry, sometimes for an hour, until he had exhausted himself. If anyone asked him why he had been crying he would tell them: because a girl he loved had been killed. And if they wanted to know more or talk on because they were embarrassed, he said he'd rather not go into it. But the way he said this was not unkind—just a straight-forward statement of the way he felt. It was wonderful. It was a sort of miracle.

No, that's ridiculous, it was nothing of the kind, and probably he hadn't changed all that much from his old self, but to me it seemed that he had; because his attitude toward me changed so noticeably—partly, I guess, due to my being there that morning we'd first met Linda. More than once he went over it with me, moment by moment. Especially he liked to dwell on the way she'd looked, her smile and the way her eyes had lighted up, when she held the unopened can of tennis balls to her ear and twisted the key, then felt the tiny rush of air.

"Do you know what she was reading?" he asked me one day, back in Glenllyn. "The book with the Polish girl in it?" I shook my head, and he held up the book in his hand: *The Rainbow* by D. H. Lawrence. "Right now it's too old for you," he said, "but maybe some of his short stories aren't. I'll give you 'The Rocking Horse Winner.' See what you think. And don't feel stupid if you don't understand it, because almost *no*body your age reads Law-rence. But try it. Write me at school and tell me what you think."

I did, and Peter replied; then I read another story he'd recom-mended (by Lawrence—or maybe Hemingway or Fitzgerald) and wrote him again. Up until then my favorite books had been *Tom Brown at Yale* and *Ted Scott over the Rio Grande,* so the stories by Lawrence and the others didn't mean all that much to me; I had to fake it a little when I wrote Peter what I thought of them, and I guess he could tell that, but he never called me on it. He seemed to feel, as I did, that writing him about the stories was a good way to get started on letters. Yet that wasn't all it was, because even when I couldn't imagine myself being any of the characters or understand why they felt and did what they did, I got a sense—sometimes a strong sense, especially from Lawrence

—of the way they let their bodies think for them; and, partly anyway, it explained the change that had come over Peter. I don't mean that he was imitating Lawrence characters; but something inside him responded to the way Lawrence felt about life, and Peter gave in to it with that slightly self-conscious intensity that characterized so many of the things he said and did. Even his answers to the most innocuous questions now had about them an alarming honesty, an almost poetic directness that was full of surprises.

"How was the dance last night?" I remember Marlie asking him, one late Sunday breakfast during Christmas vacation. Peter had gone to the Saturday Evening, one of a series which Marlie was still too young for.

"Except for an incident that happened around midnight," Peter said, "it was pretty much what you'd expect: fear on the faces of the wallflowers—canned vivacity from the belles of the ball—in-betweeners looking hungry."

"What happened at midnight?"

"A girl's shoulder strap broke and her left breast popped out. Though she was one of the wallflowers, her breast was a lovely thing to behold: not large but shapely, *promising*. It happened in the shadow of a column, under the balcony, and she didn't think anyone saw. She hurried off to the powder room and got fixed up. When she returned, she was one of the most popular girls on the dance floor, and she didn't dare guess why. She danced around and around, being cut in on by one boy after another. And she just couldn't stop smiling and at the same time she couldn't stop frowning. It was touching and sad and sort of wonderful to see. I almost fell in love with her."

Only the three of us happened to be at the breakfast table on that particular occasion, but Peter would have answered Marlie in the same way no matter who had been there. And the thing that surprised me most was that he wasn't showing off or saying things just for their shock value. Maybe there was a little of that, but mostly he was living up to some code of honesty gleaned from

Lawrence and Hemingway. If he was using it as a weapon, it was against the snobbish side of social decorum: the side of Mother that had disapproved, automatically, of Linda Mayewski.

IT TOOK HIM NEARLY A YEAR to free himself from Linda, but in June, after graduating from school, he fell in love with a girl named Liz Randolph.

I never met her, and the first I heard about her was the night he and she took off from Cathy Sturgis's deb party and drove to Wilmington. Cathy was Trishy's older sister, so Marlie was asked even though she was a subdeb, and Mother said she could go provided Peter took her and Peter drove her home by one o'clock.

Marlie arrived home at one-twenty, but not with Peter—with Graham Brownell, one of Peter's few good friends. Graham explained that Peter was helping Liz Randolph to get her dancing slipper fixed. The heel had broken, so Peter had driven Liz somewhere (Graham didn't know where) to do something about it, and had asked Graham to take Marlie home. Mother was annoyed with Peter, but only mildly; at least he had been responsible enough to see that Marlie was taken care of. She went to bed and slept.

At five-thirty in the morning the phone in her dressing room woke both Mother and Mr. Wagner. It was Liz Randolph's father, who had heard that Peter and Liz had left the dance at about twelve-thirty and hadn't been seen since. Mr. Randolph wondered whether Peter was home yet. Mother checked, discovered he wasn't, and got worried. She and Mr. Wagner sat up waiting.

At six-thirty, Peter arrived (without Liz—he'd taken her home) and walked right into their ambush. I wasn't awake to hear it but Peter said Mr. Wagner had opened the front door and greeted him with "Well, Don Juan, you seem to be a real chip off the old block. What have you done with the Randolph girl?" Then Mother burst into tears. Then Peter said, "Everybody's safe—

almost everybody is sound," and trudged upstairs before they could properly give him hell.

"Who's Don Whatsis?"

"Some hot-stuff lover boy. Look him up in the encyclopedia. Spelled with a J, not a W." I did look him up, but it didn't help much. I mean I couldn't connect it with that remark about Peter being a chip off the old block, and while I liked Mr. Wagner most of the time and tried to remember to call him Dad, I didn't think he had a right to say things like that. It made me want to stand up for Peter—and so did a remark Mr. Wagner's mother made a few days later.

ALL OF US EXCEPT PETER went to our stepgrandmother's birthday party the following Sunday. As on the few other occasions when we'd gone to Rollingmede, I was astounded by the size of the Wagner estate. It was like two, maybe three, golf courses side by side, enclosed by an elaborately spiked black iron fence twenty feet high.

"Home sweet home," Mr. Wagner muttered as we passed the Gothic-looking stone gatehouse, and the way he said it (with a touch of bitterness) made me wonder why, with all his money, he had moved in with *us* after marrying Mother.

After driving through a patch of maples and oak trees, we climbed in a slow circle to the tip of a hill from which, in the middle distance, we could see two tenant farms: one for Black Angus cattle, the other for Cheviot sheep—each farm with its own stone farmhouse, barn and whitewashed stone outbuildings. Like a toy Versailles in the distance, straight ahead, we could see the main house.

Now it disappeared, and we drove through a plantation of spruce trees. Mother put her hat on and was looking at herself in the mirror of her compact, dabbing powder on her nose. She put the compact away and twisted around in her seat to make sure we three in the back looked presentable. Marlie stuck her tongue out and Mother smiled, but there was a half-scared look in her eyes—the way she always looked when she had to face old Mrs. Wagner.

We circled past a garage and came to a stop at the front entrance.

"Good afternoon, ma'am—Mr. Francis." Mother's door was opened and held by a stocky man with iron-gray hair cut like a clothes brush.

"Hello there, Joe. Louisa, you remember Joe."

"Why, of course I do. Joe, didn't you used to work for the Glenllyn Police Department?"

"Yes, ma'am, that was some years ago, you have a good memory." His voice was a quiet growl and his speckled gray face was fixed in a slight squint, as though daylight hurt his eyes but not enough to bother with sunglasses. He wore a black linen suit. You could tell he was a watchman because his suit coat was so tight from the bulge of his gun. He helped Mother out of the car now, and we sat in the back seat watching, not daring to move until he had finished with Mother and opened our door.

The house was almost too big to stand back and look at. No one would be peeking out to see who had arrived, any more than you peek out from inside a museum. Taking our carefully wrapped presents, we followed Mr. Wagner down a glassed-in corridor with a flagstone floor. At the end of this a door opened inward, seemingly of its own accord. As I approached, I saw that it was being held by a footman with buck teeth and skin the color of milk chocolate. He stood there a little bent over, half bowing.

"Gibbons," Mr. Wagner said, nodding and smiling. The footman smiled back sadly, as though he knew some melancholy secret which he was sworn not to tell.

Once we were inside, a butler named Stone (also colored, but more dignified than Gibbons: a seventy-year-old Gary Cooper carved out of mahogany) relieved us of the birthday presents we were clutching and placed them on a polished marble table against the wall. Stone then helped Johnny and me off with our coats, and in a rich baritone whisper, asked us (Marlie and Mother had disappeared) whether we wouldn't like to wash our hands. Johnny said no thanks, he had washed them at home, but it appeared there was no question of refusing. Without actually pushing us, Stone managed to propel us across the hall and into a large coatroom, beyond which was an even larger bathroom.

Johnny threw a piece of gum he was chewing into the wastebasket and walked right out again, but I stayed and washed my hands with a round cake of amber-colored soap that had a leather smell. I wondered where Mr. Wagner had gone.

Nobody was in the front hall when I came out of the bathroom, not even Stone or Gibbons. Then I heard the sound of people talking. It came from the far end of the main hallway and off to the right, but the sounds themselves were so lost in the high-ceilinged spaces that it was impossible to tell how many people there were, or whether they were cheerful. I took my present off the marble table and started toward the talking, afraid that lunch might already have begun.

"Christy—" Turning, I saw Mother, who was walking out of still another room with (from the little I could see) huge mirrors all over. "Hi," I said. "Where's Marlie?"

"Dad took her in a minute ago. Now you'll have to take me." She reached for my hand and I gave it to her.

At the end of the hall we turned into the first of what seemed to be several large drawing rooms, and there everybody was. When they saw us, they paused in their talking and made a kind of path for Mother. At the far end of the path was Mrs. Wagner, Sr.: an old lady with bright white hair, wearing a light-gray dress and at least seven strings of giant pearls that looped nearly to her lap. Mother gave my hand a little squeeze, then dropped it and walked ahead of me, straight to the old lady.

I didn't follow her immediately because people started talking again and closed up the path. I couldn't see Johnny, and none of the grownups looked at me. My first thought was to get rid of the present I was holding, so I skirted around the knot of grownups and made my way to Mrs. Wagner. She was sitting in an armchair with a high back that was covered in heavy gold cloth. A man in a thick brown tweed suit sat beside her, on a backless seat covered with the same yellow-gold material. He was leaning backwards with his right leg raised and with both hands clasped around his kneecap. From the family resemblance, I assumed he was Mr. Wagner's brother. He had a long face, thinner and younger than Mr. Wagner's, and light-brown hair. His slightly bulging brown eyes wandered lazily about the room. There was a bored expression on his face that flickered from time to time into faint amusement. As he clasped his kneecap, he let the raised foot swing a little back and forth. He caught me looking at him. For a moment he stared back, eyes bulging; then, inclining his head in his mother's direction, he pointed to the present tucked under my arm and said: "Happy birthday, Mama."

Mrs. Wagner fixed her gaze on me. She looked as if I had threatened to throw the present in her face. "And which one might you be?" she said in a crisp, quiet voice, as though she and I were alone in the room together. "I have a difficult time keeping track."

"I'm Chris."

"Chris? That's three, isn't it, Richie?" The man beside her nodded. "I thought there were four."

"There are." He dropped his leg and put his hand up to his mouth to hide a yawn.

"Yes, of course," she simpered. "The fourth is Saint Peter."

"Peter is no saint and I'll bet neither are you," I said, blushing, "but who would want to be?"

Her eyes opened very wide, and for a moment they flashed anger; but when Richie tossed his head back and laughed silently, she took a deep breath, fingered her pearls and looked at me as though I were something she might consider collecting. I looked back at her in the same way. Her dress had rows of tiny gray glass cylinders sewn in the shape of a V down her front. Her hair was piled high in a pompadour of pure-white ringlets. Her brows and lashes were dark. Her gray eyes were large, beautiful and cold.

There were minute red veins on her nostrils, and crisscrossing her cheekbones. She noticed me inspecting her, and a twitch of a smile crossed her lips.

"Your mother tells me you'll be going off to boarding school before long," she said. "I'm sure it will do you a world of good. Now tell me—what is it?"

"What is it?"

"Yes, what *is* it?" She pointed to the present in my hand. I didn't know. Mother hadn't told me.

"A surprise!" I said, holding it out to her. "Don't you want to open it and see?" She chuckled, as if she'd guessed that I didn't know the answer to her question.

"Of course I want to open it," she said, more gently. "But after lunch, I think. Gibbons"—the rabbit-faced footman had appeared from nowhere—"take this young man's birthday present upstairs with the others. Thank you, Chris. You'll find your younger brother with some of my grandchildren, on the porch. Show him the way, Gibbons."

"Whatever did you *say* to Mrs. Wagner?" Mother asked later on, when she was kissing us good night. "From the look on her face, she certainly seemed surprised."

I didn't know how to explain without getting her upset about nothing, so I shrugged, and she decided not to pursue the subject.

Fourteen

SOME KIND OF DEMON had taken hold of me when Mrs. Wagner had made that crack about Saint Peter, and I'd liked it—*liked* talking back to her, then staring back at her. The trick was not to care. More and more, that summer up at Loon Lake, I took chances I would never have taken before. I smoked for the first time: corn silk in a corncob pipe, then real tobacco rolled with a cigarette-making machine that I ordered from a coupon in a magazine and had shipped to "Mr. Roger Townsend, c/o Christopher Hooper." One afternoon when nobody was around, I got in Mr. Wagner's Lincoln, sat behind the wheel, tried the gearshift, pretended to steer— then, before I could change my mind, turned the key in the ignition and took off. Just around the block and back, first gear all the way; but it would be hard to exaggerate how wonderful it felt. The next day a whole gang of us went on a hayride for Gary Cook's birthday party, and I kissed Annabelle Swenson—a girl about whom I'd had, until that very moment, feelings so torturously romantic that I hardly dared look at her

for fear she might catch me and frown or (more likely) sneer.
What she did—when I pretended to lose my balance on top
of the moving wagon, fell against her (missing my aim) and
kissed her on the chin—was giggle, give me a pretend slap
and giggle again. At this point I sneezed; my favorite corncob,
which I had tucked in my back pocket, snapped in two; and I
have never been able to remember what happened next.

But soon afterwards, I walked in on Miss Russell when she was
half undressed. I am at a loss to explain why, at ten and twelve
years old, Johnny and I still had a nurse, but I believe Miss Russell
was the last of them, and my impression is that Mother employed
her partly out of pity and expected her to be more of a general
help about the house than a governess. She was a sweet, slightly
sardonic, soft-spoken hunchback who had no friends on the
mountaintop and nothing different to do on her days off, yet
never complained. So when the telephone rang one afternoon and
the person calling asked for Miss Russell, I felt so glad for her that
I ran up to her room, banged on her door and opened it simultaneously, nearly knocking her down.

"Telephone for you!" I said loudly, offering urgency as my
excuse for bursting in on her. I was so surprised at finding her nose
to nose with me that I didn't immediately realize she was naked
from the waist up. She could have screamed and covered herself,
with her arms if nothing else, but she waited quietly while I
looked at her: marveled at her tanned and drooping breasts with
nipples like two large, soft, purplish strawberries. She *wanted* me
to look at her. But it didn't seem at all as though she were being
provocative. Maybe she was, but what I sensed was something
quite different: as though she was saying, "You thought I was just
a hunchback, didn't you? Well, I'm more than that. Take a good
look—go ahead, see for yourself."

When I became too embarrassed to do what I wanted to do
—keep staring—she nodded briefly and half turned so that her
bare hump was in profile for me.

"You've never had a close look at this back of mine, have you,

Christy?" she said. I shook my head and she said, "Touch it. It won't bite you. That's right. Now run the palm of your hand over it. Make friends. That's the only way to treat a hump, you know —make friends with it. Good. Now, would you please run downstairs and tell whoever is on the telephone that you're sorry for the delay, and that I'll be down in a moment?"

After that I thought of Miss Russell as someone special, someone with a special sense of her own dignity. But also there were times (particularly at the beach) when I could think of nothing but breasts; when the whole point of swimming—indeed, of Loon Lake, of summertime, of life itself—seemed to be the chance it gave you to steal glances at breasts as they moved softly about inside of bathing suits. I schemed to burst in on Marlie accidentally-on-purpose while she was in the bathtub; but the door was always locked, and after my first try, the keyhole was wadded up with toilet paper.

I had to talk to somebody about this new and infinitely enchanting reason for getting up in the morning, so I told Roger Townsend about seeing Miss Russell, and he immediately assumed his Hollywood German Scientist pose. "Yah goot, goot," he droned, pulling at his ear lobe and nodding sagely. "And vut verr zay like—how, egg*zackly*, vould you glassivye zem? De boobs, I mean."

"Classify them?"

"Yeah," he said, shifting back to himself. "*Classify* them."

"Such as?"

"Are you being my straight man?"

"No, I want an answer."

"Well, such as are these particular boobs Blips, Nubbins, Bloopers, Super-bloopers, Baby Blimps . . . or the kind like silk stockings with sand in 'em?"

"Punching bags," I said. "Slightly deflated."

"Very *good*," said Roger. "Keep it up and you may become as scientific as I am. I classify all sorts of things, you know. Such as farts. Are you ready?"

"Ready."

"Farts may be classified as follows: Fizz, Fuzz, Fizzfuzz, Blotch, Blam, Blim-blam, Baloom, Baloom-blotch, Baloom-blam, Baloom-blimblam. And Butler's Revenge."

"What's Butler's Revenge sound like?"

"Can't you guess?" I shook my head. "It's totally silent and goes on unfurling for about fifteen seconds."

ROGER AND I CONSIDERED Johnny too young to be allowed in on such sophisticated discussions; but when it came to action rather than talk—to exploits like planting a stink bomb upwind of the Sunday evening vespers held outdoors at the beach, or sneaking into the Loon Lake movie house—John was in the thick of things. His biggest flaw was being a poor liar; but in spite of that drawback he was an invaluable confederate because there was virtually nothing he didn't dare to do. Once, at school, he was "on detention"—which meant having to spend the afternoon in study hall redoing sloppy homework while everyone else was out playing games—when a baseball came through one of the big plate-glass windows and rolled along the floor to Johnny's feet. For some reason the glass hadn't shattered. There was a hole—larger than the baseball, of course, but still recognizably round—and Johnny (a commendable pitcher for his age) couldn't resist the opportunity it presented. In full sight of the study-hall master, he picked up the baseball and heaved it back through its own hole. The trouble was, he ticked the glass, which shattered the entire pane with a splintering crash, and the school (to save its own face) had to send him home for the rest of the week.

It was through such courageously executed inspirations that Johnny had earned our respect, and we weren't at all surprised when he came to Roger's and my rescue, the time we were shot at by Mr. Kramer behind the movie house.

Early in July, while looking for a tennis ball in the bushes alongside the movie house, we discovered a small window with a faulty screen through which we could slither onto end seats to-wards the back and on the right—a spot almost invisible from the place where Mr. Kramer, the owner, generally stood while the projector was running. This system worked throughout July, and got us into *State Fair* with Janet Gaynor and two Tarzan movies with Maureen O'Sullivan playing Jane. But the first week in August, Mr. Kramer found out, or at any rate repaired the screen and added an outside layer of turkey wire.

"My father keeps his wire cutters in our garage," Roger said, but all three of us knew that would solve nothing.

"Let's go to the Sweet Shop," I said, "and think."

The plan we finally settled on was not another way of getting in to see movies free (that was too much to expect), but simply a way of getting revenge for having been screened out. It was a prank, based on an idea so theatrical that we had to try it whether it worked or not.

The idea was to throw crab apples on the almost flat tin roof of the movie house, so that it would sound, to the old ladies inside, as though a typical Loon Lake thunderstorm was about to sweep the mountaintop. When thunder was actually heard, the afore-mentioned old ladies (and there were a lot of them, along with a few old men—enough to fill the rocking chairs on three large hotel verandas) would usually scurry out to collect their rain checks at the box office, then hurry on back to their hotels before getting soaked.

The show (*Flying Down to Rio,* with Fred Astaire and Ginger Rogers) started at eight-thirty. We were ready by eight twenty-five, when it was getting dark outside and, inside, people were seated but not yet captivated by the movie. One of us was posi-tioned behind and one on either side of the movie house. On signal, we let fly with the crab apples, and crude as this ammuni-tion was, it worked surprisingly well. After each of us had thrown the first half bushel or so, Johnny ran around to spy on the rain-check situation.

As he told us afterwards, John had counted eight or nine (he wasn't sure which) little old ladies who had, without question, already left the movie house and started back up the sidewalk, and he'd seen others lined up at the box office for rain checks, when he heard two shots behind the movie house and ran back to see what had happened.

Roger and I weren't there, but the rest of our apples were, and so was Mr. Kramer, wielding a pistol. "That there's one of 'em!" he shouted, shooting the pistol directly at Johnny as two men in state-trooper uniforms ran around the corner of the movie house and gave chase. John ran across the street, leaped over the three-foot box hedge around Mrs. Ingraham's rooming house, and flattened out on the other side of the hedge, hoping the darkness would hide him until he could find a safer place. It might have, too, if he hadn't been wearing a white shirt, but the troopers spotted him at once; and when Roger and I snuck back to see why John didn't join us at the planned emergency hideout (inside Crossby's wagon barn), the troopers caught us, too.

At the time, it was not at all funny. They made a great show of severity, there in Mr. Kramer's dingy office—beginning with the silent treatment. The two hulking troopers stood guard on either side of the door and we three, scared stiff, sat side by side on a small hard bench. Meanwhile Mr. Kramer (a chicken-breasted, red-eyed, drippy-nosed Pennsylvania Dutchman who wore two-tone perforated shoes, purple suspenders, and a shirt that looked like mattress ticking) leaned against his roll-top desk and telephoned Mother to come "bail out" her delinquent children. Apparently he thought Roger was one of her children too, because he didn't telephone the Townsends, and we didn't encourage him to.

When Mother and Mr. Wagner arrived, they were at first somewhat cowed and apprehensive; then Mother saw the pistol lying on Mr. Kramer's desk. "Were you *shooting* at these boys!" she cried.

"Please, Mrs. Wagner," said the older state trooper in a firm but not unkind voice. "I'd like to keep this calm and orderly—

like, you might say, an informal hearing. As far as the gun is concerned, it's loaded with blanks—blank cartridges, the kind they use to start races. Now, we will begin with the boys, each one taking a turn at having his say; then we will hear from you and Mr. Wagner; then from Mr. Kramer here; and finally from me."

"Officer," Mother said, "before we begin, may I ask your name, and your partner's name?"

"Grange, ma'am. Sergeant William Grange. And this is Corporal Ron Dieffendurfer." He spoke with quiet courtesy—a big, pockmarked, thick-necked towhead who seemed determined to be punctilious precisely because he didn't look it.

"Thank you, Sergeant. I don't know whether you're related to the great Red Grange, who was born and raised not far from here, in Forksville . . ." She paused briefly (exactly the length of time recommended, no doubt, by Dale Carnegie), and in that moment I saw the trooper's eyes light up with pleasure. "But whether or not you are related, you bear a proud name. I love that covered bridge at Forksville and have done several watercolors of it."

"Yes, ma'am, and thank you—my daddy and Red Grange are some kind of cousins. Now, we will begin with the boy on the end there," he said, looking at me. "Please state your name and age, then say anything else you like by way of explaining why you were disturbing the show by throwing apples on the roof."

"My name is Chris," I said. "I'm almost thirteen, and we were doing it just for fun."

"And you?" He looked at Roger.

"Roger," said Roger. "Thirteen. Just for fun."

"All right," the trooper said, shifting his gaze to Johnny.

"John is my name, and I'm eleven this September," he said, blushing furiously.

"Yes," said the sergeant.

"And, uh—well, the thing is . . ."

"Go on, please," the sergeant urged softly.

"We *were* doing it for fun," John said.

"But not just for fun? For another reason too?"

John nodded.

"And what was the other reason?"

"He found out about the window screen and fixed it," John said.

"You daygone *right* I fixed it," Mr. Kramer crackled, "after you kids bust in no tellin' how many times!"

"Mr. Kramer, just a minute, sir," the sergeant said, slightly annoyed. "You're out of turn."

"Sergeant Grange is absolutely right," Mother said in her take-over voice. "He began by laying down ground rules for this hearing, and I was to follow the boys—so if you'll be so good as to give me your attention, I'll be as brief as possible."

"But, ma'am—" said the trooper, who clearly wanted to pump John some more.

"It's getting late, Sergeant—these boys should be in bed, and so should I, so I'll make a very few points. *First*"—she held up a closed fist, then pointed her index finger at the ceiling like the engraving of Cicero in my Latin grammar—"no harm has been done to Mr. Kramer's property. Secondly, it is Mr. Kramer's responsibility to keep his building in shape, and if kids stumble on an open window with a broken screen, they can hardly be blamed for climbing through it once in a while to see a good movie. You, Sergeant Grange, and you, Corporal Dieffendurfer —suppose you were eleven and thirteen years old. Wouldn't you be pretty sad kids if there was a free way into the local movie house and you didn't use it when your pocket money was low and an exciting Western or a Laurel and Hardy was showing? Thirdly and lastly: I don't like to be personal, but Mr. Kramer is well known on this mountaintop for his mean ways, and I can't think of a better example than his *shooting* at these children tonight. Blank cartridges or no blank cartridges, for young boys to feel they are really being shot at, not only by a grown man but by a grown man with the approval of two state troopers, is close to criminal. I don't mean criminal in the legal sense," she added, waxing more eloquent than was her usual wont, "but criminal in what it might do to their characters—including the completely false impression it must give them of proper law enforcement."

By the time she was through, the troopers looked like contrite miscreants, and Mr. Kramer was both apoplectic and speechless. I was (to put it mildly) relieved; Dale Carnegie and I both gave Mother A+ on this challenging homework assignment.

"Well, well," said the sergeant, looking authoritatively at his wristwatch. "It's late—you kids better get home, and—"

"May I say something?"

"Sir?"

Mr. Wagner had been so self-effacing, the way he'd let Mother grab the ball (like Red Grange) and gallop downfield with it, that his question gave us a jolt. "Before we go home," he said, "I'd just like to ask the boys how many times they used that window. John?"

"Three."

"Three boys three times each makes nine free shows. And what is the cost of a ticket, Mr. Kramer?"

Since Mr. Kramer had shrunken into his swivel chair and wasn't speaking, I answered, "Thirty cents, fifteen for kids under twelve."

"We'll take the full price, thirty times nine. Well, then, here is a five-dollar bill," said Mr. Wagner, slapping it down next to the pistol. "Two-seventy for the nine tickets, and the rest for the trouble you have been caused by tonight's disturbance. I wish these boys could apologize to each of the customers who was driven from the theatre, but that seems impractical. I believe they owe you an apology as well, Mr. Kramer. I agree with Mrs. Wagner one hundred percent, but I'm sure she would agree with me that dishonesty is dishonesty, at any age and no matter how tempting the circumstances. Chris, please stand up and apologize."

One by one we stood and mumbled our apologies.

"Thank you, boys," Mr. Wagner said. "Good night, gentlemen," he concluded, shaking hands with each of the troopers. Then he turned to Mr. Kramer, still coiled in a viperous sulk. "As for you, sir," he said, in the mildest tone imaginable, "if I ever catch you doing anything like shooting at children again, I will engage the finest lawyer in Pennsylvania and sue you straight into bankruptcy."

When we had taken Roger to his house and gone home, Mr. Wagner called John and me into the living room. "I am raising your allowances," he said, "by ten cents for you, Chris, and fifteen for Johnny. You're getting a bigger raise, John, because you're the only boy who had any intention of telling the whole truth, over there tonight."

"Thanks," said John, "but the whole truth now is that I didn't mean to say anything about the screen. I'm just no good at following intentions."

Mr. Wagner laughed. "I hope you stay no good at it," he said, and gave John an affectionate shove in the direction of bed.

Fifteen

SOON AFTER OLD LADY WAGNER's birthday party, Peter had left on a world cruise—not as a passenger, as a cabin boy—and I never knew where to write him, so I saved things up to tell him when he got home in September: things I thought he'd approve of because they'd meant taking risks, and because they gave you that same feeling of exhilaration that characters keep having in the stories he gave me to read. As it turned out, Peter's cruise ship docked on a Friday and he had to register as a freshman at Princeton the following Monday, so I hardly got to say hello to him until Thanksgiving. But by then I had added something else to my list: drilling a peephole between my third-floor bedroom and the maids' bathroom.

It (the peephole) hadn't worked out quite as planned, though I'd given it a lot of thought. The hole was covered by a picture, on my bedroom wall, of Charles A. Lindbergh smiling and waving from the cockpit of his plane, the *Spirit of St. Louis.* I drilled it with an ice pick, and it came out inside the medicine closet in the maids' bathroom. I propped a broom up, with the broom part as Bridgit's head (it was about the right height), and used that to judge where the hole should be for best viewing results. I knew that I wouldn't be able to see Bridgit or Kathleen naked very often —only when one of them had just stepped out of her bath and opened the medicine closet—but on the other hand, the hole's hidden location should keep it from ever being discovered. I was not only surprised but stunned a few days later when Mother said she was moving me down to the second floor to share the back bedroom with Johnny. That was John's and my old nursery—the bedroom right over the kitchen—and it seemed odd that she wanted me to go back to it.

"You'll be off to boarding school next fall," she said, "and I'd like to do over that third-floor room for friends Peter will be bringing home from college, and your school friends too. And by the way," she added, "don't forget to return that ice pick to the pantry. It's in your top bureau drawer."

I LEFT NOTHING OUT when Peter and I finally had a chance to talk. I even told him about the next thing I planned to do: play hooky from school and go see a movie in Germantown, called *Bali-Bali*.

"It's supposed to be full of native women wearing only skirts," I said.

I expected him to be really proud of me, but he kept slowly shaking his head, half in wonderment and half in disgust.

"What's the *matter?*" I asked, louder than I had to because I felt a kind of despair wash over me.

"It's not your fault, Chris," he said. "It's probably mine."

"Fault for *what?*"

"Listen," he said. "Miss Russell's dignity is the best thing you've told me—practically the only thing you've told me that doesn't make sex seem smutty. Forget about *Bali-Bali*—or go to it if you want to, but don't think you've done anything to raise a flag about. Going to *Bali-Bali* and drilling peepholes and all that kid's stuff is no different from Mr. Wagner's crack about Don

Juan when I'd spent a few hours alone with Liz Randolph. It all amounts to one big drooly leer, as though sex were something dirty, instead of—instead of *shining.*"

I didn't say anything. I had nothing to say. I had a dead feeling, as though I might never again have anything at all, on any subject, to say to my brother Peter. I couldn't cry, but that's what I wanted to do. We were up in his bedroom. He'd brought a suitcase back from college but he hadn't unpacked it yet, and I was sitting on the floor, leaning against it. He was in the red armchair, with a glass of dark-brown beer in his hand.

"Here," he said, offering me the quart bottle. I shook my head. "Go on," he said. "It's called bock beer. You might like it." I shook my head again, then held out my hand and took it. It was too bitter, but I didn't make a face. I handed the bottle back without saying anything.

"Did you ever meet Liz Randolph?" he asked, as though he were changing the subject.

"No," I said, so quietly that I could hardly hear the word myself.

"Really pretty girl. Tall. Straight black hair, long, with a blue ribbon. Blue eyes. Lovely arms and hands. Wonderful gestures. Swanlike. That night she wore a light-blue evening dress, ridiculously frilly—maybe even with polka dots, I've forgotten. But the effect was a combination of Cinderella and Alice in Wonderland. Very deceptive. In fact she can dish up the snappiest repartee you ever heard, and her voice sounds both alert and sleepy, like Myrna Loy's. God knows why she took to a whale like me. Maybe I challenged her."

Without a pause, he began telling me about the night of the Sturgis dance, speaking in a storyteller's voice, a campfire voice, with pauses to refill his glass or think the way he wanted to phrase something, but never expecting any comment from me—wanting only my attention, as though he was telling me a highly personal parable.

They had left the party moderately inebriated, ostensibly to fix the heel of her dancing shoe, but they had hardly parked and started in necking when they decided that this was a waste of time, why didn't they get married? They had heard that there were justices of the peace in Baltimore who married anybody anytime, so they headed for Baltimore, whence, once wed, they would keep driving south until they found a grocery store open that would sell them five pounds of seedless grapes, and they'd take these to the nearest unoccupied beach, where, the sun now being up, they would eat the grapes and copulate like alligators.

"Why don't we do the alligator part first?" Liz said. "Then if the marriage thing doesn't work out because we need legal papers or something dumb like that, at least the trip will not, as they say, have been in vain."

"Brilliant suggestion," said Peter, pulling into an all-night filling station just over the Delaware line. "I'll ask this fine pumper fellow directions to the nearest seedless grape."

He also bought gas, which reduced his money-in-pocket from eighteen something to fifteen something. The gas-station attendant didn't know too much about *any* variety of grapes, but he did know of a well-disposed tourist home called Whispering Willows, some ten miles down the road, which Peter thought a suitable substitute for grapes plus beach, because by now it had, in Delaware, begun to drizzle.

That was the way Liz put it. "It has," she said to Peter upon his return to the car. "Now all together, follow the bouncing ball: It *has*, in *Del*-la-*ware*, be*gun* to *driz*zle." They said it together, over and over, driving down the highway toward the Whispering Willows. It was raining now, quite hard. When Liz complained that the phrase was putting her to sleep, they added words (ending up with: "It has, in dry, delicious Delaware, begun to drizzle dreadfully") and said the whole thing as fast as possible, proving to each other that they were not only sober but incredibly clever.

"Now," said Peter, "in order to prove precisely how sober I am, I shall reverse the syllables, beginning at the end and working toward the beginning, as follows: 'Fully dread drizzle to gun. Beware, Dela delicious—' "

"Look out, Peter! *Look out!*" Liz put her arms in front of her face. Peter jammed on the brake. The car skidded across the gravel shoulder and shuddered to a stop.

Their headlights, which had been fairly worthless through the downpour, now clearly illuminated a large truck parked not ten feet in front of them on the side of the road. A man was walking toward them, dangling a flashlight. Peter rolled his window down. "Accident?"

The truck driver nodded. He was short and thick-set, wearing a baseball cap and black rubber raincoat. "Worst I ever seen," he said. "Come take a look for yourself."

Peter told Liz to stay where she was till he saw what was up, and got out of the car, turning up the collar of his tux. "Not your truck, is it?"

"No, thank God!" The driver pointed with his flashlight. "It's right over the other side of mine."

Together they walked around the parked truck. Peter looked at the sector of road illuminated by its headlights. A liquid red substance was gradually mixing with the rain, spreading in jagged streaks across the road surface. At irregular intervals, small piles of flesh seemed to have been propped up like little haystacks. Only, Peter thought, it couldn't be flesh because the stuff dissolved and drained off into the ditch as he was looking at it.

Broken bottles and wooden crates made a crazy trail off to the right, leading to the huge carcass of another truck posed drunkenly ten or fifteen yards across the ditch. Its cab section was mashed sideways into the ground, while the trailer part tilted downward like a resting seesaw board.

Across the ditch on the other side of the road, in the darkness, was a large black car. It looked to Peter like any other wrecked car, except that the entire roof had been shaved off and lay on the grass to one side.

Peter borrowed the truck driver's flashlight and walked over.

The side was bent in like a crumpled beer can. Only a few large splinters of glass, coming out of the door frame like inverted icicles, were left of the windows. At first, Peter didn't notice any bodies at all. He shone the flashlight inside the car on five drenched corpses. They looked inconspicuous against the gray upholstery, sitting in natural, comfortable positions, as if completely unaware that their vehicle had been decapitated and their own heads mangled. The faces of a man and woman were pressed together like 'lovers.

Peter walked back to the truck driver and returned the flashlight. Again he saw the strange bloody substance, mixing now with the strips of dissolving chalk-white flesh in weird patterns under the parked truck's headlights. "That's not blood, is it? It couldn't be. None of the bodies were thrown."

"Nope. Catsup. Tomato catsup. The other stuff is flour."

"Driver get killed?"

"Sure did."

It was no longer raining. They walked in front of the headlights and waded around in the grotesque mixture, kicking bits of broken bottles and white, rain-soaked cloth sacks. Why, Peter wondered, was he doing this? How did he get here anyway?

"Peter . . ." Liz was coming down the road toward them, in her bare feet. He left the truck driver and ran over to her.

"It's nothing," he said. *"Please* go back. The road's covered with glass. Truck and car skidded into each other. We'll have to find a telephone." He took her by the arm and started back toward the car.

"Peter—that *hurts!"* Her voice was surprised.

He relaxed his grip but didn't let go. "I'm sorry, Liz, but we've got to hurry, we've got to get to a phone as quickly as possible."

"What was it you saw? Peter, let *go* of me!"

He opened the door and pushed her inside, but before he could get the engine started, she got out and was walking over to the truck driver.

"Liz, you'll cut your feet! Liz, please!" But she kept on walking toward the truck, leaning a little forward, her evening coat turned up at the neck. He didn't go after her. She was her own woman —that was what he loved about her. He just sat and watched her talking with the truck driver. The man was pointing with his flashlight; then the two of them walked over to the car. She had to see everything he had seen. Letting off the brakes, Peter pulled slowly onto the highway and drove alongside the truck. When Liz saw him, she came back. She got into the car without speaking.

The driver walked around to Peter's window. "Better get a *couple* of ambulances," he said.

Peter nodded, then drove around the catsup and flour mess and into the night. Liz was sitting up straight, looking through the windshield. Neither of them mentioned the accident.

"Sorry about the strong-arm act," Peter said. "It wasn't meant the way it seemed."

"I'd like a cigarette, please, if you . . ."

A mile or two further on they saw the sign: WHISPERING WILLOWS—OPEN—VACANCY. Peter called the county hospital, then rented a three-dollar cabin under the name of Mr. and Mrs. Anson Hunter. The bedstead was brass, almost purple with age. They undressed and turned off the light and lay naked, side by side, on top of the sheet, but they hardly looked at each other. They looked at the flaky ceiling. Their cabin was close to the road and they heard tires speeding on the wet surface, then saw the flash of headlights moving in a bright smear across the ceiling. Maybe it was the ambulance. Soon the truck driver would be able to turn on his ignition, let off his brakes and drive away—probably drive right on home to his wife or to his girl's apartment, tell her about the accident, then sleep with her. Christ, this was foolish!

Liz was moving. She put her arm across Peter's chest and he closed his eyes. The feel of her lips and then her cheek brushed across his mouth.

"Time to dress," she said. He nodded in the dark and took her head in his hands and kissed each of her eyelids. The last thing she said to him as he let her off at her own front door was "Sorry about the alligators."

WHEN HE WAS THROUGH telling me all this, we sat without talking. He finished off what was in his glass. It was only about four-thirty in the afternoon, but it was already getting dark. Outside his bedroom window, nested on the drainpipe, I could hear some birds settling down, chirruping softly, chittering.

"I'm glad you told me," I said. "Is it really true, though?"

"Why would I make it up, Christy?"

"I don't know. All the things you both said and saw and heard and stuff. How could you remember all that?"

"It's true—maybe embellished a bit, but true."

"Scary coincidence, or whatever you want to call it. Being another car accident. You know, after—"

"After Linda." He nodded and for a moment covered his face with his hands, slowly rubbing his cheeks up and down. Then he dropped his hands and frowned. "I think that's what got me most," he said. "As though it had something to do with *me*—that I was bad luck or something."

"What does that word mean, that alligators do?"

"Copulate? It means mate, couple."

"Did you and Liz ever get to do that?"

Peter nodded. "The next Sunday," he said. "Right here. When you were all over at old lady Wagner's millionth birthday party."

"Did it—"

"Chris, I'm not one of the people who likes to talk about those —those particulars—as though they were exploits or something. But in general, I doubt anything much more comes of our— whatever we had. My cruise job started almost immediately, and when I got back Liz was at that finishing school in Florence— same one Marlie goes to. But separation wasn't the real problem. I think there's a psychological moment, and for us it passed down in Delaware when she got out of the car. Or maybe when I did."

"Sort of like in Fitzgerald, you mean? *The Rich Boy*—first

Paula, then Dolly? I noticed you registered as Anson Hunter."

"Hey, you've been doing your homework."

"Yeah. But it doesn't grow me up any faster."

"What'll you do when you finally get there?"

I shrugged. "If there's still a Greenwich Village, I guess I'll go live in it."

"Like Daddy?"

"Like Daddy. But not next door."

"Maybe I can arrange for you to see him in New York."

"Forget it. Ma would never let me go near his apartment."

"Maybe something else. Let me think."

"Okay," I said. "Thanks. But Peter, why did you tell me about Liz and—and everything?"

Peter leaned forward and picked the empty beer bottle up off the rug. "Who knows?" he said, and smiled. "It might save you the price of a movie ticket."

Sixteen

IT DIDN'T. I tried to live up to Peter's standards, but *Bali-Bali* was held over a second, then a third week at the Jubilee Theatre in Germantown, and I didn't have the strength of character to resist it.

One stupid thing I had done, about a week before I had mentioned it to Johnny—not that I planned to go, but just that it would be really great if I could somehow get to see it. So when he saw me sneaking off from school before football practice, he was easily smart enough to figure out where I was headed, and began to follow me. I waited for him to catch up, then told him I was walking home early because I had a stomach ache.

"Nice try," he said. Then: "Come on, Christy—let me go with you just this once. *Please.* I swear I'll never ask you to take me along a single other time, and I'll pay you back for both of us— I've got birthday money saved up, easily more than enough, I bet."

"It's just that you always tell. You can't keep the simplest secret."

"My problem is only when people ask me, though, and I know I'm blushing and that they see me blushing, so it's hopeless to lie when they know beforehand that what I'm about to say will *be* a lie. But this time nobody will even suspect we weren't at school, so how would it occur to them to ask questions?"

"Okay," I said. "Okay, okay—but let's *shake it!*"

We got there a little late, and I don't remember much about the movie except that there wasn't a whole lot to remember—no plot, and only a couple of brief scenes with flippety native boobs, what Roger would call Nubbins and Bloopers—but it made John and me feel on top of the world just to have done it: skipped football, taken the trolley to Germantown, got past the movie ticket people without their giving us a hard time about how old we were.

Coming back to Glenllyn, we felt like clowning around and went into our handkerchief act. Johnny stuck a handkerchief in his breast pocket, got on the trolley well ahead of me, and took a seat at the back. I got on last and sat near the front. After a couple of stops, I made my way back to where he was sitting and staring out the window. When I was close enough, I began to make desperate about-to-sneeze sounds, finally grabbed the handkerchief from his breast pocket, dove my nose into it, faked a tremendously moist-sounding sneeze, wiped my nose lavishly, then rudely jammed the handkerchief back into his pocket and walked away. While all this was going on, he kept staring fixedly out the window as though nothing unusual had happened.

We had given our handkerchief performance a number of times in the past, and had become quite convincing at it—so much so that people at the back of the trolley usually chuckled and sometimes guffawed. But this time there weren't very many people near Johnny. The only one who seemed to watch the entire act was a rheumy-eyed, unshaven old wino; and after I'd returned the handkerchief to John's pocket, this bum took it out again, *really* blew his nose, then stuck it in his own pants pocket. When he did that, Johnny and I collapsed in such a helpless, shrieking fit of laughter that the trolley conductor kept a close eye on us all the way up Germantown Avenue.

IT WAS DARK, and after six o'clock, by the time we got home—too late to say we'd been kept over for an extra-long football practice. Besides, Mother (who had been badly frightened by the Lindbergh baby's kidnapping two years before) was driving around in the car, hunting for us between home and school; and Mr. Wagner, who had arrived out from town after she'd left, was torn between joy and anger when he saw us walk in the yard, still laughing.

"Hello, kids," he said, sounding determined not to lose his temper. "Come into the living room for a moment, I want to chat." He shut the French doors, then said, "Who wants to be the one to tell me where you've been? John, I hope you're still no good at following intentions. But I think Chris should be given a chance to not follow his. Chris?"

"Germantown," I said.

"But why would you want to skip athletics, leave school early and go all the way down there without telling anybody? Chris, I'm still talking to you, so don't look at John as though it was his turn."

"Movies."

"Movies. Okay, movies. But quite a few Saturdays you both manage to get to the movies. What was so special about this one?"

"He's going to find out anyway," John blurted, "so tell him, Chris—just *tell* him!"

"It's—it's supposed to be a dirty movie. It's called *Bali-Bali*. But it wasn't dirty at all, it was dumb, there were hardly any women in it who were, you know—naked on top—and it was a cheat, it was stupid, we—"

"All right, Chris, you're beginning to babble, and I can see this is more complicated than I'd anticipated." He stood up and looked through the curtains, then turned back to us. "Your mother will be home any minute, and she will be worried sick at not finding you, then very relieved, then mad as hell—just as I was—so here is what I think." He sat down again. "I think there are times when the whole truth would do more harm than good —which is going back on what I've always told you, but I'm afraid just about every rule has its occasional exceptions. Which doesn't make the whole-truth rule any less valuable, just less general. So —we will tell your mother that you went to Germantown, to the movies, but we won't say which movie or why you went. If she asks which movie and why, you must tell her, but if she doesn't, then you need not. Mothers sometimes worry too much about boys and sex, but fathers, even stepfathers, don't usually have that problem. Okay—no more talk. Upstairs, and get ready for supper. Beat it!"

THAT PART WENT ALL RIGHT. Mother was so relieved that, once she realized "Dad" had already had a talk with us, she hardly cared where we had been.

What didn't go all right was my own temper. I could feel it gathering over the next couple of days—my resentment of Johnny: resentment of the way he always got praised for saying things that put me on the spot; of his stubborn kind of courage; even of the way he looked up to me, always wanting to do whatever I did. And maybe more than all that I resented the fact that he was growing too fast for my comfort. He was almost as tall, if not *as* tall, as I was, and he was nearly two years younger. He must have put on three inches since spring, and I hadn't noticed it until we were both at the *Bali-Bali* ticket booth together and the cashier assumed we were the same age. Until then, inside my head Johnny had stayed little and pudgy.

When I finally released all this anger, it was by deliberately picking a fight with him—as though I had to prove to myself that at least I could still beat him up.

Roger had given me a full carton of Wrigley's Spearmint chewing gum for my birthday a few weeks before. I had kept careful count of the packs, and one was missing—or rather, the sticks of gum had been removed and their silver wrappers refolded, then each slid back into its own folder, and all five tucked into the Spearmint pack wrapping. So that when I looked at it in the carton I could have sworn it was real, but when I picked it up it was nothing but empty paper. And John was the only one, the *only* one, who knew where I kept the carton.

Normally I would have accused him of playing a stinking dirty trick and demanded that he replace the pack as soon as he got his allowance, but I was too ready for a fight to bother with such niceties. I discovered the missing pack before going to school, and on the way home, as John and I were passing the little park with the iron deer in it, I gave him a shove so that he fell over a low hedge. "That's for taking my gum," I said.

"Hey, Chris! Cut it!"

"And that's for sticking the pack back empty!" I said, shoving him again as he tried to get up.

"*Chris!*"

Before he could get up again, I piled on top of him. He was almost flat on his back, but his shoulders weren't pinned yet. He rolled halfway onto his left side, braced his right foot flat on the ground and tried to roll me off him while I tried to push him down flat again. For half a minute, maybe longer, we strained against each other, grunting and sweating and getting nowhere—then, to my despair, I felt him gain an inch or two on me, then a little more, and feeling myself weaken more every second, I made a final desperate, squealing effort to keep him from rolling me off him and onto *my* back, but it was no good—he had me . . . he . . . No, he *didn't! He didn't!* Just as he was about to win, his strength gave out. He flopped onto his back, helpless, and I pinned him.

I stood up, tears in my eyes, and brushed off my knickers. I felt lousy and wanted to help Johnny up, but he had rolled over and was lying on his stomach, his face in the crook of his elbow.

"Why did you *take* it!" I yelled. "I'd have given you a pack if you'd asked me!"

He shook his head.

"What does that mean? That you didn't take it? I *know* you took it. No one else could have!"

Again he shook his head.

"Come on, Johnny—get up, why don't you?"

Once more he shook his head. I walked away, then stopped and waited for him. He got up, but wouldn't move until I did, and kept well behind me all the way home.

I told Roger about it at recess the next day, and he said, "Uh-oh. You better get ready to say you're sorry to John, Christy, because *I* was the one who took the sticks of gum out of that pack, even before I wrapped it all up and gave it to you. I thought you'd recognize it as my little joke—I thought it had the unmistakable Townsend Touch."

I did tell John I was sorry, and he nodded his head and held out his hand, smiling, and I shook it. That night I stuck the rest of the carton of Spearmint in his top bureau drawer with a note saying it would make me feel better if he kept it and didn't try to give it back. Right about then I stopped chewing gum. Not only Spearmint—I stopped chewing gum altogether.

Seventeen

PETER HATED PRINCETON. Not that Princeton was to blame—
he'd have hated any college. After four years of boarding school,
he imagined that college meant freedom on a glorious scale; but
he couldn't take the courses he wanted to (even though he'd got
high honors on three of his college boards), and he had to go to
chapel on Sunday, and no cars could be kept in the area by
students. Marlie was at La Petite École in Florence, and in May,
when Mother and Mr. Wagner sailed to Italy to bring her home,
Peter fled Princeton and drove west. He'd saved enough money
from his cruise pay to get to California, and once there, he got
a job in the oil fields. There wasn't a thing Mother could do about
it, and she was wise enough not to try. Peter wrote them that he
was fine, making good money and prepared to stay as long as he
"needed" to. To me, he wrote that he was looking for "reality—
whatever the hell *that* is."

I guess he either didn't find it or found too much of it in those
oil fields, because he came back that fall in time to enter Harvard,
repeating freshman year despite his straight A's at Princeton. But

by that time I had already left for Devon School, north of Boston. I had wanted and expected to go to St. Matthew's, but whenever the subject was being discussed Mother seemed either noncommittal or against the idea. Finally I asked her why, and she said St. Matthew's wasn't as good a school.

"Peter went there," I said, assuming that was an argument in favor.

"That's partly why I don't want you to," she said. "Peter didn't make a very good name for himself. They just couldn't handle him."

"He got three highest honors on the boards!"

"Marks aren't everything, Chris. There are things far more important. You ought to be proud—you're going to Dad's old school."

"Which Dad?" I looked directly at her, trying not to blink.

"The best one you've got," she said quietly. "Your stepfather."

"Oh. Him."

"Exactly what does that mean?"

"Nothing—I guess."

"Let me tell you something, Chris. You're not very old, but you're old enough to understand this. You might not be going to boarding school at all, if it weren't for your stepfather."

"You said marks aren't everything. Money isn't either. Look what Peter did—he worked his way around the *world.*"

"And who do you think got him that cruise-line job? Just who do you think introduced him to the head of the steamship company?"

"He got it himself."

"He certainly did not get it himself. Your stepfather arranged the whole thing—paid his way to California, got him the job and gave him spending money besides."

I wanted to say *I don't believe you,* but I knew she was probably right. I was trapped.

"Why did he want to take us on, anyway!" I shouted.

"Because he loves me, and he's very fond of all you—"

"No, I mean even if he loves you, why would he want to have four children, all of a sudden like that? It doesn't make sense!"

"Four children is exactly what he *did* want. Because he wasn't very happy growing up with his own family, and I guess he dreamed of having a better time—with us."

"I still say it doesn't make sense."

"You have a lot to learn, my young son," she said, "and I suppose you'll have to learn it in your own way."

I WAS PACKING for boarding school, with John pretending to help me, when Marlie wandered in.

"At least you're not going to Italy so you don't have a passport to worry about," she said, and tossed a new leather wallet onto the bed. "That's a little going-away present," she said. "I got it in Florence but I've been saving it to give you as you went off to boarding school. I have one for you too, Johnny, so don't look so envious."

"Hey, *thanks!*" I picked it up and opened it. It was the softest leather I'd ever felt, and the most beautiful color: polished chestnut, stamped with gold fleurs-de-lis. Inside was one piece of Italian paper money. "Some present!" I said, and gave her a hug.

"Ma tells me you're unhappy about not going to St. Matthews." She pushed some stuff out of the way and sat on the edge of my bed. "You know what I've discovered about new schools? I've discovered that the things you think will matter, don't, and the things you never thought of, do."

"Guess you're right," I mumbled.

"Before I went to Ethel Walker's, I thought the hardest thing would be not being able to leave the place after classes and go to a town that had stores and movies. But when I got there, what I *really* missed was families with kids. Not a single teacher living on the school property was married and had children, and it almost drove me bananas—seeing *no* fathers, *no* brats like you two . . . just older women, and girls my own age."

"How about last year?" I asked.

"Can you guess what I expected in Florence, ninny that I was?"

"Gigolos!" Johnny said.

"Close . . . I expected to fall in love, or at least to have some romantic Italian fall in love with me. In my mind, the school was just a headquarters, a place to operate from. I thought the best thing would be to have a handsome young teacher, maybe a graduate student on the faculty, fall for me. That way we could have our little romance without any problem about where and how to meet."

"No luck?"

"*No* luck. The closest I got to a handsome young man was Michelangelo's statue of David. I liked my teachers, but they were all women—all except art history, and he was about ninety."

"Was it strict?"

"You bet. About hours and stuff. But sometimes the teaching was—well, relaxed. And you could smoke at certain times, if you got written permission from your parents, but Ma refused to let me. I hated her for that, because I was a half-year younger than most of the other girls and I didn't want them to know it. But forget that—you know what you should do, Chris? Write down the things you think you'll object to most at Devon, stick it in an envelope and give it to me. We'll open it up when you come home for Christmas, and you'll see how wrong you were. I'll get a piece of paper and envelope—you start thinking."

The three of us sat around trying to come up with the worst that could happen to me. Finally I narrowed it down to five things: no Saturday-afternoon movies; no playing with friends from Country Day, and with Johnny; being allowed to go to the drugstore only once a week, on Saturday afternoon; and two others I've forgotten. I folded the sheet without showing it to Marlie.

She solemnly licked the envelope and tucked it in her skirt pocket. "There," she said. "And the whole divinely romantic point is this: expect what you get, and you'll get what you expect.

In other words," she said, hugging me, "have a good year. And goodbye."

"Have a good year yourself," I said. "When's your party?"

"Not until December. I'll see you then." She blew me a kiss and was off to some outing or other. It was mid-September, and her coming-out year had already begun.

I WROTE PETER the evening I arrived at Devon, in our first study-hall period, and told him I hated the place—that Mother had sent me against my will. I was being honest, but as the term wore on and I made friends and played on the eighth-grade football team for the Blues, I began to like the school in spite of myself. Peter didn't answer my letter. I was hurt for a while, but then I forgot about him. There was a new boys squash tournament and I reached the finals. Everybody said I'd have won the tournament if my opponent, Putty Carleton, hadn't been ambidextrous (which wasn't true, but I didn't mind people saying it).

Gordie Trumbull, the tallest and heaviest boy in our grade, told me one evening that his father was an artist. We were in the basement, polishing our shoes. The basement corridors were lined on either side with shoe lockers. Gordie's locker was across from mine. I remember that I was holding one shoe, my left hand inside it, and was putting polish on the toe from a can on the top of my locker.

"You ought to see his studio," Gordie said. "Some of the paintings are as high as this ceiling. Murals."

"Does your mother pose for him?"

I don't know why I asked the question. It was certainly innocent enough—I knew nothing about artists, and wasn't even sure what a mural was. But the moment I asked him about his mother, Gordie walked casually over to me, drew back his fist and punched me in the stomach. The sharpness of the pain, which made me double over, gasping for breath; the feeling that I was about to vomit the canned strawberries we'd had for dessert—all this comes back to me now, but not strongly. What I feel much more sharply is the surprise, the bafflement, and most of all the conviction that what my new friend had done was so unreasonable, so far outside the code of fairness, that it blinded me with rage. I remember dropping my shoe and lunging at him, the polishing cloth still in my right hand. I took him by surprise; once I'd doubled over, he probably thought the whole matter was finished. Or maybe he didn't really want to fight; maybe he realized—as soon as he saw the hurt, unbelieving look on my face—that he'd made a mistake. Whatever the reasons, he fought halfheartedly while I saw nothing but a hulk of flesh and muscle to be torn into wildly, with all the strength I could summon. I remember being slammed against the corner of the shoe lockers, and hearing the squeal sounds come from me, and the tears of hate as I squirmed out from under his weight and tackled him, bringing him to the stone floor, then swinging at him again and again, breathing so hard my lungs burned and my muscles felt numb, out of my control, as if they had a will of their own and were making my arms and legs work entirely apart from any ability or even desire within my brain. I never did see the others gathering from different parts of the basement. The first I knew of their existence was when, with blessed relief, they pulled Gordie and me apart, holding each of us clumsily, as if apologizing for having to do something that they realized was none of their business; as if they assumed that I had some fight left, and would justifiably hate them for smothering it. I slumped against them, fighting nothing but my lungs. It was then, for the first time, that I felt the tickle at the side of my neck. I reached up and stopped it. When I took my hand away, it started again. I looked at my fingers and saw that they were covered with blood.

Dr. Allenby, in the infirmary, put stitches along the top of my ear, where it had been torn away from my head. I kept asking him why it didn't hurt—why I hadn't felt it. "You will," he said, and smiled the way judges do—the way Lewis Stone, Andy Hardy's old man, always did in the movies.

Technically, Gordie had won the fight. Aside from a swollen lip, he hadn't been damaged; and if we hadn't been pulled apart he'd have pinned my shoulders to the floor within the next minute or two. I couldn't have lasted, and he knew that; but I had fought myself out. That was what seemed to count. The reason for fighting in the first place was never asked of either of us; but Gordie didn't forget it. He came up to me one day in the gym and apologized. He said he guessed he hadn't heard me correctly; he thought I'd asked whether his mother posed for his father without any clothes on.

I couldn't see why she shouldn't, since they were married; however, neither of us ever referred to it again, and we became friends—not best friends, but good ones. Mother came up for Parents' Day. Gordie's family lived in Chicago, so I invited him to go to dinner with us, and when Mother found out his father was an artist she made such a big fuss over it that you could tell she was trying to mask her real attitude.

She said she painted, herself, *loved* to paint, and that she and Mr. Wagner had been to Italy last spring and his favorite Renaissance artists—hers too—were Botticelli and El Greco, and what did Gordie's father paint, what kind of pictures, and wasn't it unusual for a Devon boy to have an artist for a father—he must be a very *famous* artist, to be able to send his son to Devon . . . and on and on until I said, "Look, Ma, why doesn't Gordie show you some picture postcards of his father's post-office murals when he sees you tomorrow. Right now, let's talk about football or something."

When we had left her at Parents' House and were walking back to our dorm, Gordie said, "What does your mother want you to be when you quote grow up unquote?"

"Banker," I said. "Lawyer. Ambassador. Corporation executive. I can take my pick." He laughed.

"What does your father want you to be?"

"My real father?" He nodded. "Anything," I said (having no idea), "anything at all that pleases me."

"I think I'd have to give pretty much the same two answers for my parents," he said. "Mothers sure are practical people," he added.

Afterwards I wished I had remembered, there in Grand Central Station, to ask my father what he wanted me to be. It had been so long since Peter had said he might arrange a meeting that I thought he'd forgotten, but he hadn't at all. He was just waiting for me to start in at boarding school, which would mean changing trains in New York on my way from Philadelphia to Boston. What Peter finally arranged was for Daddy to meet me in Grand Central, in January, when I was on my way back to school after Christmas vacation. There was an hour or so between trains. We were to meet at the information booth at twelve-ten.

I was there ten minutes early, and I waited until one o'clock before my father showed up. Standing there waiting for him, I had wondered whether the arrangement was quite fair to Mother, and what she might say if I wrote her from school about it. But when I saw him I knew it couldn't be wrong; just as I knew, of all the people in Grand Central, that he was my father.

The first thing I noticed was that he seemed smaller than I had remembered him. He was wearing a shapeless chesterfield, and its left pocket was badly torn. I could tell from the way he walked that he was thin underneath the coat; and he had a day's growth of beard. But his eyes were the same mild gray-blue and his smile seemed even kinder because his face was sad.

He kissed me and said, "You're looking awfully well, dear. Peter tells me you're getting good marks. Did you have a nice vacation? Did you get my Christmas card? I sent it a little late." I knew he hadn't sent any Christmas card, by the way he said it and because I'd never got one from him. And I knew that the other statements were things he'd planned to say. But I still couldn't block that strong feeling of sympathy and affection that welled up whenever I saw his photograph or remembered the sound of his speaking voice.

He started to ask me something. "Chris . . . ?" he said, and stopped. I waited, and he began again: "Chris, how did Marlie look?" I must have had a puzzled expression because he added, "At her coming-out party? Peter tells me she had it two days after Christmas, and I've always—"

"She looked absolutely beautiful." I hadn't seen her on the ballroom floor, of course—only at home, before she went to the dinner; but that was what he wanted to hear, and it was true.

"I can imagine," he said, nodding his head. "Yes, yes—I can imagine."

It was time for my train then. He carried one bag while I carried the other and a pair of ice skates Mother had given me for Christmas. Walking across the waiting room we didn't say anything, and it made me feel uncomfortable because I thought, with only ten minutes together in five years, a father and son ought to have something more to talk about. I wanted to tell him the weird dream I'd had last night, about the tinderbox full of foreign coins he'd given me in Juan-les-Pins. I cleared my throat to tell him, but the whole thing seemed hopelessly complicated and childish, and it would embarrass him even more if he'd forgotten the coins and didn't know what I was talking about. I smiled, then he laughed—laughed nervously, a way I had never heard him laugh before—and said, "Did you hear the one about the Roosevelts, Chris?" I said no, I hadn't, and he mumbled a dirty joke. I was so startled at the fact of his telling it that I didn't listen, and I wasn't even able to affect a laugh. Then I tried desperately to remember one to tell him back, but my mind went blank.

All the way up on the train I could think of nothing but dirty jokes, and (if you count Roger Townsend's classification of boobs and farts as two) by the time we pulled into Back Bay Station I had remembered twenty-seven of them.

Eighteen

I wrote Mother, asking her if I could have a photograph of Marlie dressed for her own party. Mother—surprised and quite touched that I should make such a brotherly request—sent one by the next mail, and I in turn sent it on to my father, with a note saying Marlie thought he might like to have it. I told Marlie what I'd done when I went home for spring vacation. I also told her why I had done it: about Daddy, in Grand Central, asking how she'd looked.

"I still dream about him," she said. "Not all the time, the way I used to. But more than just sometimes. He brings—I don't know how to say it—a strange *weight* to my dream life, so that sometimes I get confused about which is real." Then she laughed. "Since last fall, though, I've had no trouble telling," she said. "The waking life has been so completely unreal."

"When does a debutante year end?"

"About now."

"Sorry?"

"And relieved—both. It's so self-centered that you become a little sick of yourself. Like eating too many chocolates at once.

You're both glad and sorry when the box is finally emptied." We were up in the old third-floor playroom, listening to Bach's Air for a G String. The melody began to soar and both of us stopped talking until the side ended.

"What'll you do next?" I asked, flipping the record, but not putting the needle on yet.

"I *hope* go someplace where nobody knows me, and where I have to work at what I'm doing. Trishy and I are thinking of the Virgin Islands. Going there and painting. For months and months."

"Are you that serious? About painting?"

"Serious enough to want to find out whether or not I'm serious."

"Have you mentioned the Virgin Islands to anyone?"

"Not yet—and please don't you. It will take some good timing, and a lot of luck."

BOTH HER TIMING and her luck must have been a little off, because when she brought the subject up, at lunch on Easter Sunday, Mother said she was too young to live on one of those Caribbean islands without anyone except a girl friend her own age. "If you want to paint, why not go to art school right here," Mother suggested. "To Tyler, or the School of Industrial Art. Or you could take private lessons."

"She's eighteen," Peter said. "When I was eighteen I was working in the Ventura oil fields."

"With girls it's a little different," Mother said.

"Don't you think that's a pretty middle-class attitude?"

"Do we have to spoil Easter Sunday by arguing at the lunch table?"

"Another middle-class no-no," said Peter. "The lunch table is sacrosanct. Especially on Easter Sunday."

"Peter," Mr. Wagner cut in, "your mother and I will discuss the matter between ourselves, then talk it over with Marlie. You're really not involved."

"Divide and conquer," said Peter. "A prime bourgeois tactic.

I've been thinking of writing a term paper called 'America's Bourgeois Aristocracy.' "

"Can I say something?" Everyone stopped talking and turned to Marlie, who looked at Mother. "After your coming-out year, Ma, you and Aunt Rosalie went on a four-month tour of Europe —but that was with Grandmother, wasn't it? You're probably right to worry about our not being chaperoned, so maybe Trishy and I could go to an island where you and Dad have friends who could keep an eye on us. I was thinking of the Ken Thompsons —didn't they retire and buy a place on St. Croix?"

"By golly, you're right," said Mother, "and that's not a bad idea. I'll write them tomorrow and see what they think. *Now*"— she looked around the table—"more bourgeois roast beef, anyone? Peter?"

It took them until the end of September to arrange it, but Marlie and Trishy Sturgis finally did manage to go to St. Croix, live in a cottage near the Thompsons, and paint. Johnny was at Devon by then—a first-former, and pathetically homesick. Marlie wrote each of us a flurry of postcards; then the postcards stopped and she wrote me once more—a letter. The letter said she thought maybe she was in love, so I wasn't too surprised when she cabled Mother asking if she could stay down there through Christmas and into January; then cabled again, at the beginning of February, asking permission to stay just a few more weeks. Mother hadn't even had time to answer that last request when Marlie, unexpected and unannounced, arrived home.

The next Sunday, on his way back to Cambridge after visiting Kit Heywood, his girl at Bennington College, Peter stopped at Devon to see Johnny and me—and to show off his secondhand Pierce-Arrow, an old black roadster that looked like a gangster car out of the twenties, something Paul Muni or Edward G. Robinson should be driving. I asked him what was going on with Marlie, why the sudden return? Peter said that the man she was in love with turned out to have a wife and two children tucked away somewhere—a detail he had neglected to mention until the wife showed up on St. Croix the first week in February.

The next time I saw Marlie was in early April, at the Washoe Gun Club, a tract combining several former plantations near McClellanville, South Carolina, which was jointly owned by Grandfather and eight other members—businessmen from Philadelphia and New York. Members took turns using the club, and Grandfather was usually able to take his turn during one of the hunting seasons (deer, duck, wild turkey, upland game); but this year he had it in the spring and invited us down, after school let out for Easter, to see the snowy egrets. Snowy egrets look like small, silky white herons, and every April they nested, by the hundreds, in the cypress trees of Washoe Swamp.

In those days McClellanville was not even a whistle stop—it was a dusty crossroads you reached from Philadelphia by taking the Seaboard Railroad's Orange Blossom overnight to Charleston, where you were met by the club's ancient and only motorized vehicle—a species of limousine that looked like a Model T Ford up front, but with its rear extended far enough back to accommodate ten passengers, or five on each side. It took over an hour to drive the thirty miles north to McClellanville, and another fifteen or twenty minutes, on narrow dirt roads, to reach the Washoe Club; but you needed at least that much time to adjust from the city to what looked like a primitive pioneer village; then from that to the bizarre but surprisingly smooth combination of Southern backwoods Negroes tending, in provident surroundings, to the families of white millionaires from the North.

I had never been to the Washoe Club before, and expected something like a Hollywood stage set for a Southern mansion. But the lodge, while quite large, was unpretentious to the point of being rudimentary—as though the Victorian gentlemen who had built it were determined to escape the clutter of their own town houses, and particularly determined to avoid any suggestion of feminine flounce or flutter.

Everything was of pine, nailed or fitted simply. A deep porch ran across the front of the building, and in the center of it, screened double doors led into a sizable high-ceilinged yet plain living room, sparsely furnished with a long black leather sofa and black leather armchairs grouped around a huge stone fireplace at one end, and another grouping, without a fireplace, at the other. Each grouping was arranged around a large oval rag rug, with an even larger rectangular rug between the two, at the foot of the central staircase.

On a round table in the middle of this rectangular rug was a giant stuffed wild turkey shot by Grandfather's sister, my great-aunt Olivia, and antlered deer heads decorated the walls. The staircase led to a landing, then divided, with each arm of the Y leading up to a balcony, off which were wings with bedrooms on either side of a narrow hallway. Downstairs, in one of these wings was a fair-sized dining room and pantry, and in the other were a poolroom, card room, small library, and also office/living quarters for the overseer, Mr. Ricketts, who lived on the other side of McClellanville but stayed at the club when he needed to.

There was no bar. If you wanted anything (including anything to drink), you asked the houseboy, who was always nearby or could be rung for if he was in the kitchen. The kitchen was in a building next door, reached by a short passageway which was roofed and screened but otherwise open. Behind the lodge were still other outbuildings of varying sizes and shapes, depending upon their use. Ten or twelve Negro families lived in sturdily built, neatly kept cabins dotted here and there among the trees, a half-mile away down a wagon track that wound through the woods. Once you explored further, you discovered the variety of the surrounding countryside—rye fields, swamp and brush-topped hills, as well as woods. But the first impression was of a clearing in a piney forest full of straight tree trunks rising sky-high, with no branches for thirty feet from the ground, and an occasional live oak, with low-spreading branches and a gnarled trunk that made it perfect for climbing.

When Mother, Johnny and I arrived (Mr. Wagner couldn't

take this particular time off, and Peter was visiting his girl's family in New York), Marlie had already been there more than a week. She had come down, at Grandfather's urging, with our first cousin Elaine Bouvier, who was Marlie's age and a good friend. At seventy-four, Grandfather was that rare combination: a merry, taciturn man—one who managed to radiate quiet cheerfulness while scarcely uttering a word. He'd had four daughters, who together had presented him with fourteen grandchildren, and whenever any of these seemed to be in trouble, his first thought was to avoid endless discussions of the sort which his daughters relished, and to get the afflicted grandchild down to the Washoe Club as soon as possible. There, he felt, everything healed more quickly, including broken hearts.

I looked for Marlie after we'd brought our bags up to our rooms, but she was off painting at the cabin of a swamp guide named Buddy: sketching for an oil portrait of Buddy sitting on his front step, playing a mouth organ. Lainey Bouvier and Grandfather had gone after red-winged blackbird—which meant making bird calls from a hillock overlooking the rye fields, hoping the blackbirds would descend in a feathery cloud to feed on the rye, so that Grandfather and Lainey could shoot into them and bring down enough meat for pies. Several years before, Grandfather had killed fifty-two blackbirds with one shot from each of the two barrels of his double-barreled shotgun—a record that still stood in South Carolina.

I headed for Buddy's cabin and soon saw Marlie on her way back to meet us. She left her painting gear at the foot of a live oak and ran toward me without so much as calling my name, and I ran to meet her. Up close, I saw that she was near tears, so we still didn't talk, we just family-hugged, turning in a slow circle, then let go and stood back, smiling.

"How are things, Marl? I mean—how's the painting?"

"Come see." We strolled over to the tree where she'd left her stuff, and she propped the canvas of Buddy against the trunk. It was a striking concept: partly through foreshortening, the mouth organ and the hands cupping it dominated the picture, as though the instrument were something live controlling the man, and not the other way around. It made you hear the music—that raunchy, human sound of mouth-organ phrasing.

"I hope you don't do much more to it," I said. "It's—I really like it. Just as it is."

"Maybe more work here," she said, pointing to a fuzzy patch. "But you're right. I won't fiddle with it."

I didn't want to go back to the lodge yet, so I climbed the tree —really, jumped into it, for the lowest branches were within easy reach and the knobs on the trunk were spaced just right. "Come on up," I called. "Ma's still unpacking."

She did. We sat on nearby branches, mine a foot higher than hers. My problem was not asking her about St. Croix. "Whut y'all do down heah, Miz Mahlie?" I asked in my best Southern accent. "Besides paint an' shoot blackbuhds?"

"Yesterday Buddy spotted an eagle's nest," she said. "Right at the top of a tall pine over near the swamp. He was telling me about it just now. It was the first nest this year and he wanted to see whether there were any eggs in it, so he shinnied up, and just as he reached it, the mother eagle swooped down, gripped onto a nest branch and glared at Buddy, trying to decide whether to strike with her beak or her claws. But Buddy's no dummy. He spat a cheekful of tobacco juice, got that eagle right in the eye. The bird was so surprised she fell off the branch and had to flap hard to get flying—then she took off and left the nest to Buddy."

"Did he say whether the nest had any eggs?"

"No—come to think of it, he didn't."

"Then I wouldn't believe the rest of it."

Marlie laughed. "I wasn't tempted to," she said. "But that's what we do down here, out of hunting season. Tell tall stories. Swamp tales."

"What's a real swamp like?"

"You'll see tomorrow—the egrets have arrived." She said it with a touch of awe, as though The Egrets were a royal couple, perhaps a duke and duchess come for the weekend.

We didn't say anything for a minute—just sat there, dangling our legs. Then Marlie looked up at me. "I'm okay," she said very quietly. "I'm going to be okay."

Nineteen

THAT NIGHT WE WENT on a coon hunt—my first—and I left before the end. Not because I'm against hunting—when it's fair, I'm for it: when the animal has half a chance, and you respect it because to kill it you have to learn to think the way it does. But hunting coon isn't like that; it's degrading. You do it after dark, so there's no way to exercise any skill in tracking the coon. The hounds do all that for you, chasing until they tree him, then barking at the base of the tree until he can't hold on any longer and falls off into their jaws. To consider that sport must surely take a morbid turn of mind, I thought—or make one.

Anyway, I left while they had the coon treed, their flashlight beams making his eyes two pinpoints of light, bright and cold as stars. I walked back to the lodge, expecting it to be empty, and there, lying on the sofa by the unlit fireplace, was Peter. Snoring.

I was wondering whether to wake him—whether he might want me to—when I heard someone come up the steps and start across the porch, then stop. It was Lainey.

"Hi!" she said when I went out to tell her about Peter. Lainey was a plump, pretty, enthusiastic girl who always spoke a little breathlessly. "I couldn't take it either. Seeing you leave gave me the courage to. But come here, Christy—come look at this lovely monster." She leaned back against the railing and pointed to Peter's Pierce-Arrow, which was parked near the lodge. "Who on earth do you suppose . . .?"

"Didn't he ever tell you?" I said. "Grandfather and Al Capone are friends . . . No, that's Peter's. He'd inside, conked out on the sofa."

"*That* is *Peter's!* My God, do you have any idea what a car like that *costs!*"

"He bought it at a junkyard and fixed it up himself."

"Let's wake him and go for a ride!"

"I'm awake, I'm awake." We turned and saw Peter standing behind the screen door, yawning. "But not for long," he added, pushing the screen and coming out on the porch. "Where is everybody? Hello, both of you."

"Hello," I said. "Everybody is coon hunting. How are you? What are you doing this far south?"

Peter shrugged. "How I am is dead beat—no sleep for two days. What I'm doing down here, I'm too tired to explain. Call it retreating. Lainey, what's the room situation? Is there an empty I can flop in?"

"Sure. Take—let me see—yes: the second on the right, right-hand wing. We'll tell the others you're here, won't we, Chris? And not to wake you."

"How about your suitcase?" I asked. "Is it in the car?"

"Forget it—thanks anyway. I'll bring it in tomorrow. But Lainey, do you think Grandfather—I mean, would he . . .?"

"Mind? Mind a grandchild actually driving all the way down from the frozen North to visit him at Washoe? He'll *love* it!"

He did. He loved it, and Mother was alarmed; her immediate assumption was that something must be terribly wrong. If there had been a telephone on the place, she would have called Francis long distance to find out what he knew.

"Why wouldn't Peter be down here for the same reason Chris and Johnny are," Marlie said, "because it's his spring vacation?"

"He has a college in Boston, a girl who goes to Bennington and lives in New York, and a home in Philadelphia," said Mother. "Why should he drive all this distance to be with us?"

"He'll tell us," Grandfather said. The fire had been lit and he was sitting in one of the armchairs smoking a cigar, letting the ashes fall on his suede hunting vest. He was short and roly-poly, rather like a Santa Claus with rosy cheeks and a square white mustache, but no beard. His smile was thoughtful, and he had a soft voice that nevertheless settled any matter whatsoever. "In his own time, Peter will get around to telling at least one of us. Otherwise he wouldn't have come at all," he said. "Meanwhile, I'm delighted to have the boy here, whatever his reasons."

JOHNNY AND I shared a bedroom, and he couldn't stop talking.

"Did you hear us, when the coon fell?" he asked; then described how Major, Buddy's uncle, had grabbed the coon before the dogs could tear it to pieces—held it high over his head while the hounds yapped and everybody cheered.

"Why did you cheer?"

"Because he fell, and Major got him before the dogs did. Major told me they'd skin it and give the pelt to Ma so she could have a fur piece made for Marlie. And you know what? Major says there are alligators in the swamp. Big ones!"

"Spare me the nightmares, sonny."

"Come on, Chris—why try to spoil the fun?"

"You're right," I said. "I guess I'm tired."

"Shall I tell you what else Major said about the swamp?"

"Sure. But if you hear me snoring, you'll know it's time to stop."

IT WAS THE NEXT AFTERNOON before we actually boarded our little fleet of flat-bottom boats and pushed off, heading for the swamp.

They were longer than rowboats, slightly thinner, narrowing and squared off at both ends. Most had room for three people. Johnny made sure he was put in the boat Major was paddling, and Marlie went with them, taking the bow seat. Mother and I were with Buck—a leathery old man, very dark, with a fixed grin showing two front teeth. Mother sat in the bow because she had her new movie camera along and wanted nothing to obstruct her view of the egrets. Grandfather and Lainey were in a third boat, paddled by a tall, thin Negro named Jonesie. That left Buddy, our guide, and Peter. But the swamp guide always uses a smaller boat and goes by himself; so Peter had to take a smaller one too, and do his own paddling.

Considering his responsibility for our safety (and the fact that he chewed tobacco constantly), I was surprised at how young Buddy looked: about sixteen, maybe seventeen—heavily muscled, but short, and young enough for Mother's and my paddler, Buck, to be his great-uncle.

We left from a small dock and headed straight for the swamp —Buddy first; then Grandfather's boat; then the other three with Peter last. At breakfast everyone had taken Grandfather's lead and treated Peter as though he owed nobody any explanation, and Peter was unusually subdued. The only one he said anything much to was Marlie, walking with her to Buddy's cabin, carrying her easel and paint box. After lunch Mother couldn't restrain herself any longer; she asked Marlie what Peter had talked about and Marlie, opening her eyes wide, said, "Me!"

Looking at him now, paddling behind us, I thought he seemed to be deliberately hanging back so he wouldn't have to talk . . . and then I stopped thinking about Peter because the swamp began to get me.

We had all started off like kids on an outing, calling to one another across the water; but I felt a distinct change of mood as soon as the cypress trees, with their haglike festoons of Spanish moss, closed in around us. For a short while I could still trace the way we had come by distinguishing one cypress cluster from another, but soon this was no longer possible. I personally became lost; which made me want to keep absolutely silent lest I distract Buddy, who still knew the way. The others must have felt something similar because nobody spoke; we all followed Buddy reverently, penetrating deeper and deeper into the swamp, between the cypresses, over the still, black water—water that now seemed both threatening and dead. And the further we penetrated, the more the swamp enfolded us with its own sound and silences. After a while we were no longer startled when a blue heron flew from one cypress perch to another, its slow-moving wings bowed, its head tucked back to its shoulders; or when a blunt-nosed alligator—not green, as I'd imagined they would be, but black or muddy brown—cruised by, its snout, eyes and back barely breaking the oily-looking surface.

Silence was predominant, but intermittently the air came alive with strange sounds: a loud *skyow* would be followed by a series of *kucks*, then by another *skyow* or maybe a *skewk* . . . After a brief silence, the *kucks* would begin again, and simultaneously but farther away, a flat *guark*. If a blue heron had flown overhead, from his new perch we would hear a low, hoarse *frahnk-frahnk-frawnk, frahnk-frahnk-frawnk*—then a pause, and finally the *dollp* of something entering the water. After another pause, longer than the first, the sounds would begin again—often with the *kuck-kuck-kuck*, but sometimes with a high-pitched *quak*, or even with a distant, repeated thumping . . . and always, closest by, the *frahnk-frahnk-frawnk* of a heron.

The cypress trees got smaller and grew closer together, so we had to paddle single file, watch out for snakes on overhanging branches, and be careful of stumps just under the surface . . . and here silence prevailed. There were sounds, but they seemed to be in the distance, left behind.

When we'd threaded through a mile or more of low, thick growth, the trunks came further apart and grew taller. We began to hear nearby sounds once more: *frahnk-frahnk-frawnk*, but higher-pitched than a blue heron. It increased until, by the time we reached the open water of a large clearing, it was a steady noise

—and there, in the branches of the larger cypresses, were snowy egrets by the score: maybe five hundred of them, nesting or perched or gliding solemnly overhead, their necks forming an S over their shoulders, their fragile-looking black legs and yellow feet trailing straight out behind.

How LONG WE STAYED at the nesting area, I'm not sure—it seemed nearly an hour. We talked freely, raising our voices to be heard over the egrets, and after a while we no longer felt like intruders. Mother would tell me where she wanted to go with her movie camera, and I would pass the word back to Buck, who grinned even wider and nodded his head as though he'd thought it all out and was giving his enthusiastic approval.

Finally Major paddled over to us, and Marlie, from the bow, shouted, "Ma, Grandfather thinks we should start back!"

Mother, in position for an unusually good nesting close-up, nodded her head but didn't lower her camera. *"Half* a minute more," she said.

Looking to my right, I could see Buddy beginning slowly to paddle away from the clearing, with Grandfather's boat next.

"Damn!" Mother looked over her shoulder at me. "My best close-up," she said, "and it had to jam!"

"Here"—Peter, from ten yards to our left, coasted to within reach of Mother and held out his hand—"if it's like mine, I know a trick that might work." Mother handed him the camera and he fiddled with something, tried starting it, fiddled once more, tried again, then handed it back, saying "All set."

"You're a *genius!*"

"Simple adjustment. I'll show you when I get back."

She began filming the nest again when Buck shouted something I couldn't make out, and started paddling. Mother, thrown off balance by the sudden swing of the bow, nearly dropped her camera. "What's happening!" she called.

"Buck's right," Peter answered, crossing our bow. "If we don't hurry, they'll leave without us. They think we're following!"

I looked to my right and saw that the others had already gone. Peter, paddling as fast as he could, got to the place where we'd last seen them, but they were out of sight. He hesitated, waiting for us.

"Go ahead!" Mother called. "Before you lose them completely! We'll catch up with you!"

He paddled away from the nesting area; but by the time we'd reached the edge of the clearing, he was coming back toward us.

"Lost them," he said. "Maybe Buck knows the way." Peter turned to the old man, who was still grinning but in a pained way, shaking his head.

"Well," said Peter, "there's only one thing to do."

"Stay here?"

"Stay right here." He looked at his wristwatch. "Buck," he said, "how long before the sun goes down?" Buck looked up at the sky, then held his hands out in front of him as though he was measuring a medium-sized fish. "Two hours?" Peter asked. Buck nodded, then shrugged and mumbled something unintelligible.

"What time was it when we left the dock?" Peter asked Mother. She didn't know.

"It was almost two o'clock when we finished lunch," I said. "How soon after lunch did we start out?"

We spent all the time we could on these calculations, figuring when we'd left; how long it had taken to reach the nesting area; how long we'd been here; therefore the paddling time from here to the dock, the dock back to here, then to the dock once more. The question was, could it be done before dark? How long could you allow for twilight? Suppose they discovered we were missing when they were halfway back—would Buddy be likely to take the others all the way back, then return for us? Or would he leave them at a spot he was sure he could find again, and return for us at once? Or did Major or Jonesie know their way back from some given point?

When there were no more possibilities to discuss, we sat quietly in our boats, trying not to think about what we would need to do if we were on the swamp all night, but thinking about it nevertheless. Thinking about little else. Endlessly turning it over and over, yet never really believing it possible . . .

"They wouldn't tip us over, would they, Peter?" Mother asked, breaking our silence.

"What, Ma?"

"Those darn alligators."

"No, no. They're *friendly* alligators. Just about the friendliest, most lovable alligators I've ever seen."

We all laughed, especially Buck. Every time he thought of Peter's remark, Buck got laughing all over again. After a while it became a little unnerving.

I sat on the bottom of the boat, with my head against the seat, and shut my eyes. I had no thought of dozing, but it distracted me to hear the egret colony without seeing it. I remembered how, when I was a kid and we were listening for Daddy's train, Marlie had said you can hear better with your eyes closed. I tried it, but the egrets sounded just as loud either way.

Then—I'm not sure how much later, but the sun was noticeably lower—my ears picked up a new sound. "What's that?" I asked, getting back up onto my seat. "Anyone else hear something different?"

We all listened a moment.

"I do," Mother said. "A wild turkey."

When she said that, Buck got very excited. "He comin'!" the old man sputtered. "Buddy comin, Buddy *comin'!*" With that he threw his head back and let out a piercing, unearthly-sounding turkey gobble that was answered immediately—then did it again, and got another answer. "He tellin' us he comin', he jes tellin' us, Buddy *tellin'* us," Buck said over and over, shaking his head, grinning and head-shaking and muttering to himself about Buddy this and Buddy that, and every once in a while throwing his head back and letting go with another shrill, eerie gobble, which Buddy would answer, letting us know how much closer he was than the last gobble.

It wasn't quite dusk when Buddy appeared, but I noticed he had set one lantern in the bow and another in the stern, just in case. "Okay!" he called, beckoning with his paddle. "Fast as you can!" he shouted, pivoting around and heading back at once.

Nobody spoke for the next twenty minutes or more—until we spotted, in the dusk and still at a considerable distance, lights on what must be the dock. Buddy's stern lantern was on by then. He gave a turkey call to tell them, on the dock, that everyone here was safe; then for the first time he slowed his boat to an easy coast, and we slowed behind him.

"Everything okay, Ma?" Peter asked, paddling up level with her.

"Me and my damn movies!"

There was a pause; then he said, "Don't blame yourself, it just happened the way it happened. We should have followed at once. They should have checked to make sure we *were* following. Next time we'll both do it differently."

"All right. But I feel I should apologize to someone."

"And I want to change the subject," he said, "to why I came down here." I coughed, to remind him that he and Mother weren't alone, but he paid no attention. "Are you ready for a shock, Ma?"

"After the last hour, I'm ready for anything."

"I know. That's why I'm telling you now, before we reach shore. Kit and I want to get married."

"You what!"

"We don't have to. We want to. Now."

"But you're still in college—both of you. You haven't a cent."

"If I decide to leave college, I'll get a job first. If I stay, Kit can transfer to Radcliffe. So we'd still have our college money, including room and board. Two in the same room should be cheaper. And God knows we can save on gas if I don't have to drive to Bennington every few days. In fact, I'm selling the car."

"What do her parents think?"

"That's the hooker. They're a thousand percent against it. Against me."

"Why, Peter? What have you done?"

"I have committed the unpardonable sin of sleeping with their daughter out of wedlock. And now, to make matters worse, I want to change her from student to housewife. They don't think she'll put up with college a single term, once she's married. Moreover, I am totally unreliable—I've already left Princeton, and am certain to leave Harvard, given half an excuse."

"Have they said all this to you?"

"In so many words. So *many* words. Mr. Heywood threw me out of their town house two—no, three nights ago. Which is why I decided to drive down here."

"He won't give Kit a cent if you marry her."

" 'Not one penny' was the way he phrased it."

"I don't suppose you stopped at Glenllyn on your way here?"

"Believe it or not, I did. Francis was friendly—friendlier than I deserve. He wanted a chance to talk it over with you, but I got the impression that he doesn't disapprove. Basically, I suspect he thinks marriage is the only thing that will make me simmer down."

"So do I," said Mother.

"And so," said Peter, "do I."

"Why doesn't anyone ever ask *my* opinion?" I said.

They laughed. Then Peter said, "Ma—thanks. I'm—well, just thanks . . ."

Mother might have answered, but at that moment we heard shouts from shore, then saw everyone standing on the dock, waving lanterns and cheering for us as we paddled in.

It was, I thought, the exact opposite of a coon hunt, when you cheer for the kill.

Twenty

PETER AND KIT GOT MARRIED with Mother and Mr. Wagner's full approval, but without even the presence of Kit's family, except for a favorite cousin. The wedding was in May, while Johnny and I were at Devon. They wanted to wait until mid-June so we could go to it, but Peter had a summer job in New York lined up for right after his last exam, and it started before Devon finished. He and Kit rented a place in the Village—a cold-water flat near my father. He could easily have arranged for John to meet Daddy at Grand Central in September, but Johnny wasn't interested. When I asked him about it, he said, "In a few years, maybe. Right now, I'm not all that ready."

For whatever reasons, I didn't see my father again either—not until I was in college; but through the boarding-school years he quietly magnetized my values, sometimes in the most arbitrary way. For example, I became fascinated by anything even remotely connected with the First World War—so much so that I copied a portion of Erich Remarque's *All Quiet on the Western Front* and handed it in as my own weekly composition for Mr. Richardson's tenth-grade (or fourth-form) English class.

I had, there's no getting around it, committed plagiarism. And yet it wasn't that simple, for while I had done it deliberately, a part of me wasn't really aware of having done it at all. I don't know how to explain what I mean without seeming to make excuses, but I wanted desperately to be a writer; I had read Remarque's war novel four times, my highest ambition was to write like him, and as I copied down my favorite passage it almost seemed—not almost, it did seem—as if I, and not Remarque, had written about those horses dying in No Man's Land. I was so convinced of it that I felt no guilt whatsoever. I handed in my composition with a glow of pride, even though I knew Mr. Richardson had read *All Quiet* and knew that he knew I had read it four times.

The following week he asked me to stay after class. When the others had left, he opened my composition book to the Remarque passage and I saw that he had given me an E, erased that, and marked me C. He stared at the page for a long time, as if he were considering whether to change the mark again. For a wild moment I thought he might change it to A; the writing deserved no less. Then, as he kept me standing there, it came to me for the first time: the full sense of what I had done; of why he had marked me E originally, and why I was being kept after class. I was, I suddenly realized, about to be expelled.

In a kind of fever, I watched him slowly take off his glasses, rub his eyes, put the glasses back on, turn in his chair and glare at me. There was no expression on his face, just the severity of those deep creases around his mouth and the slightly frightening magnification of his eyes through the glasses.

"Hooper," he said, "you can express your*self* better than this." With that he handed me the composition book and turned his attention to a stack of papers on his desk, leaving me to find my own way out.

MY SELF WAS JUST WHAT I couldn't express, because it was suspended between two opposite poles: Philadelphia, and a vision of Greenwich Village; conformity, and the idea of rebellion. Hemingway's *A Farewell to Arms* succeeded *All Quiet* as my favorite book, and I wanted not only to be a writer but to have a woman like Catherine Barkley fall in love with me. But another side of me would have settled gladly for law or diplomacy, kept on wallowing in parties every school vacation, and traded the adoration of a dozen Catherine Barkleys for one quick kiss from Janice Hollingsworth.

I knew damn well she was a flighty little Farmington flirt, and yet, my senior year at Devon, I was hopelessly in love with Janice —a sparkling creature exactly my own age, and therefore at least two years too old for me.

Ignoring the age problem, I had persuaded her to go with me to the Cromwell dinner-dance that Christmas vacation, and I still remember, in embarrassing detail, the schoolboy fantasies that filled my head as I bathed and dressed and late, as usual, drove out to the Hollingsworths' to pick up Janice.

I knew, as soon as I saw the cars parked in their driveway, that the Hollingsworths had guests. I turned down my lights, shifted into neutral and coasted around the circular, snow-covered drive, coming to a stop in back of a silver Buick. I switched off my engine and leaned back against the seat, taking a final drag on my cigarette. I could see lights behind the draped windows of what I guessed must be the living room. Janice was there, I thought, probably furious with me for being late when she hadn't wanted to go to the party with me in the first place and had only agreed because I'd pleaded with her, every time we danced, with that corny note of desperation in my voice. Janice was there, all right. So were her mother and father and whoever owned these parked cars. They were all waiting to see how Janice's escort would act and what he would say. "What a jerk!" I imagined Janice mumbling to her mother; then Mrs. Hollingsworth would whisper something like "Don't say that, dear, it's not polite." "Even if it *is* true," Janice would add, and she and her mother would smile knowingly at one another.

My car window was rolled down and the cool night air poured

in, but still I could feel perspiration on my brow and under my shirt collar. What was I so nervous about? If that was the way she thought of me, why waste my energy, even if I did love her? I'd recover; I'd get over it.

I'd get over it, and damn fast! In a sudden burst of scorn for my own weakness, I determined to have things out on the way to the party. I'd come right out and tell her how I felt, not daydream about it. No more of that kid's stuff: reciting lines, making up expressions in front of the bathroom mirror. I'd *say* it—"Janice, I love you"—come right out and say it, simply and forcefully. If she tried to change the subject or laughed at me, I'd tell her she was perfectly free to go home from the dance with anyone else she chose. Livvy Clarke. I personally would hand her over to Princeton's Livvy Clarke. Or to Joe Millington, or to any of those other college creeps who kept monopolizing her. I should offer to do that right here, sitting in the car, even before I started the engine. I wished she were sitting beside me this second; that I could somehow extract her from the house with a magnet.

Who was she, after all, to regard me, Christopher B. Hooper II, as an amusing child? Who was she—who had probably never even heard of Greenwich Village, never mind read *Lady Chatterley's Lover* in a smuggled, unexpurgated edition—to treat me like a schoolboy playing hooky?

As if in answer to my question, an image formed before my eyes: of myself standing in the middle of the big circle at Devon School, with snow in the air and on the ground, the School House behind me, and a stack of books under my arm. Only the School House and I were both inside a round glass paperweight that Janice held casually in her hand. Every time I opened my mouth to shout *I love you!* she would smile mischievously and shake the paperweight to make the snow fall faster.

Slowly, tenderly, I wiped across my brow with the back of my hand. Taking careful aim, I flicked the burning cigarette stub at a tree trunk five yards from my front fender. I watched the stub fall and sizzle in the snow. Then, running my tongue over my chapped lips, I pushed down on the door handle, let the door swing out, and stepped down into the white slush.

Walking carefully so as not to splash the slush over my rubbers and onto my patent-leather shoes, I made my way across the drive. As I reached for the Hollingsworths' storm door, my right foot slipped. I gave a quick jump from my left, landed in a slide, and gripped the storm-door handle just in time to keep from falling to my knees. "Holy Christmas!" I breathed, squeezing the handle to stop myself from shaking.

Inside the entryway I scuffed my rubbers back and forth on the mat, straightening my black bow tie and trying unsuccessfully to make out my reflection in the curtained glass of the front door. I wanted more than anything else to lie down and go to sleep. I yawned, raised my hand, and before I could stop myself, pressed the doorbell.

There was a sudden rush of noise and commotion inside; then a gaping hole seemed to appear in the wall of the house, right where I was standing. Blinding lemon lights tore at my eyeballs. I squinted, making a grotesque kind of smile, and stared helplessly at the human being before me.

"Evening," I heard a man's voice say. "You must be Chris Hooper. Nasty night for a party, isn't it? Come in, come in— Janice'll be right down. Went up for gloves or something." I looked for a moment at the hand extended to me; then, reaching out, I shook it. I cleared my throat, stepped into the house and said, "Mr. Hollingsworth? Glad to meet you, sir."

"Glad to meet you. *Janice!* Come into the living room, Chris. She won't be long."

"Chris." A pale, graceful woman in a mauve evening dress, with a white knitted cardigan thrown around her shoulders, stepped silently through the living-room doors and into the wide hallway. *"Nice* to see you, Chris. How's your mother? She and I are old Red Cross cronies. Won't you come in and meet—this hall's freezing, Phil," she said, turning abruptly to her husband. "I hope the thermostat's not on the blink again. Mr. and Mrs.

Girard"—she had turned back now and half entered the living room— "and Mr. and Mrs. Pope. This is Chris Hooper, Louisa and Frank's boy. He's come to take Janice to the Cromwell party. Why don't you stand by the fire and warm yourself for a minute, Chris. I'm sure Janice will be right down."

"I'm pretty warm already," I said, wondering immediately afterward why I had made such a dumb remark.

"Eric Cromwell," Mr. Girard said in a deep, genial voice. "Eric and Polly have a forty-footer—forget the name of the class—a yawl. Fast. Takes everything around Mount Desert." Mr. Girard sat on the sofa, looking, I thought, like Mr. Toad of Toad Hall.

"Does he keep her there over the winter?" Mrs. Pope asked.

"No, the Chesapeake. Cambridge? Annapolis? Around there."

"Cambridge," Mr. Hollingsworth said. Mr. Girard reached down and, with both hands, hoisted his right leg over his left.

"Who sails her down, I wonder," he croaked.

"College kids. Young Eric and his friends."

"Nephew of mine, Hobie Wright," Mr. Pope began solemnly, shaking his head. "Hadn't seen him since he went up to New Haven, so I asked him the other day, asked him how he was doing. Which half of the class was he in? 'Well, Uncle John,' he said, smiling proudly, 'I'll tell you. I'm in the half that makes the top half possible.' "

Everyone seemed to think this uproariously funny. Watching them, I smiled stiffly, afraid they might turn and ask me where I went to college. I tried to think of something I could say to distract them when their laughter stopped. Leaning forward with my hands against the back of an empty chair, I tried as hard as I could to think of something brilliant to say, something that would stimulate discussion for weeks afterwards. I clutched at the cloth design of the chair-back and thought of nothing at all. But it didn't seem to matter, for a hard, quick clacking of high heels sounded on the staircase. Mr. Hollingsworth, tall and thin with gray trousers that clung to his stilt-like legs, was standing behind me, patting me on the back, saying, "I'd offer you a drink, old man, but I think if you and Janice are going to get to The Barclay before eight-thirty you'd better push."

Turning around, I found myself so close to Janice that my coat brushed across her ruffled sleeve. She was holding a long white kid glove in her right hand. The other glove was partly on her left hand and she was tugging it, trying to pull it up to her elbow. She kept pulling at it, looking down at her arm and biting her lower lip. Then, without warning, she lifted her hand, smiled at me—brightening her eyes until I could see nothing else—and said "Here." She handed me the right-hand glove. "Hold that."

Mrs. Hollingsworth was up from the sofa now. "Heavens, dear," she said to Janice, "let me help you. Get her wrap for her, will you, Chris? It's probably on the hall table. That's fine. Now —galoshes, scarf, wrap. Anything else? Evening bag! Got it? Off with you, then. Have a good time—don't get in *too* late—drive carefully, Chris. I'm sure you will, but we mothers, you know—" The front door slammed. I held the storm door for Janice; then we were out together in the sharp night air.

"Well, anyway, it's stopped snowing," Janice said. She walked ahead of me, holding her heavy red gown in front and bending forward to watch where she stepped. I held the car door while she sat on the edge of the front seat and worked her way into the car, pulling her gown after her. Then I went around and got in the driver's seat. I slammed the door, thinking *now* I would say it. I cleared my throat, licked my lips and cleared my throat again. "Sorry I was late," I mumbled, pressing the starter.

"Don't be silly," Janice replied. "We've got oodles of time. These things never start promptly."

I'm chicken, I thought, completely chicken. Janice flicked on the car radio. So she won't have to make conversation with me, I decided. I turned the steering wheel, eased around the other cars in what was supposed to look like a highly complicated maneuver, and headed out the driveway.

Janice kept fiddling with the radio, hunting for music. As she leaned forward I could smell her perfume and, underneath somewhere, the smell of lavender soap. I couldn't just sit there saying nothing. I turned the heater on.

We were out on the highway now. Music filled the car. I rolled my window down further and stared hard at the empty road ahead. How was it I had planned to phrase it? Just the right phrase, if I could only remember it—not "I love you" or anything so stupid-corny. I couldn't think; could think of nothing at all to say except how sorry I was. Sorry for being late; sorry for slipping in the slush; sorry for forgetting to say good night to Mr. and Mrs. Hollingsworth and their guests. Maybe if I had remembered to say good night, everything would be different.

I could feel Janice looking at me. She pretended to be hunting in her evening bag for a cigarette, but I could feel her eyes on me. If Livvy Clarke were in my place, he'd probably have her in stitches by now, telling her college gags, or maybe he'd be inviting her down to a Princeton prom. I couldn't talk about books. Or seedless grapes. I felt suddenly desperate, as if everything I had ever really wanted was slipping beyond my grasp because I couldn't think of the single magic word. I had to try. I had to say something to Janice, no matter how stupid it might sound. I cleared my throat and swallowed.

"I guess Livvy Clarke and—and all the gang will be there tonight," I said.

"*That* jerk! Just because he hits a little black rubber ball around a little white wooden court, he thinks he's God's gift to Philadelphia womanhood."

I turned to look at her and almost lost control of the car. She couldn't have said that—but she had, she *had*. I felt mildly dizzy and sort of reckless. "That's a swell dress," I ventured. "You look terrific in red."

"Really? Do you *really* like it? I bought it yesterday," Janice said, as if she'd been waiting since yesterday for a chance to tell someone, "at that new shop in Ardmore, the what-is-it, I can never remember the name. Anyway, Mother doesn't approve at *all*, she thinks it's too brazen and too sophisticated and not sophisticated enough and a thousand other things. I just let her talk and talk until she was utterly talked out, then—"

"Light?"

"Thanks—then I calmly told the salesgirl to wrap it up, and by that time poor Mother was too exhausted to *care!*"

Maybe the love thing could wait. It would sound all wrong if I brought it up now.

"Well," Janice went on, "she *cared*, but I guess she saw *I* cared more, so—" She shrugged. I felt wonderful; I don't think I had ever before felt this wonderful. "I mean," she added, "what the heck—I have nice shoulders. Haven't I?"

"Yes"—I held the flame to my own cigarette, then snapped the lighter shut and tucked it back into my vest pocket—"yes, old girl, as a matter of fact you have."

MY EUPHORIA LASTED through the dance (where Janice had a little too much to drink and I had more than that) and through driving her ever-so-cautiously home. Parked in the Hollingsworths' turnaround, we had a last cigarette and talked in an easy, relaxed way—among other things, about Marlie and Janice's cousin, Donny Hancock, who had been going around together steadily since September.

"What's he like?" I asked.

"Don't worry," she said, "he's a good one."

"Is it serious? Do you think they'll get married?"

"Donny's serious, I'd say. He's been out of college since June, so that isn't a problem." Janice took her boot off, then her shoe, and rubbed the top of her foot where the strap crossed. Seeing her foot made me think of Liz Randolph.

"Sore?"

She nodded. "Little bit."

"Let me rub it for you." She leaned sideways, against the door, and stuck her foot on my lap. For a minute I rubbed softly, feeling her ankle and instep—their perfect, delicate shape.

"About Marlie and Donny," I said, "let's beat them to it. Let's get married. Right now, hey—tonight. Let's drive to Baltimore and get married."

"*What* are you trying to make me do?" Janice said, taking her foot back. "Flunk my midyears?" She slipped on her shoe; then her boot; then she leaned toward me, closed her eyes, pointed to her lips and said "Exactly one, please?"

Twenty-one

THAT SPRING, on Easter Day, Grandmother died. She had suffered toward the end and was released by death from all that. If you believed in Heaven (as her family most fervently wished to and no doubt did), she went off to live happily ever after. But it shook me more than I would have thought possible. Like the Parthenon, my world was held up by a certain number of columns, and while she was only one of them, her going weakened the whole structure. Wherever she was, the colors must be blue and peach and, of course, white. I hoped they provided enough pillows so she could prop herself up and read comfortably; and that Mims would eventually join her; and my grandfather, carrying a humidor filled with the finest cigars. I've heard that when children are very young (is it less than three months?) you can't play peekaboo with them, because when you duck your head or cover your face with your hands, they think you have disappeared entirely and, until proven otherwise, forever. But when they get a little older they can hold your image in their minds until you show your face again, and thus they can anticipate your reappearance, which is the point of the game. I was like the younger child, so far as Grandmother was concerned. Because she had disappeared from view, I thought she must vanish altogether—cease to make a difference. It took me a while to realize that this wasn't the case at all.

For that reason, I have blocked out her funeral and burial service from memory. I know the Romanesque-looking city church she had attended and which then attended her; and I have been more than once to Laurel Hill Cemetery, that Dickensian promontory overlooking Philadelphia's Thirtieth Street Station railroad yards as though it were not a burial ground at all but an underground platform where the quietest of passengers await their perpetually late ghost train. I know these ceremonial places, but I don't connect them with Grandmother. What comes back to me instead, from that Easter vacation, is a strange evening spent with Marlie—at supper, then at her art class—two days before the funeral.

The others were all over at the Bouviers' or maybe the Ashmeads', in any case rallying around, keeping themselves and Grandfather distracted. Marlie had stayed home because her studio class met in town at eight o'clock and she very much wanted to go to it, but didn't particularly want the aunts and uncles to know that. I arrived home after the rest had left, and decided to keep Marlie company at supper. It was easier. Besides, I hated officialized gloom, or what was almost as bad, its conscientious avoidance at a family gathering.

At first Marlie and I were a little self-conscious—because we weren't with the rest of the family, but also because we so seldom saw each other alone like this that neither of us was any longer sure what the other thought about. I had scarcely seen her for the past two or three years—since our week at the Washoe Club. She had outgrown me in some ways and I had outgrown her in others, so we had lost our earlier familiarity. Partly, the problem was that (except for the St. Croix episode) she had—or I felt that she had —gone the full, consuming Philadelphia social route: after boarding school and the Italian finish, having her coming-out year, followed now by art school combined with football games, skiing weekends, house parties; and scheduled to culminate this June in a lavish wedding to Janice's cousin Donny Hancock, a nice new Yale graduate with an advertising job lined up for after their Bermuda honeymoon.

It's easy and pleasant to wish such people well, but difficult to know what to talk to them about; and I guess, for different reasons, Marlie felt the same degree of confusion about me. But it didn't last long; like two friendly foreigners, neither of whom can speak the other's native tongue, we experimented until we found a third language held more or less in common—in our case, the subject we hit upon was art.

One of Devon's Saturday-evening slide lecturers the previous term had been an art expert who specialized in detecting forgeries, and I began telling Marlie about him. He'd shown us slides of a fake Rembrandt, a fake Gauguin, a half-dozen others, and not one of the forgeries looked at all like paintings by the artist they were supposed to have copied. The "Rembrandt" was muddy; the faces of the "Gauguin" natives looked more French than Polynesian. Yet the most distinguished art professors, critics, curators and collectors had in their day accepted these fakes as authentic. The question our lecturer had raised was why? How could all those experts have been fooled by such obvious fakes?

"I'll bet he left you dangling right there," Marlie said, "told you to think about it and come to your own conclusions. That's what our art-history professor in Florence was always doing. It's called 'stimulating their minds'—like winding up toy people— and it always gets the professor off the hook."

"This guy was different," I said. "He had an ingenious answer, and he wanted us to credit him with it. And I don't blame him." I paused, to see if she wanted me to go on.

Marlie reached across the table and covered my hand with hers. "You're a master of suspense," she said, giving my hand a squeeze. *"What was his answer?"*

"Okay, here goes: that every generation looks for different things in a great artist, depending on what that generation needs. One generation might respond to the sentimental, wherever it appears. Another might reject the sentimental and respond to something else, something more severe. A great artist offers the sentimental, the severe—many other ways of being seen. But a forger, even a great forger, can only copy what *his* generation sees in a particular artist. So every twenty years or so, when the next generation clicks into place and the needs change, museum directors have to take another look at their collections and cull the previous generation's fakes, which by now seem obvious."

"Hey, I like that. That rings true. Japanese madonnas always look Oriental. African madonnas always look Negroid. Flemish ones like *fräuleins*. The Christs on Kathleen's kitchen calendars always look like a gentle Irish tenor with a brand-new beard. The way we see does just what your speaker said—it reflects our own needs, the way we see ourselves."

"But then how do you ever get to be an art detective?"

"Right, *right*—good point! The art detective has to step outside his own generation, but how can he do that? And which way does he step: forward, backwards, sideways?"

Supper dishes came and went, food was passed, seconds served —I was hardly aware of eating, Marlie and I got spinning so fast.

"Listen," she said, finally looking at her watch and sipping the last of her coffee, "why don't you come to art class with me—they won't mind, and you'd have fun, I know you would."

"Drawing oranges?"

"Not drawing, oil painting—and it might be oranges, but it also might be an old lady or an overcoat or a traffic cop. He never tells us beforehand. Come on, Chris—keep me company."

THE CLASS WAS NEAR Temple University, in a room that looked as though it had once been a small gymnasium—the kind with an oval balcony banked for runners. There were at least two dozen students setting up easels in a semicircle around a raised platform, on which sat a plain but pleasant-looking silver-blond woman, naked under a blue-green kimono. No one turned around when Marlie and I came in—they went on getting ready for work. She whispered about me to a fellow student with a bushy red mustache, who went somewhere and returned with a smock, easel, palette, box of paint tubes, two or three brushes, and a palette knife. He handed these to me with a welcoming smile and pointed to a spot marked on the floor, where I was to set up my easel. Marlie had already set up her own on the other side of the red mustache, too far away for me to talk to her.

I was just as glad, especially right after the model disrobed; though my surprisingly slight embarrassment at being there with Marlie soon disappeared entirely, for the class emanated a no-nonsense atmosphere. The model—who was a little thick in the waist, young-matronly—sat on a stool, settled into a comfortable position, then said, "How's this?" An older man with a beard, whom I took to be the teacher, said, "Could you raise your chin a little, Vicky, and look slightly to the left? Good." No one else said anything. They painted. I painted, or pretended to, using the palette knife so I wouldn't mess up their brushes. The teacher wandered from easel to easel, only occasionally saying anything and then in a low voice, privately. At regular intervals the model rested—putting on her robe, lighting a cigarette, sitting on the platform and either flipping through a magazine or talking with one of the students closest to the platform.

When two hours had passed, the teacher went to the platform and said, "Okay, that's it for tonight. Thank you, Vicky—next Thursday, same time?"

Vicky said that would be fine, and put her kimono back on. "Okay if I—"

"Sure!" he said. "Help yourself—to yourself."

She smiled, stepped down from the platform and began touring the room as students cleaned up their brushes and put tops on their tubes. She glanced at every canvas still on its easel, but seemed deliberately careful to keep her face expressionless, at most smiling noncommittally, and the students seemed not so much disinterested in her opinion as unconcerned about anyone's at this early stage. It wasn't until she got to Marlie's oil sketch that the model actually said anything—then, with an intake of breath, she clapped her hand over her mouth as if to prevent herself from shouting, took a step back, opened her eyes very wide and said, "Kiddo, you *got* it!"

"*Thank* you, Vicky," said Marlie, blushing like a pleased little girl, chewing on her lower lip and brushing back her curl with the back of her wrist.

"She *got* it, Diamo," Vicky said, turning to the teacher, who had come up behind us.

Diamo—hefty, bald, very florid, with a square-cut gray-brown beard and no mustache—stopped abruptly and squinted at Marlie's canvas. She had worked on it for almost two hours, but it looked like a quick *watercolor* sketch done in fifteen or twenty minutes; yet it had an extraordinarily complete quality. It was as though she had painted a shadow body, but with the shadows themselves subtly undershadowed, colored so that by some optical trick you were encouraged to provide the solid flesh yourself, from remembered images of bodies in an identical pose. The stool was there, but as three or four modulated slapdash lines which, like the seated figure, made it seem both solid and ethereal.

Diamo finally nodded his head. "Every damn time," he muttered. "Every goddamn time." He turned to me. "She your sister?" I nodded. "Lucky kid," he said, and walked away without saying a thing to Marlie herself.

"He's shy," said the model. "He can't stand to look anyone in the eye when he says something nice about them."

On our way to the parking lot, Marlie and I stopped at a bar and grill kind of place at the end of the block and had a beer.

"Has Peter ever seen any of your paintings?" I asked her.

She nodded. "He likes them. A whole lot." She took a swallow of beer and licked her upper lip slowly, thinking. Then she smiled sadly, looking down at a filled-in beer ring, a kind of liquid mirror on the table where her glass had been. "He thinks I'm a jerk to want to marry Donny, and that Donny's a jerk, and that I should leave this philistine prison and go to New York and take a cold-water flat in the Village and paint, paint, paint"—she slapped the palm of her hand onto the beer ring and dropped her forehead onto her knuckles—"paint, paint, paint"—her shoulders were shaking, but the sobs were still barely audible—"just paint—and paint—and *paiiint!*" She cried—plain cried—for a half-minute or so while I patted her helplessly on the back; then without raising her head she held out her left hand for a handkerchief. I gave her mine, and she sat up, drying her eyes, sniffling. "Peter's theory," she said in a perfectly controlled voice, as though she had never broken down, "is that quote suffering is necessary to achieve artistic greatness unquote. And do you know why I can't buy that?" I shook my head. "Because I've used up my capital, as far as certain kinds of suffering go. I just can't afford it."

I FELT IT THERE in the Temple Bar and Grill, and even more so two months later, at her wedding, when she walked up the center aisle of St. Mark's toward Donny Hancock: felt how much I loved her—how intensely she had attracted me every minute of my life —how truly glorious the nonexistent prospect of incest was and always would be. After she and Donny drove off to the airport, I started drinking with Johnny and Graham Brownell (one of the many Marlie had rejected) with the idea of achieving stupor—but after three drinks I stopped. It seemed pointless, and a little disgusting—as though what really mattered was how drunk you could get.

Twenty-two

I STARTED AT HARVARD that fall, and was cramming for my midterm hour exams when Mother telephoned to say she would pick me up the following morning, Saturday. We'd both drive to Devon together; see Johnny play in the season's last football game, against St. Matthews; take him out to dinner; spend the night at the Devon Inn; and return to Cambridge Sunday afternoon.

"Ma, I'd love to, but I just can't do it. I'm studying for exams."

"You have to, Chris," she said. "I don't want to talk about it over the phone, but it's a crisis. John might not be allowed to go back to Devon next year, or to graduate. I need your support and your advice. Bring your books along."

"Why doesn't Francis?"

"Dad is in New York—one of those three-day family business conferences."

"Okay, I'll bring my notes. Is it a *behavior* problem?"

"No, nothing like that. Academic. I'll tell you tomorrow."

She arrived at ten-thirty, dusted my room with a dirty shirt, made the bed, cleaned a few windowpanes; then we went to a student joint for early lunch. On our way out I couldn't avoid introducing her to my American history section man, a dyspeptic scholar with a congenital antipathy to idle chatter, and she spent ten minutes telling him about her Boston ancestors. As always, it embarrassed me; but at the same time I loved the way she was so totally unconcerned with where angels do or do not fear to tread.

Halfway to Concord, when she finally got around to John's "crisis," she came at it obliquely. "Tell me about the Rector," she said. "In all the years you were at Devon, I never got a real sense of him, and I'll have to face him right after lunch tomorrow. Is he as frightening as he pretends to be? Read that letter in my handbag and you'll see what I mean."

To those unfamiliar with Devon, I should explain that it is what used to be called a New England church school: that is, an Episcopal boarding school modeled on a composite of English public schools. A Boston Frothingham, the Rector (whose first name was Lucius) had been born just before the Civil War; was educated at Cheltenham and Trinity College, Cambridge; had been ordained upon graduation from the Harvard Divinity School; and was then assigned for several years to putting the fear of his God (missionary, football star and sheriff, divinely combined) into the residents of Nugget, Colorado—a period in his life about which little is known but much may be imagined. He returned to Massachusetts, married his cousin, and founded Devon School around the time Grover Cleveland first went to the White House—and now, more than fifty years later, he was still headmaster. Six foot two, two hundred and ten pounds, built along the general lines of an oak tree, at eighty years old he was what is known as an institution, if you define "institution" as someone everyone is a little afraid of, who seems to have been in authority forever.

The letter in Mother's handbag was terse almost to the point of rudeness. It said John's academic performance had dropped seriously below Devon standards, that there was a definite possibility he would not be asked back next year, and that it would be advisable to arrange a conference in order to discuss his future.

"What do you think?" Mother asked when I'd put the letter back.

"It sounds serious, all right; but one thing I wouldn't take too seriously is the tone of the letter. The Rector sometimes seems rude when he only means to be terse. It's his style to be abrupt."

"Is he a reasonable person? Does he play fair?"

"Fair? Reasonable? I'd rather say he is always *just*. I think that might be why so many people are afraid of him."

"Are the masters afraid of him?"

"The most forbidding masters. The most high-powered parents."

"I wish Francis were here, I do indeed. What does the Rector do to people? What should I expect?"

"Somehow he makes them feel like shaky children."

"But how? What does it have to do with his being just?"

"Let me think a minute before I answer that one."

Actually, I had already given the matter years of thought. Being a bona-fide shaky child when I first arrived at Devon, I'd been in an ideal position to develop theories on the subject of the Rector's impact, and toward the end of my second-form (eighth-grade) year, I had concluded that he scared people because he was too just—inescapably just—more just than humans ought to be.

I had come to that conclusion on a Saturday in mid-May, shortly after the Rector had finished saying his good nights. He said these after prayers, each evening at eight-fifteen, to every member of the Lower School, in the north hallway of Prebble House. Evening prayers were always short, almost offhand, as though their effect were meant to be cumulative. When the bell ending evening study hall rang, the master in charge would throw open the doors and there, coming from his quarters, would be the Rector, moving brusquely yet without haste, prayer book in hand. He would proceed to the master's desk platform at the head of the room, kneel down—kneel right on the floor, in his perfectly tailored dark-gray worsted herringbone tweed suit—open his prayer book to the red silk marker, find the exact place on the page, raise his eyebrows and glance suspiciously at us as we sat at our desks (the way a pitcher glances at the runner before going into his wind-up), then look back at the page and read the prayer in a rapid mumble, so that no matter how hard you listened you couldn't connect more than two out of every three sentences. You knew when he had reached the end because he snapped the prayer book shut, grabbed the edge of the master's desk, pulled his huge pachyderm form to a standing position and lumbered into the hallway to a spot near the stairs leading up to the first- and second-form dormitories. Then we lined up row by row inside the schoolroom to file out, shake his hand and enunciate our "Good night, sir" in response to his "Good night, Hooper" or (if he momentarily forgot your name, which was unusual) "Good night, boy."

On this particular May evening, a surprising thing happened. Instead of saying good night to me when I stepped up and shook his hand, he muttered, "Wait over there, boy." Stunned, I went and stood by the stairs. Soon I was joined by another second-former, then by a first-former. By the time the Rector was through with his good nights, there were half a dozen of us lined up at the foot of the stairs, limp with uncertainty. Because I was nearest, he came straight over to me, leaned forward in his massive, stiff-backed way, and said, "Breathe." I exhaled vigorously through my nostrils and he growled, "No, no—in my face, boy." He looked quite a lot like the bust of Caesar Augustus in the School House. If he had asked me to untie his shoelaces with my teeth, I would have done so, solemnly. I opened my mouth and breathed full in his face. He nodded and moved on, making each of us repeat this mystifying performance, then turned abruptly and left.

The next day I was told (by whom, I forget; there seemed always to be someone who knew such things) that we had been suspected of drinking. All six of us were sopranos in the choir. The choir had sung at the wedding of one of the Lawrence girls— whose brothers and father had all gone to Devon, and who had an enormous dairy farm near the school. After the wedding, which had been held in the school chapel that Saturday after- noon, the choir was invited to the reception, and I for one had consumed a fair quantity of cookies and fruit punch. There was another punch, well spiked, across the lawn from our bowl. I suppose some guest thought he had seen one of the boys dip into it and had told the Rector so. The Rector made sure for himself.

What struck me at the time was that he never said a word about it to us: no moralizing preamble, no threats about what might happen, not a hint as to what he was inspecting us for. He just smelled our breaths, grunted his satisfaction and—pigeon- toed, leaning a little forward—barreled down the sixth-form study hallway toward Headmaster's House, leaving us to piece the puz- zle for ourselves.

"That was great for us," I said to Mother after describing the incident to her, "because we were innocent, and we didn't have to listen to the kind of speech that makes you feel guilty even if you're not. But when I thought about it a little more, it worried me—never getting the chance to speak up, even the chance to be asked 'Did you do it?' so I could say 'No, I didn't.' Because just suppose I *had* drunk from the wrong punch bowl, but by mistake. And suppose that I hadn't reported my mistake to any of the masters because I was afraid to. Or because I didn't think I had to. Or because I felt dizzy and wasn't thinking straight. Would the Rector, after smelling liquor on my breath, have expelled me without a word spoken—or would I have been given a chance to state my case?" I didn't know. There was no way to be sure. But ambiguity (I told her) is not the Rector's strong point, and if the moral scales became hard to read, I doubt you could expect much sympathy or compassion. "Whatever he de- cided would certainly be *just*," I added. "But kids aren't always profoundly interested in justice, and neither are grownups. Fairness, yes—the word you used. But not justice. Because as a kid, too often you are either actually or inadvertently in the wrong. You need room to wriggle. What I'm telling you is, the Rector has an extremely limited appreciation of wriggle room."

"Chris," she said, "you have given me exactly what I needed— a key; a key I can use. The Rector sounds like your grandfather —the way your grandfather used to be before he retired and became so mellow. Basically, it's the Victorian businessman's approach—so now I know what I'm up against, and I think I know what to do about it."

JOHN PLAYED BEAUTIFUL FOOTBALL. From the moment we arrived at the school, it was impossible to imagine his having a problem of any kind. The grandstands were filling up, the St. Matthews team was already on the field, the Devon squad jogged out from its dressing room amid shrieks and cheers, and there he was—Big John, my baby brother, still only a fifth-former, another full season to go, but already star left end of this year's undefeated team, out there somersaulting, jumping in place, kidding around with his teammates as though this were a midweek practice session about to begin and not the big game of the year.

I lost track of how many passes he caught and how many interceptions he made—never mind the spectacular tackles and flying blocks. At times it seemed he was the whole team, like a one-man band, and the others—including the entire backfield— were his instruments; and when the grandstand began shouting "*Hoo*per-*Hoo*per-*Su*per-*Su*per!" faster and faster, louder and louder, Mother took her handkerchief out and proudly bawled.

The score was 27–7 for Devon; all parents and guests ate dinner (roast beef, and vanilla ice cream with butterscotch sauce) in the school dining room; right after that, the traditional victory bonfire was lit, and the cheering and the tossing of people into the air went on until bedtime. There was no question of chatting with John—we were lucky enough to sit with him at dinner—and the next morning, breakfast was followed by chapel, which was followed by lunch. We saw him (so to speak) in the interstices, but he wasn't really reachable, and it finally dawned on me that one reason must be the election: the squad was due to elect next year's football captain at four that afternoon.

"He should get it," I said to Mother when we were alone for a moment after lunch. "But can he accept it?"

"Not if he's not here," Mother said. "But he will be, and he'll graduate. Mark my words!"

"Does he know why you're really up here?"

"Not a thing about it."

"When's your meeting?"

She looked at the big clock on top of the School House. "Twenty minutes."

"All set?"

"You *bet* I'm all set."

"What's in the envelope?" I asked, pointing to a big brown folder tied with string, which she had kept close to her all during lunch and now hugged as though it held the maps to Treasure Island.

"Documents," she said. "Financial documents."

ON OUR WAY BACK TO CAMBRIDGE, Mother told me something of what had happened during her confrontation with the Rector; but Mother is no raconteur and it wasn't until several years later, after the Rector had retired, that I was given a full, more or less objective account of it by Mr. Rainsford, the assistant headmaster. Mr. Rainsford—a quiet, small, pink, rather Martian-looking man with a relentless sense of humor—had answered the doorbell and conducted Mother to the Rector's study. It was a large study —more like a Georgian living room, big enough for over a hundred schoolboys—and the Rector's desk was at the center of it. He was expecting Mother and rose to greet her, glancing as he did so at the folder under her arm. She had considered mentioning John's football prowess during the brief hellos, but rejected the tactic as too transparent. She had also considered and rejected mentioning that her family, the Langdons, were related, through marriage in the early part of the nineteenth century, to his family, the Frothinghams. It was, she told me, hard for her to resist bringing that in, not only because it would have been so natural, so true to her own nature, to do so, but also because her intuition signaled her that this was the sort of thing Lucius Frothingham was slow to discredit: bloodlines. But she discarded all such ploys in favor of the frontal attack, and elegantly prepared, carefully memorized phrasing.

"May I put my case directly?" she said, before he had even had time to offer her a chair. "I have read your letter. We both know John's academic situation—I in a general way, you in detail. But what I have to say has less to do with John than it has to do with your school, and I would like to feel that you will welcome my being absolutely forthright."

The Rector had of course had considerable experience with distraught and even irate parents—usually the fathers rather than the mothers, but never mind. He had discovered decades ago that the less he said at the beginning, the more the parents could get off their chests, and therefore the less they would have left to say at the end.

"Absolutely, Mrs. Wagner" is what he said now. "But do sit down—please make yourself comfortable."

"Mr. Frothingham," Mother said, ignoring his offer of a chair (thereby making it too rude for him to sit at that imposing desk), "what would you say, sir, if you had invested more than five thousand dollars in a company you believed to be the best of its kind, received nothing but reassuring reports from it over a period of more than four years, and then, without any forewarning *whatsoever*, were told that your entire investment was down the drain?"

"No doubt I would be livid," said the Rector, still forced to stand, and now forced to stand back a foot or so while this vigorous lady whipped papers out of her folder and lined them up on his desk blotter—an area never before disturbed by anyone, including his beloved wife and the servants.

"Here," she said, "are my bills and receipted checks to Devon School for John over the past four years and two and one half months. And here," she added, putting down another paper-clipped pile, "is every report card, every letter, every Devon School communication of any kind concerning my son John Hooper over the same time period. The bills add up to more than five thousand dollars—probably much more, if you count trans-portation and all the inevitable extras, plus annual donations through the parents' committee. The report cards and letters add up to a sunny picture of a growing boy doing nicely—not bril-liantly, perhaps not even *very* nicely, but nicely. That is the picture they give, until this letter," she said, pulling the villainous missive from her handbag, "received"—and she took a closer look, to make sure of the date—"approximately one week ago. *Now*, Mr. Frothingham, I will be delighted to accept your kind offer of a chair."

He sat also, taking several moments to flip through her bills and Devon's report cards. Then he placed his right elbow on his desk blotter, and with his first two fingers softly tapped his lower lip —something he frequently did when he was about to take his audience by surprise. "Mr. Rainsford," he said, "it appears that Mrs. Wagner is very much in the right. Have you anything to say?"

"*I*, sir? I'd need time to look into the matter further, sir," said Mr. Rainsford, feeling exactly like a shaky child. "But offhand, I'm afraid the answer is no."

"Nor have I," said the Rector. "Nor have I. So"—he turned to Mother and smiled—"we must start from there."

JOHN ENDED UP BEING TUTORED during Christmas and Easter vacations, and going to a tutoring school from mid-June to mid-

August; but he returned to Devon, just as Mother had predicted; and he graduated with headroom to spare.

More important to him at the time, he was unanimously elected football captain (not that it isn't always unanimous, once it becomes clear who will win), and he never suspected the part Mother had played in his Devon football career.

I was walking him back to his study, as we were about to leave, and while I am nearly five foot eleven, I felt so small next to him it seemed inconceivable that I had ever thought of him as a pudgy shrimp. For the briefest moment I felt a stab of jealousy, not only for his size but also for his well-deserved popularity, and for the easy way he wore it. And possibly also for Mother's considerable efforts on his behalf, wondering whether all her sons would have received the same special treatment.

Then the ugly feelings passed, and I wanted to wipe away the fact that I'd felt them. "Remember," I said, "remember that last fight we ever had, the time I thought you'd stolen my pack of Spearmint?"

"Sure," he said, shaking his head. "Some things I guess you don't forget."

"Well, I've often wondered—didn't you *let* me win that time?"

"And some things," John said, slapping me on the back, "you just never can seem to remember, no matter how hard you try."

Twenty-three

I DID PRETTY WELL on my hour exams, but most of what I was learning was outside of classes. It was 1939—the fall the Second World War began—and it's not hard to recall the excitement of starting college then. Archibald MacLeish had something to do with it: he made a speech to the new freshmen the night we arrived, stating with severe finality that one out of every five listening to him would be dead within ten years. That thought, combined with the natural ideals carried over from school and the intellectual curiosity charged by the new student's conception of Harvard, catalyzed me into a sort of insatiable fervor that I had never felt before and have certainly never felt since. Every idea was worth arguing, every thought worth expressing, every person worth making an intimate friend of: every moment was priceless. The goddesses we worshipped were Imagination, Spontaneity, Sincerity and Verbosity. We had metaphysical discussions over scrambled eggs at five in the morning, and worked off our hangovers by writing bad poetry.

Through some bizarre transformation, my father became central to all this ferment: the symbol of everything bohemian that Mother rejected. Bless her, she told off headmasters, chaired charity committees, ran centennial celebrations. She was the arch example of matronly energy focused on Victorian objectives; her aims for her sons were staunch character and material success, and the first must necessarily precede the second. She insisted that we start early to take responsibility, worried a little if our friends were eccentric, and made sure that we answered our dinner-dance invitations on time. If a store purchase was unsatisfactory or a clerk disagreeable, she was prone to call for the manager; but she was just as quick to praise the praiseworthy, and store managers loved her. D. H. Lawrence would not have. Once I gave her *Sons and Lovers* to read and she couldn't force herself to continue past the second chapter. She had of course never heard of Jonathan Edwards or Henry James—never mind Rivera or Bergson or Engels. Which did not disturb me in the least. What I objected to (in spite of all the things I loved her for) was Mother's tendency to plan your life in terms of her own goals, and the corollary to that: her assumption that anyone in his right mind must see things pretty much as she did.

My father, on the other hand—I had learned more about him over the years, from Peter—seemed a bold, free, expressive personality. He not only lived in Greenwich Village, but lived there with a woman named Tina, who was his common-law wife. He'd had many jobs, from manual labor to selling first editions. Part of me sensed that neither he nor his constantly changing jobs were particularly bohemian—that, if anything, he was in most ways quite conservative: a sweet, lovable, alcoholic failure. But I was careful not to focus on these suspicions, because I needed a rebel camp to head for, and my father's was the only one available. I convinced myself that I could understand why he'd never been able to live with my mother happily.

He wouldn't, I reasoned, allow himself to be tied down to the Philadelphia suburban existence: the five-fifteen; golf on Saturday; church Sunday. He was a deposed prince, a sand artist, an officer courier to extinct Balkan countries. If he wanted to tell me a dirty joke—even one about the Roosevelts—he had a perfect right to tell me a dirty joke. His license was the license of mystery and of impulse. By sophomore year that was something I could easily understand, from the front bedroom of my rat house, while reading Molly Bloom's soliloquy or taking notes on Nietzsche.

I lived on Mt. Auburn with three or four fellow club members, but I hardly ever saw them except at club meals because I spent so many of my waking hours at the *Crimson,* Harvard's undergraduate daily. I was going out with a Radcliffe girl who had costarred with me in the Dramatic Club's production of Noël Coward's *Family Album.* Her name was Barbara Kingsford, and she was unlike any of the girls I had grown up with: intense. Intense about acting, intense about the sociology course we both took with Professor Sorokin, intense about hot jazz, intense about everything.

She had light-brown hair that she wore in a loosely fluffed, carefully abandoned Marlene Dietrich fashion; a complexion that contradicted the siren image because it almost squeaked with health; and penetrating, blue-flecked gray eyes that she blinked at regular intervals when she was thinking. She wasn't *from* anywhere, in the usual sense. She was American but had been born in Germany, where her father was a well-known (I gathered) foreign correspondent after the war and into the thirties, and she was depressingly well-informed about practically everything. As a young girl—an only, and late, child—her parents had taken her with them to nudist colonies outside Berlin, and she had absorbed an uncomfortably objective attitude toward sex, which she recognized in herself and tried to overcome by an earnest but oddly utilitarian indulgence. We indulged before our play's dress rehearsal in order to enhance and electrify our performance. We indulged during exam period to relax ourselves. We indulged after special evenings at downtown Boston nightspots, where we had listened to Bunny Berrigan or Duke Ellington, or had gone to a get-together (occasionally in somebody's hotel room) arranged by Pee Wee Russel and Bud Free-man—fornication becoming the final high-flying solo to cap every jam session. When Berrigan died, we held a student wake, and later on indulged in his honor. Through her father—now retired, but a kind of Delphic oracle—Barbara seemed to know everybody worth knowing, at least well enough to remind them of whose daughter she was; and she could talk the ambiguity out of ideas, or the mystique out of rituals, the way a taxidermist stuffs animals.

"Take your debutante custom," she said. "It's really just a glorified marriage market, beginning with those dancing classes you went to at age—what was it, eight? Nine?" It was midday and we were lying on my studio couch, partly clothed.

I reached up for a cigarette, on the bookcase hanging above and almost over us. "Did I ever tell you about the time at the Saturday Evening—that's one of the pre-deb subscription dances, held at the Warwick—when the main chandelier turned into a shower? A pipe had burst in the ceiling, and the first thing we knew bits of plaster began falling onto the dance floor. Then—"

"You're changing the subject, Christopher, because you don't want me to squeeze the juice out of your precious adolescent memories. But that isn't what I really want to do. I just want you to concentrate on me—because how else will I ever get to come?"

"What do you mean, ever get to come?"

"Never mind that. As I was about to say, the debutante ritual is amazingly efficient, despite being expensive, because look at all the priceless—to those involved, priceless—things it does at once. It boasts and confirms the family's social status—same as with Ruth Benedict's Kwakiutl Indians. It forms a financially support-ive inner circle—the fathers of debutantes giving each other big business. It provides a way to keep excess earnings away from the government. It ensures that the rich will marry the rich. What else?"

"Speaking of marriage, in tomorrow's *Crimson* there's a story on Radcliffe that has some interesting statistics. Did you know that nearly seventy percent of Radcliffe girls marry Harvard boys?"

She blinked at regular intervals, then haunched herself around and propped her chin on her hand, so that we were very close, our faces a few inches apart, looking into each other's eyes.

"Okay," she said. "You're right. I guess just about everything, for at least ten years after puberty, could be broadly classified as a marriage market."

"Frig sociology. What was that about if you ever get to come?"

Her eyes suddenly filled with tears, yet no tear fell. "I thought you knew," she said. "I have never actually come, with anyone. Never. Not once."

We saw no less of each other after that, possibly more; but I was haunted by what she had told me—it made me alternately excessive and inhibited, as though I had an obligation I resented and could have walked away from, had my own pride not been involved. At times I longed for the glow of innocence that Philadelphia represented, and thought I was still in love with Janice, but Janice's father had been appointed something high up in the State Department and they were spending the war in Washington. Though even if she hadn't moved to Washington, I'd probably not have seen much of her except (of course) at parties. I went to more of those than ever, on vacations; but my college world scarcely overlapped with the Philadelphia party life and Loon Lake summers that had absorbed me almost totally during boarding school. Out of sentiment and a longing to hold onto some part of childhood, I still went back to Loon Lake for part of every summer. I even had a licit, necking relationship with Martha Ballard (my mixed doubles tennis partner in the Labor Day tournament) and one or two other budding Venuses who summered on the mountaintop and wintered at Farmington or Foxcroft or Westover. But the longer I lived in my rat house on Mt. Auburn Street, the more patronizing I felt toward the self that, once upon a time, had never heard of Cambridge.

Then the last week in September, junior year, the whole thing with Janice revived when the *Crimson* sent me to Washington for a conference, and I arranged to stay at the Hollingsworths' overnight.

At the time I told myself that the Hollingsworths were a pleasant convenience, a way to avoid paying a hotel bill; but I knew the real reason why I wanted to see Janice again in spite of—maybe because of—the yearning intensity and sophisticated intelligence of Barbara. It had something to do with the Sleeping Beauty tale. My assumption was that if we spent the night (some night, any night) together, Janice would become miraculously transformed into everything I had always wanted in a woman: warm, witty, crazy, slutty, elegant—the best of Philadelphia fused with the best of Greenwich Village. She would prove Barbara wrong about my Philadelphia—my childhood: wrong in writing it off as a sociological freak, a fatuous phenomenon. If Janice would only sleep with me—only *allow* herself to be awakened!

IT WAS A TWO-DAY CONFERENCE, sponsored—indeed, thought up—by Mrs. Roosevelt, and called something like the International Student Assembly. The point, according to the invitational literature, was to get "thinking" young people from every available country to thrash out their hopes and fears for the postwar world so that we could prepare now to solve such problems after the war was over and won.

I went down on the train with Marquis Johns, a Negro with an impeccable Oxford accent. When he came to the *Crimson*'s editorial room to suggest that we make the trip together, I said, "Of what country, Marquis, are you a thinking young person?"

Instead of answering me directly, he took several large white envelopes from his inside pocket, shuffled them for a moment, making sure they were all there, and handed them to me in ceremonious silence. The first was a personal letter from Mrs.

Roosevelt, the second from somebody in the British embassy, the third from the French embassy, the fourth from a Haitian dignitary. It appeared that Marquis's father owned half of Haiti and had been instrumental in bringing about that republic's recent declaration of war on the Axis powers.

"Looks as though you really rate," I said, handing the letters back.

"Rate?" He sat perfectly still, but I could tell he was expectant from the way he suddenly folded his hands and started cracking his thumb knuckles.

"It means they really want you; they're counting on you to show. Show *up.*"

"Oh." He nodded humorlessly, riffling the letters and returning them to his coat pocket. "Well, yes—I should hope so."

A few days later, when we left on the night train for Washington from Boston's Back Bay Station, he kept patting his inside coat pocket to make sure he hadn't left the letters behind. His clothing was as impeccable as his accent; he wore a pinstriped blue suit, a light-gray tweed coat, pearl gloves and a gray fedora. Furthermore, he had hired two porters to carry his four large suitcases.

I looked at him—small as a schoolboy, his shiny black face chubby yet serious, with large, alert eyes—and shook my head in amazement. "Why all the bags?" I asked. "We're only staying two days and one night."

"Do you think it's too much luggage?" he replied. "I wondered about that, and I decided Americans always take lots of luggage. It's a *nice* custom. Adds immensely to the ritual of traveling, don't you agree?"

It was the same two-porter routine when we changed to the Pennsylvania Railroad in New York, and again the next morning when we arrived in Washington. Marquis had the porters check his four bags at the Union Station, and we went out to hunt up some breakfast.

I forget the name of the place we decided on. It had booths

for table service. We were both somewhat groggy and took a booth instead of sitting at the counter.

I was groggy, anyway; Marquis was looking around like a kid about to have his first meal away from home. "What's that!" he squealed suddenly, pointing at my feet.

I looked down on a large black bug, squashed symmetrically two inches from my right toe. "Cockroach," I said.

"Incredible!"

I didn't see the waiter until after I'd heard his voice. It was not a loud voice, but it was perfectly audible, for he clipped his Southern accent in an unusual manner, managing to sound monotonous and impatient at the same time.

"Sorry," he said, "you can't eat here."

Marquis and I looked at each other, then back at the waiter. I tried to think what I could say, how I should handle the situation. Clearly it was up to me to handle it; it was my fault for forgetting, for bringing Marquis here in the first place.

But before I could say anything, Marquis had pulled out his letters. "Here are several references that might interest you," he said, taking the documents out of their envelopes and handing them one by one to the waiter.

The waiter was young, with light, colorless hair and a shaving cut on his neck. He stood with his starved-donkey profile to me, glaring at Marquis. He glanced briefly at the first letter, then dropped the lot on the table. "Don't cut no ice heah," he said. "Sorry, you'll have to go. *You* can stay," he said, turning to me.

"Come on, Marquis," I got up. "It's pointless to argue."

"One moment, Chris. Would it," he said courteously, "be possible to speak to your proprietor, your manager?" His tone was so disarmingly polite and his accent so undeniably upper class that for a few seconds the waiter was dumbfounded.

"Let's get out of here," I said, but Marquis never took his eyes off the waiter's. He sat there and calmly, graciously repeated his request, as though the problem was not one of having it granted but of making it understood.

"Hey, Eddie!" The waiter shouted to a pockmarked, redheaded man in a white linen coat and chef's hat who was leaning against the counter, chuckling at something he'd just heard. "Come here a minute!"

Marquis didn't wait for Eddie to get to our booth. He rose, stepped politely around the waiter and went up to the redheaded chef. The chef squinted his eyes, rapidly examining Marquis: down, then up, then down again.

When Marquis spoke, his voice was expertly controlled. "Your employee," he said in a confidential, advisory tone, "has been endeavoring to persuade my friend and me to stay and have our breakfast here. May I suggest"—he lowered his voice even more and pointed to the squashed cockroach—"that instead of using persuasion to keep your customers, you institute a policy of cleanliness?" Then, with perfect timing, he turned on his heel and marched out.

I caught up with him halfway to the corner. For a minute I couldn't think of a thing to say; I just patted him on the back, shook my head in amazement and patted him on the back again. But we still had the problem of breakfast. "Let's go back to the station," I suggested. "There must be a place to eat there."

"You go, Chris," he said, "I'm not hungry. If I was," he slapped the letters against the flat of his hand, "I'd eat these."

"That isn't by any chance a joke, is it, Marquis?"

"Yes," he said. "Yes, I think it is." He looked mournfully at his credentials, as though he couldn't decide whether to tuck them safely back inside his coat pocket or to toss them into the street-corner trash container. "They have lost their magic," he said softly and crumpled them in his hand. But instead of throwing them away, he jammed them into his pocket.

I must have looked surprised because he smiled at me and patted his pocket. "A souvenir," he said. "A reminder that in an advanced civilization one cannot use magic to ward off evil. What is required is a sense of humor!"

I TOLD JANICE about the incident that evening, when we were in the bar of one of those minute ultra-fashionable restaurants, waiting for a table.

"You're the only person I know whose one Negro friend is bound to be an *aristocrat*," she said. "How do you always manage to achieve these weird and wonderful mixtures?"

"Will you be one of them? Will you be my rebel debutante?"

"Post-debutante."

"Doesn't sound nearly as dashing—rebel post-debutante."

"It all sounds too much like the Kentucky Derby for me. What precisely did you have in mind? Not driving to Baltimore to get married? Surely your thinking has progressed in the last year or two."

"Stop laughing at me, you know how sensitive I am . . . Quite —well, now. Did you ever notice how sensitive Britishers are always saying 'Quite—well, now'? But I digress. The point is, do you have a girl friend you can stay with in New York?"

"Yes, several."

"On the last weekend in October? That's one month from now, the weekend of the Harvard-Princeton game."

"Funny—Daddy always calls it the Princeton-Harvard game. But yes. So much for the debutante part. Where does the rebel come in?"

"It doesn't matter how you refer to the game—we wouldn't be going to it."

"Ah-*ha*. Yes, indeed. I begin to see. You borrow an apartment for the night. I am ostensibly staying with, let's say, Maggie Trowbridge and am going with you to the football game, but I am actually sharing your friend's apartment with you and not seeing the game at all."

"You said it, not me."

"But you thought it up and are fully prepared to execute it?" I nodded. "*Fully* prepared?"

"*Semper paratus*. Like a marine." The major-domo sidled up

through the almost-impenetrable atmosphere and signaled that our table was ready. "Let's eat on it," I suggested before she could say no.

Neither of us returned to the subject during dinner or between acts at the ballet, but it was on both our minds the entire evening and it would have to be settled one way or the other that night, because I'd be up and off to the second day of the conference by eight-thirty the next morning—then taking a late-afternoon train back to Boston.

It was now a little before midnight, and we were in the Hollingsworths' kitchen drinking a glass of milk and eating cookies, like good children. We sat side by side on the big blocky kitchen table and looked at each other sidewise.

"Um," said I.

"Um," said she.

We both laughed.

"You go first."

"Okay," she said. "Why do you want to?"

I nodded. "Good question, as they keep saying at this conference. I take it you really want an answer. Not 'Because I love you' or something squishy like that, but a real answer to the real question, 'What would be the point of a one-night stand?' "

"Yup."

"None," I said. "There would be no point—and *that's* the point."

"You mean you want to find out if there is such a thing as a rebel debutante?"

"Yes—who can make love shine."

"That takes care of Saturday. What do we do on Sunday, and Monday, and Tuesday, and Wednesday, and . . .?"

"I'm not sure about the weekdays, but Sunday we could go to see my father—my real father—in Greenwich Village."

"Do you remember Livvy Clarke?" I nodded. "I'd be cheating on him."

"Are you—does he—"

"No, we haven't. He's much too stuffy."

"Then—"

"Then I'll let you know in the morning, Chris, Oh, hell, I know the answer now. I'll go. I'll go to New York, but don't ask me to guarantee any more than that. You'd better get tickets to the football game, just in case."

"In case what?"

"In case you forget to bring your rubbers, or I lose my overshoes and get cold feet. And don't look at me like that, it gives me butterflies. I think we'd better go to bed, separately and at once, before something entirely predictable happens. Good night, Chris. Have . . . a . . . good . . . night." She kissed me after each of the four last words, then jumped off the table and ran out of the kitchen without looking back.

Twenty-four

THE LOGISTICS OF MY carefully prepared October weekend in New York were more complicated than I'd hoped they would be. I had borrowed the apartment easily enough, but I could only have it through Sunday morning. John was a freshman at Harvard now, and we shared a car. He had driven it to Philadelphia for the weekend to take his girl to a party, and would pick me up in New York at noon on Sunday. Neither of us had Monday classes, so we planned to spend Sunday night at my father's and Tina's in the Village (Peter made that arrangement), then drive back to Cambridge together the next morning.

As for Janice, she would be pretending to stay on 72nd Street with the Trowbridges, but the football-game excuse had been dropped because (for reasons I've forgotten) she couldn't get to New York until late Saturday afternoon, by plane. Besides, she didn't need any elaborate explanation—just told her mother it was a shopping visit, and that she'd be staying with her old Farmington buddy Maggie Trowbridge.

With so much depending on so much else, I panicked

when the phone rang and I wasn't even inside the apartment to answer it. I had run across the street to the corner drugstore for a pack of cigarettes, and had just walked back into the apartment building when I heard it. It was five-thirty, about time for Janice to call. For a moment I stood there in the vestibule, mesmerized, unable to move. Then I sprinted up the stairs to the second floor, jammed my key into the lock, shoved the apartment door open with my shoulder, and pounced on the telephone.

"Hello!" I was trying not to shout, trying to sound cheerful and suave. "Just blew in," I said, grinning at the ceiling. "Heard your ring as I was crossing Park and Fiftieth and ran the ten blocks to my borrowed digs—pause; laugh."

There was a long silence, then a girl's voice said, "Hello, Christy."

"Why, hello," I said, wondering who, outside my family, would be calling me Christy.

"I guess you didn't get the—"

"*Mar*tha! I thought you were at Westover."

"Well, I—"

"For a second there I didn't know your voice. I mean, I guess this is about the first time I've heard you on the telephone."

"That's right," Martha said. "I thought of that before I called. I wondered if you'd . . ." The sound petered out.

"Martha?"

"I'm still here," she said. What the hell, I thought. There was another pause. Then it came: "You didn't answer my letters—my last letter. But I had a weekend permission and was coming to New York anyway, to stay with a classmate. Johnny said you were at this number, so I thought I'd just—see how you were."

"I'm glad you called. It's wonderful to hear your voice, Martha." I cleared my throat. "How long did you people stay on the mountaintop?"

"Till the middle of September."

"Did you win the mixed doubles tournament?"

"Didn't even enter it."

"How was the Labor Day dance?"

"Wonderful. No, it wasn't. It was lousy. Chris, can I see you?"

"Well, the thing is, I—"

"Can I see you for just a minute—ten minutes—any time this weekend?" The urgency in her voice was so pathetically obvious that for a moment I wished, sincerely wished, that I still felt the same way about her.

"Sure, Martha. Sure," I said, looking at my wristwatch. I should have known it wasn't Janice—she probably wouldn't even be in the city for another ten minutes. Besides, she would never be the one to call me. "How about right now?" I said into the telephone. "Where are you?"

"Sixty-eighth, between Lexington and Third. You don't have to, Christy."

"Don't be silly, I *want* to. If I weren't so tied up, I'd—between Lex and Third? I'll hop a cab and be right over."

"I could come to you, if that would—"

"Don't be silly," I said, thinking, *That's twice I've said that.* "Be down in a few minutes. Goodbye, Martha."

"Goodbye, Chris. *Chris*—"

"Yes?"

"You don't even know my address."

"Gad, that's right. Shoot."

SHE CAME OUT OF THE TOWN HOUSE as I was paying the cabdriver, and I thought, with relief, that at least I wouldn't have to meet the family she was staying with. *I'd like you all to observe Chris Hooper, my summertime doubles partner, my seasonal love . . .* but she didn't look bitter. She looked as she had always looked— sweet, enthusiastic, ready for a fast set; the straight-backed, big-boned, windswept type that always seems so lost in high heels and tiny hats.

"I have to be back in five minutes," she said, smiling as if she were prepared to spend her life handing me gifts she couldn't afford.

"You promised me ten, remember?" My tone was exactly right: affectionate but brotherly. I smiled, took her head between my hands and gave her a kiss on each cheek. I felt a little awkward doing it, but she must have got the point; she frowned when I had finished, then looked abruptly down, fumbled in her purse, brought out a minute handkerchief and blew her nose. I looked casually over my shoulder at Lexington Avenue, then back toward Third. "Let's try Third," I said, offering my arm. "The bars there are so noisy they're private."

"Bars?" She snapped her purse shut and looked up at me as if I'd said something quite profound that she couldn't fully grasp. She smiled uncertainly and took my arm. I gave her hand a slight squeeze, intimate but measured, and began walking.

We both looked straight ahead. The clack of her heels sounded lonely on the cold pavement. I fished a cigarette out of my coat pocket and paused, without letting go of her arm, to light it. When I looked up she was gazing at me with unashamed adoration. Now was the danger point: right now.

"I'm sorry," I said in my most rigorously honest voice, "about not answering your letters. Things have been kind of hectic—going to this Washington conference last month, and—"

"Please, Chris—"

"No, I mean it. Those were wonderful letters, and I should have answered them."

"It doesn't matter now."

"But it does matter, Martha. Even friends—"

She reached up and put her hand over my mouth, just touching my lips with her fingertips. "Not yet," she said, scarcely breathing the words. "Not this second. Not for the next ten minutes. Eight minutes. Whatever it is."

"Funny—" I said, as we began to walk again.

"Me?"

"How different you are, here in New York."

"I know. I belong any place else—beaches, mountaintops—"

"I didn't mean it that way."

"Of course you didn't, darling. *Look* at that enormous baby carriage abandoned right on the street corner. I wonder if there's anything in it—anything alive."

"Martha—"

"Yes, darling? You don't mind if I call you darling, do you, darling? It's just a manner of speaking—some people do it to everybody."

"Martha, listen to me—"

"It doesn't mean anything, it's just a habit I've picked up working backstage on this play at school—the backstage type, that's me all over . . . What were you about to say, darling? Oh, *buy* me one of those stuffed pheasants someday," she cried, wheeling me around to face a fly-specked shop window. "That's *exactly* what New York makes me feel like: a stuffed pheasant in a Third Avenue junkshop." She slipped her arm out of mine, and taking my hand, held it in both her own. "But go on, Chris, darling— I'm listening. I really *am* listening."

I looked past the pair of pheasants and saw a man peering at us from the dimly lit shop: a shabby, aged leprechaun who, as soon as he caught my eye, began to make his way forward between the umbrella stands and the Franklin stoves. I looked over his head to the clock on the wall. Six-seventeen. Janice had already arrived at the Trowbridges'. I turned and gazed anxiously across Third Avenue, scanning the signs. "Let's duck in there," I said.

"Where, darling?"

"That bar over there."

"Do we have to, Chris?" she said. "Can't we just walk around holding hands? Must we really spend our last few minutes in a dreary little booth, burying the corpse?" She dropped my hand and covered her face, as if by pressing hard enough she might stop herself from shaking. "I think you'd better take me back," she whispered.

"Martha—don't."

"I wasn't supposed to. I—"

"Listen to me, Martha—now listen," I said gently, taking her by the shoulders, pleased with the mature tone in my voice. "This is not the casino overlooking Loon Lake. Those are not Japanese lanterns—they're streetlights. And this is not August. It's New York in October, and I am in love with a girl named Janice. Janice Hollingsworth. She's just arrived from Washington, and she flies back tomorrow, and I have to call her. Now. Before doing anything else I have got to cross this street and go into that bar and pick up the pay telephone and call Janice Hollingsworth."

She nodded, then took her hands away from her face. She was blinking, but there was, incredibly, a smile on her lips—not wistful or self-pitying but a smile of resolute good sportsmanship: the girl who lost the finals. "All right!" she said. "But I still have a few minutes, a few hundred seconds left. When they're up, I turn back into a stuffed pheasant."

I PILED MY CHANGE on the narrow shelf under the telephone, flipped through my wallet until I found the match cover with the Trowbridges' number on it, slid the door of the booth shut and began to dial. I made a mistake on the third digit, then dropped my nickel as I was gouging it out of the return slot. I could see it on the floor between my feet, but I couldn't pick it up without either opening the door or stooping in my heavy overcoat. Rather than waste the time, I took a dime from the pile of loose change and started over again. My hand was trembling. I forced myself to dial slowly, looking at the match cover for each separate digit. When the telephone began its ringless ringing inside my ear, I leaned against the door of the booth and held my breath.

I was staring through the glass at Martha—Martha Ballard: a tall, athletic-looking girl in a ridiculously small hat, wearing one of those tweed overcoats (blue) that flared out from the waist. It calmed me to watch her. She was not bad-looking, really. Handsome rather than beautiful—like the head of Liberty on my dime.

Thick wheat-blond hair, cut short and naturally curly; broad shoulders; a slightly over-full figure, beautifully carried; surprisingly slim ankles for so large a girl. If I did say so myself, I'd had pretty good . . .

"Good evening, Mr. Trowbridge's residence."

"Hello—good evening . . . Could I speak with Miss Janice Hollingsworth, please?" I might have guessed there'd be a butler. "She was supposed to—"

"Who is calling, please? Might this be Mr. Hooper?"

"That's right. I'm Chris Hooper. Has Janice—Miss Hollingsworth—has she arrived yet? I was to call her here."

"Yes, sir, she arrived this morning. She and Miss Trowbridge were taken to the football game, I believe, but they're back in the city now. They telephoned less than half an hour ago and left a number for you to call. Would you like me to—"

"*What* football game?"

"I beg your pardon, sir? Oh—the—I believe it was between Princeton and—now let me think a moment, sir—"

"Harvard," I said. "Harvard-Princeton," I repeated patiently.

"I believe you're right, sir."

"I am. You say they left a number?"

"Why, yes, sir, they did. Would you like me to—"

"I wish you would."

This time there was no mistake in my dialing, and my hand didn't tremble, but I had a lightheaded feeling, as though the phone booth and I were a foot or so off the ground. I counted the rings. There were eleven of them, so that their being finally answered at all seemed an act of calculated condescension.

"Hullo!" It was a half-drunken voice—male, undergraduate—shouting over party sounds. "Powell, get your fat—hullo, *hullo!*"

"Is Janice Hollingsworth there?" I asked. There was a sharp click, as though the phone had been dropped; then whoever picked it up again began singing into the mouthpiece, imitating Al Jolson: "*How* I love ya, *how* I love ya—My dear old . . ." "I'm sorry, pal," the first voice cut back. "Who was it?"

"Janice Hollingsworth. Janice . . . Hollingsworth!"

"Hold it, I'll take a roll call . . . Has anyone seen The Face?" he shouted into the room. "Lad here wants to talk to The Face!"

"Princeton or Harvard?" someone shouted back.

"Don' mean to be personal," the voice said into the telephone, "but would you min' giving your credentials, mate?"

"God! Look—"

"Sir-*rossis* U.," the voice announced. "Shall I *cutimoff?*"

"*How* I love ya, *how* I—"

"She's not available," the voice told me; then "Hold it, hold it—don't make a move, here's Maggie. Maggie's my personalized secretary. If you're a *very* good boy, she'll—"

"*Give* me that, you ass . . . Hello? Chris Hooper? This is Maggie Trowbridge. Janice isn't here right this *second*, Chris, but this thing won't last much longer—God, it can't—and we're all going over to Le Petit Navire for supper, so why don't you meet us there in about, say, three-quarters of an hour? Would that be all right?"

"Sure," I said. "I'll try to make it."

"I'm terribly sorry about the mix-up. Janice was here just *two* seconds ago. Wait. Has *anyone* seen Stony and Jan?" she asked, holding the phone away. "They *were* on the balcony," a girl said. "Look"—Maggie Trowbridge was back on the phone—"if she shows up, where shall I have her call you, Chris?"

"Let's leave it the other way," I said. "I'll meet her at Le Petit Navire."

"Well, if—sure, I guess that would be best. I can almost promise you she'll be there. In an hour or so. If she *isn't*, you'd better —let me see—yes, you'd better try here again."

BEFORE HANGING UP I had seen Martha leave—could still see her, a block away, walking slowly in the direction from which we had both come. Maybe I should catch up with her; take her out to dinner . . . No, after dinner—to a movie. I knew where she was staying. I could go around this evening. First, though, I had to see Janice—just for a minute, ten minutes . . . The whole thing might, after all, be a hoax, a practical joke: what the butler had said, the party, everything . . . In a state of mild delirium, I opened up the fat Manhattan directory and began flipping through its pages, wondering whether Le Petit Navire would be listed (if it existed at all) under L or P or N.

On the balcony with Stony, she'd said—who the hell was Stony? *Stony!*—Sweet Jesus, that's what they sometimes called Livvy Clarke. His first name was Livingston.

I slammed the telephone book shut and stomped out of the booth—then went right back again and telephoned Peter. This was one of those times when he had to be there; had to let me come talk to him; had to be a *brother.*

He was—all those things. Come right out . . . Supper . . . Bed for the night . . . Just talking about me, wondering how I was.

I got elaborate directions for the subway and bus, then said screw that and took a cab the whole way. What else was there to spend my money on?

PETER AND KIT WERE LIVING on Long Island now—next door to La Guardia field. After graduating from college, they had floundered around for a year or so in Manhattan. Then Peter took Mother's advice: he signed up at an advanced aircraft training school for a two-year technical course (paid for by Francis) that, should he graduate well, would qualify him for a lucrative job in the aircraft industry. He led his class the first year, and was now most of the way through his second. I had met Kit a number of times, of course, but always as little brother. I had only seen her when she was visiting us; I'd never stayed with them in New York, and I wasn't even aware that Kit was pregnant.

They both met me at the door of their ground-floor four-room, barracks-like apartment; and after I'd hugged Kit carefully (her stomach stuck out so far), she said, "Want to feel it kicking?"

That's the thing I'd forgotten about Kit—that she was so immediately personal; that she enfolded you so joyously. She was tiny next to Peter—tiny and lively and exquisite, and on top of that, somehow voluptuous. I loved the way she stood with her feet planted apart and her head tilted a little to one side when she asked a direct question. And while you were answering, she looked at you as though you were really special, really important. And her reply was to what you hadn't said, to your unspoken attitudes, as well as to what you'd said.

Peter was different—different from Kit, and different from his usual self. He got me a drink, but not one for himself—there were a couple of crucial tests on Monday, and he had at least an hour's more studying to do tonight. Kit had been the original rebel debutante—my God, Peter had *lived* in her college room for days, maybe weeks at a time. Surely, between them, they could give me faith or strength or whatever the hell it was I needed after this day. I had come ready to drink and talk until dawn—to dump all my troubles in their laps and watch, a silly smile on my face, while they sorted them out for me. And Peter sat there watching me nurse my drink, getting up to set the supper table before I'd half finished it, glancing surreptitiously at his desk with the open course books on it—even though he had all tomorrow to dig into them.

"What do you think you'll do after college, Chris?"

"I tell everybody I'm going to be a labor lawyer, but I really have no idea. Peter, do you remember—"

"Stay away from labor—the CIO, the AF of L, they're all poison, Chris. Law, yes. Labor law—forget it. Bunch of thugs, in the aircraft industry anyway."

"Well, you may be—"

"Corporation law, now that's something else again. You take Pratt and Whitney, any of these big aircraft companies. They have whole law departments, guys who get thirty, thirty-five thousand a year for doing nothing *but* handling company cases. Patent law. Infringements. Defending against workers who sue when they've got hurt due to their own carelessness. I'm talking like a G D capitalist and I know it sounds funny coming from me, but —Kit, are there any more noodles, see if Chris wants more noodles. What was I saying? Oh, yes: you've got to specialize, Chris, and I'll give you a, well—a sort of a tip. There's a kind of plane that can hover almost like a hummingbird—called an autogiro, invented by a fellow named Cierva—and it's going to develop someday into an important piece of military equipment, and what you should do when you're in law school is become *the* expert on the law having to do with that kind of plane, and when you graduate, believe me . . ." I'm not sure exactly when I stopped listening, but I wasn't obvious about it: I nodded at the right places, made the right murmurs and even asked a couple of questions.

Kit asked me twice to please spend the night—we could explore La Guardia together in the morning while Peter studied for Monday's big ones. But at ten-thirty I persuaded them to call me a cab.

"You came here looking for something," Kit said, standing with me in the cool night air, watching the cab pull up, "and we couldn't give it to you." She blinked, then smiled wistfully and hugged me. "That can happen. It's because Peter and I have too much ourselves, right now—and because we're guarding it too closely." She patted her stomach. "Try us again in a few months, Chris—when Peter is through with this damn school, and Cherub has arrived."

BACK IN THE APARTMENT, I poured myself a drink from the bottle of bourbon (Janice's favorite: Dant's) that I had so craftily supplied for our orgy; and I thought about Peter, about how ironically he had changed. And then it occurred to me that maybe he himself hadn't changed at all. Maybe he'd just changed in relationship to Mother. He had started off in the fold—as her boy protector, her confidant—and now, after a few wild side excursions, here he was back in the fold. But back on his own terms;

not in reaction to my father or stepfather or anyone else, but able, now, to go about his own business—which seemed, from this evening's monologue, to be aircraft technology. Still playing, by Jesus, with his electric trains!

Maybe before you were free to go about your own business, you had to do what Peter did—come back to the fold, but on your own terms. I drank to that—my own terms, whatever they were —then corked the bottle and went to bed.

Twenty-five

JOHN RANG THE APARTMENT BUZZER around noon. We had a sandwich at the drugstore across the street, went to an early-afternoon movie (Zasu Pitts, bless her ugly puss and pine-board figure), then drove down to the Village and cruised around, looking for my father's apartment.

"Do you feel as weird as I do about this?" John asked.

"Not weird, exactly," I said. "More scared, I think."

"Scared of what we'll find?"

"Or what we won't find."

IT WAS AFTER FOUR when we arrived at the address on Houston Street. The building bearing my father's number was a narrow brownstone apartment house with a grocery store on the ground floor. I looked at John and he shrugged, then cleared his throat and said, "Well—what are we waiting for?"

There was a step up and then a typical little dirty marble entryway: marble like the floors of men's rooms in movie theatres. Under the built-in mailboxes were name tags. It seemed incongruous to see MR. AND MRS. CURTIS HOOPER on one of them—as if an imposter had picked the worst accommodations in the city and used our name out of spite. I'll have to admit there was an element of distaste, probably based on shame or snobbery, in my immediate reaction; but it was mixed with wonder, with curiosity and most of all with anticipation.

I pressed the button and got an instant return buzz from inside. Pushing open the door, we were admitted to a narrow wooden stairway that smelled the way a telephone booth does if you close the door and smoke a cigarette all the way through. For a moment I forgot John was with me and began climbing toward the uncovered light bulb at the top of the stairs as if that held some inexplicable salvation: as if getting to the light bulb had been the purpose of my trip to the Village.

We had not covered more than half the distance to the landing when a woman appeared at the extreme front end of the second-floor hallway. By the sunlight that cut through her opened door and sliced across the hallway banister, I could see that her face was both soft and heavy. Auburn-red hair, uncontrolled masses of it, struggled about her plump shoulders. Her body was big and almost shapeless under a cheap green kimono which burst open below her freckled neck, revealing a tight pink brassiere that was doing its feeble best to restrain her spongy bosom.

When she first saw us (we were, after all, creeping up the stairs), I expected her to scream something derisive and duck back into her room. She didn't. Her movements were undeniably toward John and me. "Oh!" she uttered in a parrotlike squawk. "These must be my boys!" Rubbery pink arms, the color of flesh as it is usually painted rather than as it actually is, protruded from her short sleeves, and I saw that she was fumbling with the top button of her kimono. "Of course they are, of *course!* That's my Johnny-boy, and you must be Chris. Ooo, Johnny-boy, you're even better looking than your daddy! Come here, the two of you come quickly and kiss Tina before she knocks your blocks off!"

John and I bounded to the landing two steps at a time, shouting

"Hello!" and "Tina!" and "For gosh sakes, it's wonderful to see you!" as if we'd have been disappointed by any less energetic a reception from such an old and dear friend. Once within reach, we were swallowed in her fleshy smotherings: together (there was sufficient surface), then one at a time, so vigorously that I dropped the car keys which I had neglected to pocket.

As I stooped to pick them up, Tina held John at arm's length. "Johnny-boy," she said, shaking her head and squinching up her face, "you're so damn good-looking—Oops! I swore, didn't I? Tina swore. Tina swears too goddamn much. But," she added, "people should be allowed to swear in a world like this. Oh, God! God! They should be *forced* to swear! I'd rather swear than drink. No, I wouldn't. Anyway," she concluded, giving me a quick pat on the cheek, "I can do both today, can't I? Because you're both so good-looking—oh, that Johnny-boy!—and you are both here and, *and*, Tina loves you both!" With this she sucked in her breath and threw her arms around us once more, swooped us into her apartment, and slammed the door.

Once inside, she inspected herself in the vestibule mirror. "Good heavens!" she said, affecting a British accent. "I do seem to look a positive mess, don't I! Your daddy brought me this from Paris," she explained, fumbling again with the top button of her kimono. "You can't *imagine* how old the miserable thing is . . . But I still look lovely in it, don't I?" She twirled clumsily into the center of the room, screwing up her face like a gargoyle and addressing us in a scraped, coaxing voice: "*Don't* I?" she repeated insistently, pirouetting in the opposite direction.

But before we had time to reply, a wire-haired terrier pushed through the kitchenette door and began scampering about the square room in a dizzy, circular manner—from bed to windowsill to card table to couch and back to the floor, barking as hard as it ran. "Oh, youuuuuu!" shouted Tina, lunging at the animal. When she got within reach, the terrier jumped onto the sill, then sprang to the floor again and began zigzagging behind her on the rug. She swirled around, and the circular chase was repeated until the dog allowed itself to be caught on the bed.

Having gathered him up, Tina pressed his wriggling form to her and gulped for breath. "Now, Champ," she gasped, "for Christ's sake hold still while I introduce you to Daddy's boys. This is John Channing Hooper. And this is Christopher Boyd Hooper the Second. And *this*"—she held the animal at arm's length and shook it gently—"is Champ, which is short for Champagne Hooper Vingt-whatever-it-is. Weet. He was nursed on a case of Pommery your daddy bought before he lost all his, shall we say, money—weren't you, baby! Weren't you! Yes, you were. Oh yes, yes, you were! *Jesus,* he smells." She relaxed her hold and the dog pounced to the floor, prepared to continue the sport.

This ceremony completed, Tina repaired once more to her buttons while John, taking off his coat, sat down on the daybed and quieted the dog by stroking him. I looked at my younger brother, sitting there on the bed with the mussed bedclothes under him and the panting terrier on his lap. Tina—grotesque and, I was beginning to think, enchanting—stood on the other side of the room, also looking at John. He *was* handsome— conventionally handsome, but something more than that. Mother's suntanned complexion and deep brown eyes were combined with my father's firm jaw and cheekbones. The whole set of his face was strong—manly in an almost Hollywood way. But like my father, he was just saved from being a cigarette ad by some indefinable vulnerability about the eyes and mouth that always seemed to say, "Tell me what to do. Tell me what *you* would do." I had the uncanny feeling of seeing my own brother for the first time—then a siren screamed quite close by, drawing my attention to the window.

It was a beautiful fall day, mild and clear, so that each outside noise could be heard separately and each object inside seemed covered with its private share of sunlight. Without haste, I took in the furnishings of Tina's and my father's apartment—so complete in their disarray that they required no organization, or perhaps they had a subtle organization of their own: the fake fireplace, its cheap tile hearth littered with cigarette butts; the big brown couch covered with old newspapers, victrola records and overflowing ashtrays; the warp-legged card table, staggering under the weight of a dusty typewriter, piles of magazines and more piles of yellow writing paper. The aging sun of Indian summer gilded each spectacle, and nothing seemed to need relation.

For a minute Tina said nothing. She appeared to be looking at a spot in front of John's shoes. Then she turned and shouted at me: "Chris! Take off your coat! I know damn well you're hot, and if you're hot in your own real father's apartment, for God's sake say so, and then for God's sake *do* something about it! Oh, I love you, darling Chris, Tina loves you, but she honestly can't stand to have you sitting there looking so Christly hot. That's right. *No*, there isn't room in there—if you open that door any further, fifteen years of junk will pile onto the floor. Clear some of that stuff away, they're only my stinking literary efforts. I write, you know. Tina writes. Did you know there was talent in the family? Which reminds me—we've got to celebrate! But first, tell me. What do you think of Tina? What do you think of your daddy's wife?" With mock dignity she sat down on the sofa, crossed her legs and reached for the silver cigarette box. "She's been stewing all afternoon, planning to receive you with appropriate—Well, anyway, now she wants to know what the h-e-double-l you think of her." She tapped her cigarette on the top of the box. "Pleasantly surprised? Or unpleasantly unsurprised? Of course our butler just joined the army, our silverware was pawned last week, and we're fresh out of crumpets, so we can't *possibly* serve tea."

"We think," I said, "well, what the hell—we think just what you wanted us to. You're obviously terrific."

"Ooosh"—she rushed at me—"I'm mad about you! But that bastard brother of yours"—she squeezed me—"that Johnny-boy—"

"Wait a *minute*," John protested. "Chris just spoke before I did. Chris always speaks first. That doesn't mean anything. Golly—"

"Golly-golly-golly-golly-golly, I rate a golly from Johnny-boy. And sober, too. Tina must be good." She propelled herself to the daybed, ballooned hesitantly over John, and bending down, kissed him facetiously but nonetheless passionately on the mouth, then swirled back to the middle of the room as if nothing special had happened. "Johnny-boy," she said, "throw Champ out the window, will you please, and get some glasses, darling, and ice and a few Cokes. They're in the refrigerator. Other way. That's the bathroom, you can go there later. To the left of the door. Got it? Just yank the trays out. Sit down, Champ, you can go out in a minute." John slammed the refrigerator shut and there was a noise of water splashing against metal.

"What kind of things do you write, Tina?" I sat on the windowsill and looked down onto the pavement. A smashed dixie cup stared back, leaking strawberry ice cream. I propped my foot up on the sill and looked over at my stepmother—then past her, to the mantelpiece, where I had just noticed the photograph I'd sent my father years before, of Marlie as a debutante.

"In the bathtub," Tina sighed, sinking back and throwing her arms along the tops of the sofa cushions. "I fill the bottom of the tub with cold, cold water, then I put a board—that board there, by the fireplace—across the rims of the tub and the typewriter on the board. It's the only way to write, the *only* way. Don't take so long, Johnny-boy," she jerked forward and shouted sideways, "and bring the doodad, the—what the hell is it?—the *opener,* or a knife or something. Because we're going to open a new bottle."

"New bottle of what?" John appeared in the doorway holding a tray of ice and Coca-Cola and glasses.

"Rum. Behind the refrigerator." She sank back again and beatifically regarded the ceiling. "What do I write? I write," she said, "Tina writes detective stories."

IT WAS LONG AFTER DARK and we had almost finished the bottle of rum before my father arrived. There was a click, a key click in the door, and then he was standing there, just inside the apartment, holding a brown paper bag in his arms. His gentleness and the quiet, affectionate way he greeted us were in such contrast to the past few hours that I sobered up almost immediately. He made no apologies, except for being late. "Couldn't get away," he said, and cleared his throat and began again: "Couldn't—impossible . . ." He seemed about to go on, but decided against it and broke off with a helpless little shrug. Then he took John and me by the hand and suddenly, perhaps because of the forced smile on Tina's face, it occurred to me that he was drunk and needed us to keep him from losing his balance. He smiled—a charming, resigned smile—and said, "I'm all right now," and let go of our hands. It was as if he assumed our acceptance of these surroundings, of his wife, even of his condition, just as he had accepted them. And sensing this, we went further; we regarded them as something better than anything we had yet known.

We heated and ate the soup and spaghetti he had brought in the paper bag, and we kept drinking. Tina dominated every turn of conversation, alternating between magnificently strung oaths and soap-opera sentiment. Afterwards we walked to Sheridan Square to a cellar nightspot where Tina became very drunk and wept profusely over the performers, over us, over the war in Europe, and over a baby she had lost early in her first marriage. My father drank a lot—his capacity seemed limitless—and hardly said anything, but now and then I would catch him observing John or me, and then he would smile. Once when I asked him whether he liked his job—representing a publishing company, Tina had explained it; actually he was going from door to door selling encyclopedias—he rubbed his chin, and speaking slowly, carefully, said, "Yes—kind to me, Chris. *Kind.*" I felt like throttling all the encyclopedia publishers in the world.

When we returned to the apartment it was early morning, sometime between three-thirty and four. I remember pulling a bed down from the wall, undressing and falling into it. My father and Tina slept across the room, but when I lay down they were still up. A big alarm clock was ticking loudly on the mantelpiece, and an all-night record program was playing on the radio behind the couch. My father was sitting on the couch, smoking a cigarette and looking straight ahead. I half expected him to lean forward, point at me and say, "Did you hear the one about the Roosevelts, Chris?"

He either didn't hear me or didn't understand me when I said good night. Tina was in the kitchenette. I felt John get in bed beside me. I moved over a little and turned on my side. He settled with his back to me and then I closed my eyes.

How long I dozed I do not know. I was awakened by a quick, repeated sound. My stepmother was slapping my father. He was still sitting on the couch, facing ahead, and she was kneeling in front of him, slapping him hard, back and forth across the face. "Wake up, Curtis! Wake up—for *Christ's* sweet sake, wake up! Open your goddamn mouth and speak to me!" She kept slapping and slapping him. Then she dragged him to the other bed and set him down and placed his head on the pillow and his feet up and covered him with a sheet. After that I heard her moving around, and I think I dozed again.

The next time I awoke she was sitting on my brother's side of the bed, shaking him gently and whispering. She was in her slip and she was smoking a cigarette, whispering to John, shaking him between whispers. He turned over on his back and he must have opened his eyes, because she began carrying on a conversation. It took a little while before he answered her; I guess he had been asleep. "Johnny-boy," she whispered, "are you sicky? Do you feel bad, Johnny-boy, see spots or anything? Here, let me rub your forehead." The all-night record program was still going on and the clock was ticking, and she would take deep puffs on her cigarette and blow out, completely emptying her lungs. John answered her incoherently and she went on. "Look at me, Johnny-boy," she whispered, faster than at first. "If you only knew, baby. You *must* know. Move over a little for Tina, honey—just a little?" She took a last puff and threw her cigarette away. I felt that side of the bed go down and then her fingers accidentally touched my back as they went over John's stomach. Now John was saying, "No, Tina —get out, Tina, there isn't room for you here. Please get out. I'm tired, Tina, please!"

The radio was playing "Easter Parade" and it ended and the announcer began talking tired humor and for a minute Tina didn't say anything or move, but I could smell her perfume. It smelled sweet, like cheap pastry; like strawberry tarts. Then she said, "Johnny-boy, Chris would be just as comfy on the couch, wouldn't he? You wake him and ask him to sleep on the couch. Will you do that for Tina? Will you?" John whispered something to her which I couldn't hear, and Tina said, "All right, baby, all right, Johnny-boy," and I could tell she was excited.

There was a lot of shifting around while she got out of bed and went into the bathroom and closed the door. I tried then to be asleep. For a few seconds I concentrated hard on sleep. I thought of sand: of the bed sinking down and down and washing lazily out to sea.

When the bathroom spigot turned on, John shook me. "Have you been awake?" he asked. I sat up and rubbed my eyes and grunted. "Have you been awake the last ten minutes?" he repeated. I nodded. "Let's go," he said. I nodded.

We both dressed quickly and quietly, putting on everything but our shoes. My father was still lying on his back, breathing deeply. His left arm stretched straight out beyond the edge of the bed. I thought how cramped he would feel in the morning and considered placing his arm back on the bed, and then I thought to hell with it. I could hear Champ growling to himself in the kitchenette as we opened the apartment door. Just before leaving I changed my mind, went back and eased my father's arm over so that it lay across his chest. The door closed with the slightest of clicks. We put our shoes on downstairs.

The unexpected brightness of the night was refreshing. I

looked up at the two open second-story windows as we pulled away from the curb. Tina must still have been in the bathroom, because there was no commotion of any kind: the apartment was silent, except for the faint, late music of the radio.

JOHN DROVE, heading for Sixth Avenue. I was wide awake now, but I didn't want to talk or think about Tina. On Mac-Dougal, our headlights picked up an old man in an engineer's cap walking toward Washington Square, wheeling a battered-looking bicycle—using the handlebars for support as he walked. I hadn't thought of M. Debreaux and his circus for years, but suddenly I could visualize him clearly, halfway through the V of his bicycle, holding very still while the town clock struck eight times.

"Johnny, do you remember that one-man circus we saw in France? You were pretty young."

"Sure. Wasn't there an old geezer on top of some tables, doing something with my brand-new bike?"

"No, the chauffeur used your bike to get a jack for the flat tire. But the old man fell—remember? And Ma wanted to stop him from trying again. Why would she do that—Ma, of all people?"

"Stop him? I thought she offered him ten bucks to give it another try. Here's Fourteenth. Left?"

"Left—all the way to the river."

Johnny's version made more sense than mine: Mother wanting the old acrobat to try again. Certainly she and M. Debreaux had stubbornness, persistence, *vitality* in common. For a ludicrous moment I imagined Mother herself in a striped bathing suit up there on the balanced bicycle, correcting the wiggle of her front wheel while a crowd of Glenllyn and Loon Lake well-wishers looked on from the playground below. If marriage was like threading your way through the V of a bicycle, she had fallen the first time, picked herself up and immediately tried again.

Fourteenth Street seemed eerie in its broad emptiness—and getting harder to focus on every second. I closed my eyes and leaned against the seat, testing it with the back of my head. Not good. I found a raincoat on the floor and bunched it up for a pillow.

"How long a drive do we have to Cambridge?" John asked.

"Four, five hours. Maybe less, this time of morning."

"Shall I wake you if I stop for coffee?"

"Unless I'm out cold."

"Sack out. We'll trade in a couple of hours."

"First, I almost forgot—thanks. For getting us out of there."

John gave a soft groan but didn't say anything. It occurred to me that tonight, for the first time within my memory, he had deliberately told an outright lie. He'd lied like an expert, to get rid of Tina. Thank God. But he couldn't have wanted to. In a sense, he was forced to—he was a victim. The victim of two people who were obviously themselves victims. And so it went.

We are all victims of victims, I thought—liking the sound of it inside my head, seeing it there in flashing red neon, wondering whether I was quoting somebody. A momentous discovery. If I weren't suddenly so sleepy I'd say it aloud. Come to think of it, however, I would have to add that we are all beneficiaries of beneficiaries. I'd tell Johnny that when I took over the wheel. Tell him, moreover, that we are also victims of beneficiaries, and (so help me) beneficiaries of victims . . . Through repetition, the words were losing their meaning, but I couldn't stop juggling them.

Opening one eye, I saw that we were on the West Side Drive, approaching the George Washington Bridge with its graceful swags of light spanning the Hudson. I waited until we had passed it; then, to help block out Greenwich Village and put myself properly to sleep, I tried a variation on the paperweight once held by Janice, sweet Janice-not-mine. Shutting my eyes, I imagined a glass paperweight some eight thousand miles in diameter (precisely the size of the earth), and inside it was a person shaking a slightly smaller paperweight, containing a person shaking a still smaller one, containing . . .

"WAKE UP, CHRIS!" I heard John say from a great distance. "Time to change!"

ABOUT THE AUTHOR

George R. Clay
was born in Philadelphia in 1921,
educated at Groton and Harvard, then (after three years
in the Navy) took writing courses at Columbia. Aside from articles
and reviews, he has published short stories in a number of magazines,
including the *New Yorker* and *New World Writing*. Two of his works have
appeared in Martha Foley's *Best American Short Stories* anthologies;
six have been listed in that anthology's Roll of Honor; and he was
a finalist in the 1977 University of Iowa Short Fiction Contest.
Family Occasions is Mr. Clay's first novel. With his
wife, Ann, and two of his seven children,
he lives on a farm in Vermont.